THE RIDDLE OF THE TRAVELING SKULL

BOOKS BY HARRY STEPHEN KEELER

THE RIDDLE OF THE
TRAVELING SKULL

BY
HARRY STEPHEN KEELER

EDITED BY
PAUL COLLINS

THE COLLINS LIBRARY
[A DIV. OF McSWEENEY'S BOOKS]

To Harry Blythe

McSWEENEY'S BOOKS
826 Valencia Street
San Francisco, CA 94110

Copyright © 2005

www.mcsweeneys.net

The Collins Library is a series of newly edited and
typeset editions of unusual out-of-print books.

Editor: Paul Collins
Assistant Editor: Jennifer Elder

The Riddle of the Traveling Skull
Copyright 1934, By E. P. Dutton & Co.
All Rights Reserved

Collins Library edition published September 2005
by permission of E. P. Dutton & Co.

The sonnet entitled "If His Love Dies... So Mine!"
appearing in chapter IX, and attributed in the story to Abigail Sprigge,
was written for this story by Hazel Goodwin Keeler.

ISBN: 1-932416-26-9

ABOUT THIS BOOK

There are mystery writers, and then there are writers who are themselves a mystery. Harry Stephen Keeler is truly and gloriously both.

Born the same year as Agatha Christie, Keeler (1890–1967) was for a time an even more prolific writer of mysteries, publishing from the 1920s to the late 1940s over fifty of the most eccentric novels ever written. In a Keeler novel, you're liable to find yourself tracking an escaped lunatic alongside a narrator who constantly shifts identities (*The Mysterious Mr. I,* 1937), solving a murder with a Sherlock Holmes-like detective who is in fact a retarded janitor (*The Green Jade Hand,* 1930), and pondering a suspect in the form of the "Flying Strangler-Baby" (*X. Jones of Scotland Yard,* 1936)… this being a midget who, dressed as an adorable little tyke, swoops down to garrote his victim from a miniature helicopter.

Keeler is sometimes called the best worst writer ever—the Ed Wood of the mystery genre. His plots consist of one jaw-droppingly unlikely coincidence after another; his writing reads like a drunken translation, filled with clangorous similes and characters spouting loopy "dialects" that, though they may be ostensibly German or Cockney, seem to originate primarily in Keeler's own cracked imagination. But the combined effect of his writing is, strange to say, joyous.

Among those lucky few who have known and relished rare old copies of his out-of-print work, you find many writers and editors, precisely because Keeler does everything you are never supposed to do as a novelist. Want tight plotting? Forget it: you can read a Keeler ten times and still not figure it out. Want believable characters? Meet Screamo the Clown, Scientifico Greenlimb, and Legga the Human Spider. And remember that old saw about how you introduce all the characters in the first third of the book? Well, in one Keeler novel, the killer is introduced in the last sentence of the book.

But then, every Keeler novel is a sucker punch to the reader. It was brilliantly cruel of Keeler's publisher, E.P. Dutton & Co., to insert at around page 200 of his mysteries an illustrated promotional page proclaiming: "STOP! At this point all the characters have been presented. It should now be possible for you to solve the mystery. CAN YOU DO IT?"

Well... no. As a matter of fact, you can't do it.

Yet there is a design within Keeler's chaos. He kept thick files of odd stories that he clipped out from newspapers and magazines; to start a novel, he'd grab random fistfuls of them and then attempt to somehow madly tie all their threads together. Keeler explained his approach to plotting in "The Mechanics and Kinematics of Web Work Plot Construction," an April 1928 article for *Author and Journalist* magazine, and illustrated it with a plot diagram of his 1924 debut *The Voice of the Seven Sparrows*. His resulting schematic plot drawings are so furiously tangled that they resemble nothing so much as the Tube Map for the London Underground.

What Keeler grasped is that readers will allow a plot to be endlessly folded and mutilated as long as it is attached to the spindle of a recognizable genre. In *The Skull of the Waltzing Clown,* the plot barely happens at all, as most of the book consists of a shaggy-dog backstory related in the living room of the narrator's uncle; in a touch worthy of *Tristram Shandy*, the old man spends one entire chapter lecturing his nephew on the history of safes and safecracking. The following year, even the narrative itself was jettisoned. By *The Marceau Case* (1936), Keeler had embarked on a trilogy of "documented novels"— these being evidence dossiers of photographs, torn fragments of notes, telegrams, and maps—that left the creation of the narrative up to the reader. It was a technique that put Keeler at the edge of the Modernist avant-garde, right alongside John Dos Passos and his "newsreel" technique in *The Big Money* (1936). But because Keeler was a pulp mystery writer pounding out a new book every few months, his wild experimentation went largely unnoticed.

Examine the mystery novel, and you begin to see how Keeler might be the Platonic ideal of the genre—the truest mystery novelist who ever lived. Why? Because in the real world, a crime is almost always reducible to the simplest answer. The husband did it—the angry neighbor did it—the guy packing a gun in the nightclub parking lot did it. But a mystery plot depends on an eccentric outsider running around insisting that unlikely conspiracies and coincidences are in fact the only truly logical explanations. The mystery is an insanely paranoiac construction that cleverly masquerades as the height of rationality.

Chalk it up to Edgar Allan Poe, beloved godfather of the mystery—and a writer, not coincidentally, whose specialty was in creating insane narrators who insist on their own rationality. When he invented the detective story in *Murder in Rue Morgue,* he had his protagonist Dupin come to the most demented solution possible by determining that a murder had been committed by an escaped orangutan imitating a barber with a razor. Not to be outdone, Dupin's next case turns upon a letter hidden in plain sight. For all the clever interpretations found within *The Purloined Letter*, Poe was above all an inveterate hoaxer: the whole thing is a sort of epic joke on readers and upon the very idea of expecting logic in fiction.

This is the mystery of Mysteries: it is a completely compelling literary genre conjured out of pure humbug. Harry Stephen Keeler takes the implicit absurdity of the mystery and makes it explicit—and he does it so ecstatically, and with such utter belief in his creation, that it becomes a thing of wonder.

Paul Collins
Iowa City
July 2005

CONTENTS

CHAPTER I

A CHINAMAN HE CATCH
HIMSE'F A LIGHT!

I knew full well, when the Chinaman stopped me in the street that night and coolly asked me for a light for his cigarette, that a light for his cigarette was the last thing in the world he really wanted! I knew, in short, that he was up to something! For Chinamen, even in Chicago, that strange London of the West where most anything can happen, do not stop white men on the street and ask for lights—even though the said Chinamen are garbed in American apparel—as this particular one was when I first had dealings—of a sort—with him.

And it was for that reason, when I turned in response to an impudent tap on my shoulder and the curt request: "Match, please," issued in a guttural rasping voice which I was to know much later was no more the speaker's natural voice than a bullfrog's croak was a nightingale's song, and found at my elbow an individual, whose face, partially illumined by the street light at the corner, showed the unmistakable squat features of an Oriental, that I watched him with feelings that were a mixture of irritation and curiosity both. But the moment that the match from the box of such that I handed him, had flared up, I caught sight of a long, livid scar traversing one of his cheeks from his ear to the corner of his mouth. And I knew him then to be no other than the fellow, of some twenty-eight or twenty-nine years of age as I made him out to be, who had been seated seven or eight seats back of me on the northbound Broadway car, and who had stared more or less fixedly in my direction during the entire ride. Evidently then, he had dismounted from the car directly behind me, and, with soft shoes that made not a sound, had followed me up to the very steps of the Essex, where I lived.

For a bare second he drew on his cigarette, handing me back the box with his free hand. Then he raised his lighted match a few inches, looking me over quickly—and thoroughly—from head to foot. Which done, he tossed the splinter of wood away, at the same time bowing slightly in acknowledgment of the favor. And, with a parting glance at the lighted transom which showed the tall ornate gilt numerals "1515" marking the number, on North Dearborn Parkway, of the Essex, he passed on.

Slowly I ascended the tall brownstone steps, pondering over his peculiar actions. At the top, I transferred my black overnight bag to my left hand, and presently opened the front hall door. No one was there—thank the Lord—to greet the returning traveler—home from the far Philippines. I might have come from no further than Gary, Indiana—for all the commotion my return was occasioning. Which suited me quite perfectly. Within a fraction of a minute I was seated in my chintz-trimmed room on the second floor—good old cheerful old cozy old comfortable old American room!—Oho, confound her!—my landlady has dared to shift my chiffonier, in my absence, over to the other wall—I'll move that back tomorrow, if it's the last thing I ever do—but there I was, anyway, seated in my room, and, strangely still thinking of that impudent Chinaman—still seeing in my mind's eye that utterly immobile yellow countenance—with the scar on the right cheek.

What the devil, I wondered, did he mean by his presumptuous actions? Was he the house-servant of someone who had moved into this neighborhood during my seven weeks' absence on pure business in the Far East? Was he really minus any matches? Yet, why had he stared at me so queerly on the Broadway car?

He irritated me, strangely. And in the hope of getting a line on the source of his abnormal interest in me, I began to review the events—such as they were—which followed my exit from the big new Union Passenger Station at Randolph Street and Michigan Avenue. For it must be remembered that at the time I knew quite nothing, naturally, concerning Milo Payne, the mysterious Cockney talking Englishman with the checkered long-beaked Sherlock-holmsian cap; nor of the latter's "Barr-Bag" which was as like my own bag as one Milwaukee wienerwurst is like another; nor of Legga, the Human Spider, with her four legs and her six arms; nor of Ichabod Chang, ex-convict, and son of Dong Chang; nor of the elusive poetess, Abigail Sprigge; nor of the Great Simon, with his 2163 pearl buttons; nor of—in short, I then knew quite nothing about anything or anybody involved in the affair of which I had now become a part, unless perchance it were my Nemesis, Sophie Kratzenschneiderwumpel—or Suing Sophie!

Thus, my review of those events. The events comprising my arrival in Chicago.

I had been clear across the Pacific Ocean for my employer, Roger Pelton, the wholesale candy manufacturer, whose home up just north of Lincoln Park, at 303 Diversey Parkway, saw me more than frequently—considering that I was engaged to his only daughter Doris Pelton! My mission in the Isles had been successful—for I had tied up old Eustaquia Revariantos, the only native planter in Luzon—in fact, in all the Philippines—and incidentally the most wrinkled old baboon I had ever surveyed with my two eyes outside of a zoo—the only planter in the Isles, as I started to say, who knew the ins-and-outs of the cultivation of the rare Julu berry: and he had put his name on the dotted line to sell us all his Julu berries for ten years to come. Now we had an organic color basis for not only the most marvelously-hued purple jelly beans that ever were munched by a king—but for purple-colored confections of all kinds, and a dye moreover that was acceptable as a pure food product by the American Bureau of Standards! But what was most important was that we had practically a strangle-hold on a new and weird and engaging candy flavor that caused every tongue over which it trickled to hang out for more, more, more! Thus my trip to the Isles. Thus my trip back from the Isles. Except, of course, that on the backtrip there had

been Sophie Kratzenschneiderwumpel! Though, to be sure, it had
been farewell, Sophie, at San Francisco! Or at least I so felt and
believed. And then, in due course, I had gotten into Chicago—from
San Francisco—and just a night sooner than I had notified anybody
I would be in, by virtue of taking a train directly after disembarking
from my boat, instead of working off my sea legs for twenty-four
hours in a San Francisco hotel as I had wired various persons I would
do. That is, to be sure, I had notified one person I would be in—had
wired him, later in fact, from the train at Salt Lake City, that person
being John Barr, my closest friend and companion—and incidentally
the owner and patentee of "Barr-Bag," which article proved subsequently to be at the bottom of this strange Chinaman business. And
so, unknowing then of the simple explanation which lay back of that
fellow's interest in me, I kept on following up events in my mind to
try and illumine matters for my benighted intelligence. On reach-
ing the city—that was at 7 in the evening, of course—I had walked
towards State Street from the big depot on the lake front, with the
intention of calling Doris up by telephone from some drug store and
drinking in the cadences of her voice, but only to find, however, that
the only cadences I was to enjoy this evening was the Pelton butler's
frigid announcement on the wire that both she and her father had
gone to a dinner party on the North Shore and would not be back till
after midnight; and also to discover, as I raked my pockets for the
nickel with which I called, that the total wealth on my person, as
I struck the city I called "home," consisted of one letter of credit—
and exactly thirty-five cents in change; with the result that
I had dismissed certain ideas about taking a taxicab home, and had
climbed aboard a more modest equipage—a Broadway car going
north on State at Randolph Street.

   And then—let's see—the car was pretty full, and I had taken the
only vacant seat I could then find—one by the side of a portly looking gentleman of about fifty-five, in the garb of a clergyman. On
account of the lack of space, I had placed my black overnight bag
under the seat. Exactly beneath myself, to be precise. In due course
nearly everybody piled off the car—that was at Ohio Street—to be

sure, the big Medinah Temple one block east—some big Masonic doings there tonight, of course!—leaving the car less than a quarter full of people. I had stayed right where I was, however. And shortly after, I began to be conscious, every time I casually glanced around, of a pair of eyes looking forward up the car at me—a pair of eyes belonging to a Chinaman who sat several seats in my rear.

But how was that now? First, he was up in front of me—then, a short while later, he was equally far in back of me—oh sure, that was it—the motorman had burned out his controller-box near the Holy Name Cathedral, and had had to turn his juggernaut entirely about by way of the switch-tracks at Chicago Avenue and then proceed north by the use of what had formerly been the rear controller-box. Only, thanks to all of us passengers turning about, also, it had become the front controller box. Nothing out of the way there—and it accounted for nothing at all.

Except for the way in which that Chinaman with the scar jumped from the front of the car to the back of it without even getting up. Except—that is—getting up long enough, as we all did, so that that German conductor could swing all the pivoted seat-backs to the opposite sides of the seats.

So that was that. And thus I'd ridden north. More or less lost in my thoughts and the realization that Chicago was not an iota different than the night I'd gone to the Philippines. And then I'd heard the German conductor call out "Burton Place." And I had jerked my overnight bag out from under the seat—from under myself, to be exact—and had made a hasty exit from the car, walking eastward in the direction of North Dearborn Parkway. I had turned there, and finally reached the steps of the Essex, that dignified old mansion-like rooming-house which spelled H-O-M-E for me. And then it was that I had felt that tap on my shoulder and had turned to discover, a second later, that my street-car Chinaman was at my side.

It was certainly odd! Had he deliberately followed me? Outside of my $15 Bulova watch, I never wear jewelry. There was nothing about my general appearance which might have indicated that holding me up would produce anything of value to anyone. In fact, all

I carried was that black bag, and it resembled exactly what it was and what John Barr, its manufacturer, intended it to be: a mighty convenient and efficient handbag for travelers—and not a case such as diamond salesmen might carry.

It lay on the chintz-covered bed where I had tossed it immediately upon entering the room. It suggested, in fact, the desirability of a clean collar—considering that no less than 1,000 men had jammed into that washroom, to change collars, in the Pullman coming in. But nevertheless I looked first in my chiffonier drawer. No collar! No clean collar, that is. But fourteen soiled ones. All carefully and neatly stacked. For seven long weeks. What a homecoming for a world traveler! Fourteen soiled collars—neatly stacked.

But never mind. My bag had practically everything in it I or anyone else could need, except perhaps an elephant's monocle, or a clay tablet from Babylonia. So I crossed the floor and put my key into its lock. And turned the key. Except that—it would not turn. And twisted it—except that it would not twist. Impatiently, I jerked at it. Strange! 'Twas the brand-new bag, all right, that I had bought myself in 'Frisco on my arrival, bawling aloud its merits so that everyone in that particular store might know that my friend John Barr made bags—and good ones, too!

I took it up and looked at it. And though it was brand-new— I suddenly became conscious that there were all kinds of curious nuances in newness! And that I had the wrong new bag! Now I began to see some strange connection with the matter of that Broadway car's reversing its direction. If—for instance—that clerical-looking gentleman who had sat by my side, reading his prayer book, had also had a "Barr-Bag" underneath his seat—underneath his portly self, in fact—then when the car reversed its direction— and we all stepped out of our seats a moment, and the backs of the seats were all flopped across—then—no, by Gosh, it wouldn't make a particle of difference! For he'd resumed his same seat next the window—and I mine on the aisle. And we would each have still been sitting right over our own bag.

But staring at the telephone on the wall, from which I had cut off the incoming service when I had left for the Philippines, but which naturally still had its outgoing service so that the phone company would not lose some errant possible nickel, I decided to solve the matter of that bag once and for all. And stepping to the instrument I dropped in a nickel and dialed it for the operator. "Give me the Diversey car barns of the Chicago Surface Lines," I told the girl. "I have no directory here."

In a second I had them—or at least a foreman in them.

"When Car No. 1515," I told him, and added: "I happen to remember it because it's the same number as my house number—comes in, will you have its conductor call—"

"1515? Up for repairs. Burned-out controller-box. Schmidt," he called out, "yer wanted at the phone."

And in a second I had the yellow-mustached conductor of that Broadway car—which I had ridden home.

"This is a passenger," I told him, "on your Broadway car No. 1515 tonight, Mr.—Schmidt, is it? Do you remember when the front controller-box burned out and we backed up on Chicago Avenue to reverse?"

"Yah. Shure I do!"

"And we headed north, the motorman finally using the other controller-box? Well, do you remember when you roused what few passengers were on the car, out of their seats, seat by seat, and switched the seat-backs over?"

"Yah. Shure I do."

"Well—for some dam' fool reason, Schmidt, I got somebody else's bag!"

"You dit? But you shouldn't! You zee, ven I flopped dot zeat-back ofer, unt you unt dot odder chentleman vot vass sid next you, vass climb back in—I see two bags unter dot zeat. Dot iss, ven I vass go to flop dot next zeatback ofer, see? De vun now behint you bod'. Unt I know dot you two don't zee dot your bags iss now geshifted, mid dot car uf ours now going der odder vay so I chust stoop down, unt shift dem two bags—mofe each aboud-d, zee, each vun in de odder's blace."

"Why—you unmitigated idiot," I told him, "changing our direction of travel, and flopping the seat-back over—didn't change our bags. Confound it, we each continued to sit over our own respective bag—regardless of what direction we were facing! But now, thanks to your geometry, or logic, or whatever you call it, that man and I have each got the other one's bag!"

I could literally hear him scratching his head on the other end of the wire.

"Vell," he said, unconvinced, "I can't zee it! De vay id looks to me, now, if effer'putty durns arount—unt all de zeat-backs dey go across—den—"

"Oh—applesauce!" I said. And hung up. And realized then that I should have had myself transferred to the lost-and-found department of the Surface Lines and reported the matter.

I went back to the bag grumpily, and hefted it on the palm of my hand. A little bit lighter it was, I could see now—just a little bit, than my own.

And then I thought of the old bunch of suitcase keys laid away somewhere in the bottom drawer of my chiffonier. In a jiffy I had the drawer open. And amongst a lot of trash, I found them. Then I commenced trying them on the bag, one by one. The fifth key turned in the lock as slick as the proverbial whistle. I pulled the jaws of the bag apart. And peering in, gave a start of amazement.

For looking up at me was a human skull. A grinning, leering skull. That, and nothing else!

CHAPTER II

THE CONTENTS OF A BLACK BAG

I say nothing else. But I should include the nest of heavy well-packed excelsior on which the skull lay. A nest just high enough, and compact enough, too, so that, when the bag was closed, the skull was kept nicely wedged against the top of the satchel, and hence couldn't roll or bounce about.

And I perhaps should include also the broad rubber band—at least three-quarters of an inch wide—which, tightly stretched, passed under the lower jawbone and around and over the semi-spherical dome of the skull, and which—in lieu of the usual springs and pivots found, on such anatomical exhibits in physicians' offices—kept these two gruesome things snugly together.

And I should also, no doubt, include the brand-new demijohn cork which was stuck in the vertebral foramen of the skull—the opening where, in life, the spinal cord runs up into the brain—and for a reason which I was to discover later.

Yes, I should include all of these—in stating the contents of that bag. These—and even certain other things!

As soon as my first feeling of revulsion toward the unsavory object had evaporated—as well as my surprise at finding such a thing in a clergyman's traveling bag, I reached in gingerly and took it out. My thumb in its eyesocket, my index finger curled around its dome-like rear.

And the tip of that index finger touched something cold. Metallically cold. At which I turned the skull about. And found that this was no just-ordinary sconce. For in the back of it sat a circular, bright, shiny silverlike metal plate, or plug, or disc, or something, about an inch and a quarter in diameter. And below it, an inch or so, was a clean-cut hole—a hole about the size of a pea—or better—a bullet! The small hole, giving in evidently to the black cavernous interior of the skull, had a truly sinister aspect. But I was not particularly interested in it. Because it was only a hole. The thing I *was* interested in was that circular plate above it. For there were words and numbers etched on the surface of the latter, crudely, as by hand. And tilting the skull slightly so that the light from the overhanging electric fixture above the bed fell on the plate with the proper angle, I read the words and numbers easily. They ran:

> M. PRIOR
> No. 82
> 9-17-'14.

A strange thing, a damned strange thing, I thought, to be traveling in a clergyman's bag. Though—had I known what I know today—no more strange, at that, than the swift drama that was to center itself about that skull in my hand. And which drama was already, at that moment, under way!

I put Mr. Skull down reverently on the bed.

That is, Mr. Skull and his rubber-attached boon companion, Mr. Jawbone.

And looked within the bag again.

But, as I have said before, there was nothing whatever in the bag but that closely packed excelsior nest. Which had kept Mr. Skull from being frolicsome, as it were—and bounding and romping about.

I picked him up again.

A fine set of teeth he had. Both uppers and lowers. All present—and no bridgework. Just a few fillings. That was all. I pulled open his lower jaw, which worked smoothly from the points where its pronglike extensions contacted their eyelet-like sockets under his cheek bones. And looked within his osseous mouth, which was, of course, empty. And, as I released that lower jaw, his teeth snapped together viciously, thanks to the tightly stretched rubber band connecting jaw and skull. He could have, dead as he was, bitten clear through a peeled banana.

I turned him around once more. And marveled again at the remarkably perfect aperture that had been seemingly drilled through his rear wall—and at the decided bevel in the edges of that aperture—at least where it was visible above the surface of the metal plate—a bevel which made it possible, apparently, as I saw by tapping the plate with the end of my fountain pen, for the aperture to clamp that round piece of identifying metal more tightly than a Chicago politician's teeth clamp onto a free five-cent cigar. Puzzled, too, I surveyed the nice new wine cork stuck into what I have already referred to as the vertebral foramen of the skull. And wondered, naturally, why—

But, no sooner wondered, than I withdrew the cork. And looked in the aperture which it had been plugging up.

And saw, with considerable further bewilderment, that the inside of the skull—the brain case, in short—was stuffed, apparently, with scraps of torn white paper, loosely put in. I pulled a couple out. They were blank. Torn from, or out of, blank sheets. Of ordinary bond typewriting paper. Now I pulled out a whole tuft of them. They were all like the first two. Blank.

Curious thing, that, I thought. The skull stuffed like that. Packed, in fact, just like a shipping basket in a department store sending a nickel bottle of Carter's Ink out to Ravenswood. Were those scraps of paper put in there to pack something inside this convenient receptacle—so that it would not rattle—bound about— break—or what? And why hadn't the white stuffing been visible through the pea-sized aperture underneath the silver plate? I took a slender pencil from my vest pocket, and poked it through that aperture. Though hardly had it traversed the bony thickness of the skull's wall itself, than it broke through a flimsily thin stratum of some inky black paper—carbon paper, quite evidently—which had blocked that other end. And whose jet surface had first given me the illusion that the skull had been empty inside—that a vacant cavern lay at the other end of that hole. Which decidedly was not the case.

I turned my attention back again to the larger opening—that vertebral foramen—and withdrew a really generous tuft of paper fragments this time. A chunk of carbon paper came forth on this attempt. Also a piece of a printed magazine page, which, judging from its fine typography and its glossy surface, was obviously part of a page from *Hearstmopolitan Magazine*. Another tuft, now. And this tuft contained, I saw, a couple of fragments of paper on which there were carbon-imprinted words. Made by typewriter. Evidently the copy of some letter. In fact, it seemed that everything at someone's hand had been used to stuff this skull neatly—blank paper—magazine page—carbon sheet—copy of a letter. But what was encased therein?

I got myself a buttonhook now from my chiffonier drawer, and, as a rake and general poker-out of stuffing, it proved very useful, aided by a bit of shaking of the skull now and then. And I had emptied the skull practically of its entire paper contents before it gave up the article it was sequestering. Which article, followed by a shower of two or three fragments of paper—the final pieces, in fact, left in the brain case—tumbled forth of its own volition—and weight—upon my bed.

And it was a bullet!

Not a bullet ensconced in a brass cartridge shell, containing powder and percussion cap. But a fired bullet. Just the lead, in short. Or rather, to be precise, some peculiar alloy of lead—for it possessed a pronounced greenish hue when held at one angle with the light—and an equally pronounced yellowish hue when held at a different angle. And it smelled decidedly acetic, as I found by sniffing at it, as though it had been cleaned of oxidation or something else by being scrubbed with slightly acid solution made from vinegar and water. And it was mushroomed a bit, too, where it had bored its way through futilely resisting bone. I laid its nose against the neat round hole beneath the plate. Even mushroomed as it was, the lead slug cleared the sides of that hole—just and no more.

This, obviously, was the bullet that had imbedded itself within the pulsing, living brain this skull had once contained!

M. Prior. No. 82. 9-17-'14. That no doubt held the answer to this thing. That, and a comfortable-looking clergyman who read a prayer book or Bible on a Broadway car. For a few minutes I stood staring glumly at the skull. Then I spoke. "Number 82," I said, "I don't exactly relish that look on your face. But I can't help but wonder what kind of look will be on your master's face when he gets you back— your master who was reading Deuteronomy—or Genesis—on a Broadway car!

"For undoubtedly," I went on to the leering skull, "if he doesn't get my handbag open tonight, with a bundle of extra keys of his own from some cabinet or closet or tool drawer, and find those seven or eight cards of mine, with that rubber band about 'em, and 'The Essex' printed on 'em, he'll put an ad in the paper about you.

"So back you go—paper stuffing and all. For you can't sit on my chiffonier, baby—not for a single minute. Back you—"

But I stopped, for while I had been addressing No. 82—as I was beginning now affectionately to regard him—I had suited gesture to word and fished up a handful of his stuffing. Only to upturn a particularly long fragment of carbon-imprinted paper, whose typewritten words arrested me for their bitter poignancy. For they read:

his heart's whole, and mine

No prosaic business letter, that!

I relinquished my handful, and raked about again. And found another, which read:

He's gone

I shook my head. And raked some more. And found more evidence of something sinister. Simply the word

wounded

A tough epistle, all right. I looked at the skull. Skull?—letter?—letter?—skull?—were they connected? Was the skull, by any chance, "him"—or was this just a fortuitous coming together of part of a dead man—and a letter about a dead man?

I unearthed another piece.

anguish, through each hour

Truly, truly spoken, I told myself. Those four words in that piece of a line. I had lost plenty of loved ones of my own. Father, mother, brother. The anguish of it all rushed back over me with disconcerting suddenness.

I tumbled forth another piece. Which read:

he might remember

That was warning—somebody! He might remember what?

I had to scrape a long time before I unearthed another one. 'With words on it, that is. And its words conveyed a sinister fear. On the writer's part. For they read:

every hour is filled with

Filled with what?

I found the companion piece immediately; at least a piece whose left-hand edge fitted its right-hand edge exactly, and furnished its continuation on that line. The two together now read:

every hour is filled with fear for me

Mighty, mighty queer, all right. The tenor of those comments. Running comments—about somebody dead—accusations—recriminations. How long the letter had been there was no telling; but quite obviously one sheet, at least, of it had become inadvertently torn up to help make the packing that should hold that bullet snug and immovable within the skull.

And I decided forthwith to do something that a second before would have been furthest from my thoughts.

Indeed, I did it. For I pulled the pillowcase from one of my two pillows. And raked into it that entire paper nest! Every last fragment thereof.

And rolled the pillowcase up into a small compact ball. And put the ball into my lower chiffonier drawer. Some Sunday afternoon, I told myself, when I was particularly bored, yet in a mood where I could endure sad things, I'd have a jigsaw puzzle to work out. Even though it was but a page from the carbon copy of some recriminatory, dejected and dolorous letter. After all, somebody had received the original of that letter; so I wasn't robbing its rightful recipient. And the Deuteronomy-reading clergyman who no doubt had had the best reason in the world for carrying them, would get his skull, jawbone, cork, and bullet back, so—so—so—

But I did, at that, feel just a little bit sneakingly contemptible.

However, I forgot my feelings. For the time being. For I had to make up a new brain stuffing for No. 82.

Which was not very difficult. In my third chiffonier drawer I found half a ream or so of white typewriter paper. From days when I had had occasion to make carbon copies of certain city-sales calls reports.

And for a minute was busy tearing up at least enough to stuff that brain cavity with.

And when I saw that I did have enough—and more—dropped Mr. Bullet back in—heard him fall against the roof of the skull with a quite resounding "plunk" and commenced wadding in paper. With both fingers and buttonhook. Paper from my new supply, that is. And kept on wadding. And shortly was up to the vertebral opening. Whereupon I re-inserted the wine cork.

"And there you are, 82," I said, with more or less of a forced cheerfulness. "Your leaden brain won't rattle now. Which seems to be the idea back of all your stuffing. So be in with you! For, as I told you before, you're not going to sit on my chiffonier. That's—that's final."

With which I inserted him back on his excelsior nest—and bearing down on the hinges of the bag heard its jaws click together tightly on him. And followed that sequestration operation by turning the key which so fortuitously had fitted the lock of that bag, its full 360 degrees around in the lock. And I put the key on my ring, and the bag on the floor underneath my front window-sill. And went forth into the night on the prosaic errand of engaging an expressman to bring my trunk and label-plastered suitcase from the station.

I met Mrs. Winterbotham-Higginsbottom downstairs in the hall. Mrs. Winterbotham-Higginsbottom was my landlady. She was dressed in her white hand-knit shawl exactly as she had been the night I went to the Philippines. From the total and persisting absence of any changes in anything, I was beginning more and more now to believe I never even had left Chicago. I got over the usual questions about how hot the Philippines were not, whether I was seasick going or coming, etc., and etc., told her very briefly about the Chinaman and received the further interesting information in return that there were no Chinese whatsoever in the neighborhood either as servants or laundrymen, borrowed $20, proving to myself thus that I was a star roomer in fact and not in theory, promised to return it as soon as I had drawn some money at the plant, and then cautioned Mrs. W-H very particularly about Suing Sophie.

For Suing Sophie was not just Suing Sophie. Suing Sophie was a sort of problem I had brought back with me to Chicago. I expected for a while to be telling a number of people about Suing Sophie. And putting them on their guard. Mrs. Winterbotham-Higginsbottom heard me through unsmilingly, and replied to my warning—or injunction—or whatever it was.

"I'll be extremely careful, Mr. Calthorpe. You say the inquiry may come from the South—or Southwest? Well—don't worry. Neither Suing Sophie nor any of her lawyers will outwit Mrs. Hannah Winterbotham-Higginsbottom."

And thus, with Sophie Kratzenschneiderwumpel—about whom I shall go into later—disposed of for the moment, I went forth into the night.

I didn't get back for two hours.

The reason? Ridiculous, I know. But I went in to view a film I saw advertised out in front of the Windsor Motion Picture Theatre, near Clark and Division Streets, just off from the express company where I gave in the order about my trunk.

The title of the film was: *The Philippine Islands: A Remarkable Travelogue, Faithful to Every Detail!*

But that's humanity. If a man came back from hell, he would probably spend all his life poring over Dante's *Inferno* and the catalogues of the American Radiator Company.

When I did get back, Mrs. Winterbotham-Higginsbottom met me in the hall, and informed me that I had missed my friend, John Barr; that he had called just about forty-five minutes after I had left; had waited for me upstairs in my room for nearly an hour and had then departed for home, asking me to give him a ring.

Which I did not, for I suddenly woke up to the fact that I was dog-tired, and had cleared some 1000 miles in the last twenty-four hours. So I went upstairs and turned in, mentally resolving to search the *Tribune* in the morning for one ad for one overnight bag containing—well—what would its ecclesiastical owner claim it contained?

But my awakening came much sooner than any arrival of any *Tribune*. Thanks to nothing else than the skull itself!

CHAPTER III

AT 1 O'CLOCK IN THE MORNING

I had been sleeping quite soundly for what I judged might have been two or three hours, when, suddenly, I opened my eyes in the darkness and heard someone knocking on the door of my room. My first thought was that John Barr had again dropped back to see me at this late hour. So, after slipping into my bathrobe, I flung the door open. But instead of greeting my old friend as I had expected, I saw in the hall, clad like myself in bathrobe, no other person than Mrs. Winterbotham-Higginsbottom, her face carrying a look as though she too had been awakened from a sound sleep.

"Someone wants you on the phone, Mr. Calthorpe," she told me. "A man. I don't know who he is."

"Good Lord!" I said. "Somebody, already, representing—representing Suing Sophie! For none of my friends here in Chicago even know I'm in town."

"No, it's a man who's got one of your cards that shows you live here at the Essex. When he told me that, I knew it was somebody who had rightful business with you—so I had him hold the wire."

"Well, I guess it's all right," I told her. "I'll come down."

She pattered down the hall and disappeared by a rear stairway. I found my slippers, and made my way down to the first floor. On the way I passed Mrs. W-H's tall grandfather's clock which stood in the hall. Its hands showed the time to be ten minutes of 1. Shortly

I was at the telephone, and took up the waiting receiver.

"Hello ?" I said experimentally—for I wasn't sure yet that Suing Sophie, or some legal representative of the lady, hadn't somehow found me.

"Am I speaking to Mr. Clay Calthorpe, at the Essex, on North Dearborn Parkway?" replied a polite voice.

The Essex business solved the matter. For Suing Sophie would not have any knowl—

"You are," I said. "And who is this?"

"Ah!" he ejaculated. "So happy to have you on the wire. Well, Mr. Calthorpe—it happens that you do not know who I am. But my name is Duncan Craig—Pastor of St. James Church."

Now at last a light began to dawn on me. This undoubtedly must be the clerical-looking man whose bag I had carried off.

"Mr. Calthorpe," he was saying, "when I arrived at my home tonight with an overnight bag I was carrying, I found myself unable to open it with the key provided for it. Verily, I was like one of the victims of those lawyers whom Our Lord—if you remember your eleventh chapter of Luke—chided for having taken away the key of knowledge. I seemed to have the key—yes—but no longer the knowledge of how to operate that key. But nothing daunted, I got hold of a number of old keys to various bags and suitcases, and trying out several, managed at last to open the bag. And lo—I discovered that I had another man's bag—for the contents were not my own at all! I took the liberty of searching through it and finally came upon a small packet of calling cards bearing your name, and some address known as—er—the Essex, and the phone number I am now calling." He paused. "Now could it be possible, I am wondering, that you yourself have not yet discovered the mistake?"

I might have been on the up-and-up with him then and there, but I was certain that I detected a pronounced note of uneasiness in the voice of the Rev. Duncan Craig—a note which betokened a hope on his part that I had not yet made the discovery of what was in his bag. So I determined to spring it on him face-to-face only—and not over a telephone wire! And so I answered in such a way that I could do exactly that.

"You have knocked me for a row, Reverend," I told him. "For I was so busy unpacking my trunk tonight—you see I just got into Chicago tonight from a trip—that I didn't even try to unlock my bag. Hrrm! And my key, then, wouldn't have worked either. Of course—I have an old bunch of suitcase and valise keys somewhere around—" I paused gently, and did not finish.

And when I should see the Reverend, I would tell him that I unlocked his bag with that bunch of keys!

But the Reverend Duncan Craig had no intentions, apparently, of my holding on to that bag. Or else, just as he next expressed it, he was leaving town himself.

"My dear fellow," he said genially, "I'm going to ask a most tremendous favor of you. One that I can't repay, perhaps, unless some day I marry you—free of charge. Now how would you like that?" I liked it—particularly as the thought came to me that the other party to such marriage would naturally be Doris Pelton. He went on. "You see, my dear fellow, I'm leaving for New York on that special plane going out at 3 a.m., which will carry a number of pastors there in time for them to be at the opening tomorrow morning at 10 a.m. of the Episcopal Convention there. And I must—I *must* have that bag! Do you suppose you could charter a cab, at my expense, and bring it to me? I haven't even my man with me tonight, to send for it. I'm all packing just now—and in such a beastly mess trying to get away—oh by Jove—I—I haven't the right to ask you this, have I?

"Of course you have, Reverend," I assured him. "I was first off of that Broadway car tonight—and so I walked off with your bag—and not you with mine." I didn't lay it on the conductor yet. "And anyway I want my own bag, Reverend, as bad as you want yours. Now where are you located? If you belong to St. James Church—you must be, of course, on the Near North Side. I'm at 1515 North Dearborn Parkway, as you naturally know."

"And I'm not even ten minutes walk from you, my dear chap, in

case you can't find a cab at this hour. 1870 Lake Shore Drive. One—
eight—seven—oh. Just dismiss your cab—that is, if you come in
one—walk up the steps, ring the bell at the side of the door, and
I'll answer in person. For I'll be in my study, packing, but I can hear
the bell perfectly. And don't leave your cab waiting—because you
and I shall sample a bottle of rare old Amontillado I have here—
Coronation 1911, dear chap, vintage of 1865! For wine maketh the
heart of man glad—if you've ever read your 104th Psalm. And thus
I shall meet you—which I must do, since I've contracted to marry
you—and to christen all your young ones besides!"

"Well, Reverend," I told him, "about the young ones—it's a
little premature yet. But I'll take you up on the marrying part."

"Good. And may I expect you then—in say—twenty minutes?"

"Right," I assured him. "For I can dress in nine-and-a-half! 1870
Lake Shore Drive, you say? All right, I'll be there—and—and don't
mislay the corkscrew, Reverend!"

He chuckled genially, as he hung up.

I returned to my room. He seemed a sort of a regular fellow at
that, I reflected, as I dressed quickly. Then I took up the black
satchel from where it sat on the floor underneath my window sill,
and tiptoed down and out to the deserted North Side streets.

There were no cabs anywhere to be seen, and I didn't bother
with any. For I could walk that short distance as fast as a cab could
bring me there.

I made my way northward along Dearborn Parkway until I saw
by the low street lights that I had reached the 1800s. Then I turned
east, and within four minutes had struck Lake Shore Drive, more
commonly known as "The Gold Coast." Here I proceeded more
slowly past tall towering apartment buildings which at this hour
did not have the least sign of their usual liveried footmen outside,
and past smaller brownstone and grey-stone residences sandwiched
between—residences which once had been mansions—but which
now waited only the sale of the valuable land beneath them to
become apartment buildings themselves. Finally I stopped in front
of one such. It was of beautiful brownstone, and its front shades—of

aristocratic blue—were all drawn. A solitary concrete lamppost in front of the house showed plainly its number: 1870. Up the stone-balustraded steps I marched and into the gloomy vestibule. Gloomy because the heavy right-hand outer oak door cut off the rays from that streetlight, and I had to grope around the side of a pair of crystal-leaded inner doors in search of a push button.

But suddenly a dark figure which stood within the further corner of that vestibule stirred. I heard the sound of the stirring a second before I apprehensively turned my head—and saw the dark figure itself. Instinctively I raised my free arm—but too late. Something descended on my head so forcibly that millions of spots of light seemed to dance before my eyes. In fact, in that immeasurably short interval of time I must have reeled violently and sickeningly to the dark side wall of the vestibule—for I felt both of my hands flat against it, trying to hold me up. The satchel—Lord knows where it was! Where I had dropped it, I guess. Except that, just as I turned my head about, and unconsciousness folded in on me, I saw that satchel going out of the vestibule under the arm of a man who looked leeringly and appraisingly back at me for just a second in the part of the open doorway that was lighted by that bright streetlight. And the man's eyes were almond-shaped; his face was yellow—and he had a long livid scar covering his right cheek!

CHAPTER IV

TRICKED

When I regained consciousness, I found myself with a throbbing head, lying on the floor of that same vestibule where I had fallen. The bag, of course, was distinctly *non est*.

By slow degrees I rose to my feet. The first thing I did was to feel for my $15 Bulova watch, and the $19 and some odd cents from that $20 Mrs. Winterbotham-Higginsbottom had advanced me. The watch was in my watch pocket, and the money in my right trousers pocket. Obviously then, the scar-faced Chinaman who had struck me down had done so with the object of getting that bag only—and not for any motives of ordinary robbery.

My first impulse, more or less, was to shake up the Reverend Duncan Craig from that downstairs study where he was still packing, blissfully unconscious of events taking place in his own front vestibule, and ask if I could now have my drink of Amontillado to rub on the back of my head instead of putting it within my stomach. But I knew that if I once began trying to explain everything to the Reverend, that scar-faced son of a Chinese sea-cook would be outside a certain police-radio zone in which several hundred squad cars were cruising around tonight.

Which I didn't intend to let happen!

And so I let the Reverend Duncan Craig go right on with what he was doing. And staggered down the front steps.

35

A taxicab slid up in front of me and came to a stop with a screaming of its brakes. Its driver quite obviously thought he was picking up a drunk. And I told him where I wanted to go.

"East Chicago Avenue police station—and hop on it, buddy."

And we were off. I glanced at my Bulova watch by a passing streetlight. Its hands showed the time to be only nineteen minutes after 1. So I couldn't have lain stunned, all in all, for over four or five minutes.

From the severe ache at the back of my head, I knew that I had suffered a terrific blow. But when I passed my fingers gingerly over its site, they came away unbloodied—and I realized that the pill which had put me into dreamland had been an ordinary leather blackjack.

Within two shakes of a lamblet's tail, we had drawn up to a curb off from an arched stone doorway over which hung two purple lights that reminded me, somehow, of two great Julu berries. The police station it was, all right. I paid off the driver and forged in. In the office I found a sleepy bushy-browed desk sergeant nodding over a newspaper, and a pair of plainclothesmen evidently on their midnight lunch hour, sitting astride a bench back of him playing two-handed honeymoon bridge.

"I'll bid four in hearts," one was saying. My entrance caused no stoppage of the game, as was to be expected, but part of the sleepy look on the face of the desk sergeant seemed to vanish.

"Sergeant," I announced, "I've just been robbed. Ten minutes ago. And I want—"

"What kinda car did they drive? How much they get?" He reached over for a pad of blank forms. "How many in th' gang? Describe—"

"Wait!" I said. "No car. No gang. One man. And he didn't touch my money. Nor my watch. All he took was a traveling bag—which belonged to somebody else."

His pencil was poised above his paper.

"I don't getcha, buddy. Give me th' details."

"That's exactly what I'm here in person for. Instead of calling up.

I want this bird's description put on the radio. He sloughed me from here to Jericho. He—"

"Yeah—and who are you?"

"My name is Clay Calthorpe. Employed—sort of general sales manager—for the Pelton Confectionery Company. Austin Avenue and the L-Road. Struck town tonight from—from a business trip. Rode home in the same seat with a clergyman. His name is Duncan Craig—of St. James Church. When I left the car, I got his bag. By mistake. A Chinaman, about twenty-seven years old, with a long ugly scar down his right cheek followed me from the car and asked me for a match just as I turned in at the Essex. Where I live. 1515 North Dearborn Parkway."

"And he up an' sloughed you? What—"

"No, he didn't. Not then. For that was hours and hours ago. Just a while ago the Reverend Duncan Craig called me up by phone and told me he'd found my card in the bag that he got. Asked me to bring the bag to his home at once. So I dressed—and hurried over there with it. 1870 Lake Shore Drive is where he lives. And this confounded Chink must have either been tapped into the phone wire of the Essex tonight, or known positively I would be coming there to the Reverend Craig's sometime tonight—"

"Why—an' wherefore?"

"Me bid is in shpades," said one of the plainclothes-men.

"Because the minute I went up the steps of No. 1870, and tried to grope around in the vestibule for a push button, the house fell on my head and I traveled through space with the square root of minus one—"

"What's that?"

"That's the speed of light, according to Einstein," said the other of the plainclothesmen. "He's persiflageous, Sarge! And how do you like that ace, Hennesy?"

"Well, I'll state it simpler, Sergeant. When I woke up, I was on the vestibule floor. And no satchel."

"And how th' devil do you know that this Chin—"

"Yes, I know what you're going to ask. Because just before I slid into dreamland, I saw him beating it out the vestibule with that bag. Come on—feel—if you don't believe. I've a bump back there as tall as the skyride tower in the old World's Fair of eight years or so ago."

"And what was in that bag?"

I pondered deeply now for the half of a second. After all, I thought, I didn't have quite the right to toss the personal affairs of the Reverend Duncan Craig squarely into police limelight without his permission. Maybe he had all the good reason in the world for transporting that sku—

"I don't know what was in it, Sergeant," I said. "For I hadn't tried to unpack it yet. And if I had, my key wouldn't have fit it. The bag weighed about two pounds—but then it's made of tough thick genuine leather with heavy metal framework. It was a Barr-Bag."

The sergeant turned to the two plainclothesman. "Cut out that damned bridge game—both o' you. I can't sleep a wink around this place with you two perpetually bidding against each other. Hennesy, drive over to 1870 Lake Shore Drive with this fellow—and interview the Reverend Duncan Craig. In short, find out what was in that bag. If the Chink was an ordinary heister, he'd have frisked this man. And he'd have been using a car too. Although maybe he was. And now I'll be sticking him on the radio."

"What you say, Sarge," said the plainclothesman who had no brogue, "to my tipping off Fatty to stop over? Stories with Chinks in 'em is his meat."

"Listen you," retorted the desk sergeant darkly, "if you was in this place a hour ago when I give them leg-men th' dressin'-down of their lives, you wouldn't talk Fatty to me. You leave 'em be right where they are. Swilling beer up at the corner. I wouldn't give 'em a story tonight—not even the story, if—if you went out and bit a dog!"

"Oke, Sarge. I'm going out now and bite one. A hot-dog at Gus's place."

And he vanished.

Hennesy and I hurried out of the station. He evidently owned the small blue flivver that was parked up the street a ways.

We were crossing Clark Street in it in ten seconds.

You have to hand it to the Chicago Police Department! By the time we were crossing Rush Street, the radio on Hennesy's little car began to intone:

"Calling all cars—calling all cars! Look out for a Chinese. With a scar on his cheek. Carrying a traveling bag. Probably afoot. Holdup, on the Near North Si—"

"That'll do ye," said Hennesy peevishly, and shut it off with his foot. "I've heard the shtory wance."

It was twenty-five minutes to two when we reached the steps of the Reverend Duncan Craig's residence. Up we went—and I let Hennesy lead the way. There was no telling about anything. For this was Chicago—London of the West. And the next man lurking in that vestibule might be a one-eyed Arab, armed with a kris.

But no, the vestibule was quite empty. Hennesy groped about and found the push button that I had not found. And gave it an energetic push. From where we stood we could hear a bell ring. Loud and long. But no one came to the door. Nor did the sign of a light show back of those leaded panes. Suddenly Hennesy ejaculated.

"Hrmph! What's this?" He drew from his pocket an electric flash lamp and projected its beam on the vestibule floor at the base of the door-jamb. A white card lay there, its four corners entirely torn away. He ran the beam up the jamb of the door—and then, for the first time, I saw four neat tacks, each tack holding a corner of that card.

He picked the card up. And focussed his light on it. And as he read its typewritten inscription, I also did the same over his shoulder. It read:

TO PERSONS REPLYING TO NEWSPAPER ADS CONCERNING THIS HOUSE:

This unfurnished house is for rent, but not for sale.
The owner now resides permanently in Europe.
For arrangements, see agents:

HARRIS AND SMITH, Capital Building.

Caretaker on premises daily and Sunday till 6 p.m.

"Humph!" he grunted, "there ain't no such a person as th' Riverind Duncan Craig. Yer Chineeman an' his pals hung wan ahn ye, me fri'nd—they hung wan ahn ye!"

CHAPTER V

DORIS AND ROGER PELTON

When I discovered that my little adventure had petered out, so to speak, leaving me with nothing but a bump on the back of my head and something new in the line of experience, I did what any sensible person would have done under the circumstance. I returned to the Essex, slapped witch-hazel on the bump, and tumbled with celerity into bed. No, I didn't get out that pile of rolled-up paper fragments in my chiffonier drawer, and fish around a half hour for pieces containing carbon-imprinted words on them—and then work another half hour putting them together. For, by suggestion of the plainclothesman who claimed that he had worked for ten years with an ambulance surgeon out of Maxwell Street Police Station, I took fifteen grains of multiplonal, which I bought—and downed by help of a glass of charged water—in the same all-night drug store where he was vainly looking up the name of Duncan Craig, D.D., in the directory—and finding that no Duncan Craig, D.D., or otherwise, even existed. For multiplonal—or rather the long profound sleep it created—was, he said, the one thing that would ward off brain concussion—although he called it just "scathered wits."

And it had commenced to work even by the time I reached the house. Which fact left me in no mettle for jig-saw puzzles! And the last thing I remember pondering groggily upon, as I lay in the dark frowning and feeling the tentacles of that multiplonal creeping over my entire nervous system, was whether that Chinaman really had a white confederate, and how in the devil—if it was the Chinaman himself who had decoyed me to that vacant house—he had ever been able to spout the Bible so fluently; and the first thing I knew when I woke up was the mathematical fact that one grain of multiplonal creates practically one hour's sleep—for it was seven in the evening—of the next day!

What a sleep that was! I felt fit as a fiddle. With not an ache in my head. And now I was officially back in the city, according to the way my wire to my employer had been worded—and I prepared to go up and make the call I had specified in that wire.

I dressed, by dint of some clean linen I unearthed on a closet shelf, and went downstairs, where I borrowed both Mrs. W-B's morning *Tribune* and her evening *News*. And, on general principles, looked in the lost-and-found columns of both. I hardly expected to find anything in the *Tribune*, as the exchange of bags had taken place too close to its want-ad deadline. And, as a matter of fact, I found nothing concerning bags of any kind in either paper. The nearest that even came to my case were two frantically worded ads, in the evening *News*, of two women who had accidentally carried off each other's French poodles the previous afternoon in the Boston Store.

All of which left me none the wiser than when I had last gone to bed.

I ate a good dinner up the street in a basement tea room, and at 8 o'clock was bowling along atop a Diversey Boulevard bus to Roger Pelton's home just north of Lincoln Park. At the old three-story home of grey Bedford stone, with its curved glass windows, I rang the bell and waited. And neither maid—nor Filkins, the butler and man-about-house—answered the door. For it was opened by no less a person than Doris herself, who marched out onto the narrow front stoop—looked up and down the street to make sure that there were not more than twenty-five or thirty people at most in the vicinity, flung her slender arms about my neck—and kissed me squarely on the lips.

Sweet that kiss, like our butter-cream-center bar. And blonde she was, like our Crispo Taffy. With eyes as blue as jelly bean No. 18—which goes in the jelly bean mixture No. 9. Dressed all in pink silk, as pink and as crisp as our Silko-Spun Crunch.

But I'm talking in crude trade terms—about something too fine to compare with mere candy.

"Come in, Clay," she said gayly. "Father's waiting to greet the victorious traveler—home from the wars!"

I held her off at arm's-length, however, enjoying to its full extent the luxury of feasting my eyes on this delicate, blonde being of nineteen summers—and twenty winters!—after my long seven weeks' absence. And as I stood there, I found myself wondering something that I had often wondered before: how I could ever adjust myself to life again, if something should come between us—something that should prevent our marriage. Then, since there were still no more than twenty-five or thirty people, at most, passing on both sides of Diversey Boulevard, I kissed her again. And we went in.

Roger Pelton rose and greeted me warmly, with outstretched hand, as we entered the parlor, with its soft monotone rug and its rose-colored lamps. A dignified sort of man he was, though not at all a forbidding one; about fifty years of age—with well-defined grey in his hair. He wore a velvet smoking jacket tonight. And it seemed to me that he looked a trifle careworn, worried, which his next words quite belied.

"Well, Clay, I'm glad to see you. We're getting orders galore for Julu-flavored candy. I went out after them the minute I got your cable."

"Which," pouted Doris, "was practically four long weeks ago. What on earth, Clay, ever induced you to come back by such a slow passenger steamer?"

"Passenger steamer?" I echoed with a laugh. "It wasn't even that. It was a freighter that took occasional passengers. No radio news. No orchestral din. Just sweet peace. Calm water. Rippling moonlight. And—and Sophie!"

"Sophie!" This from Doris. "Have you been philandering on me, across the Pacific, Clay Calthorpe?" But the tone of her words showed that she knew the mysterious Sophie was no rival of hers.

"I fear I have," I said darkeningly. "But let's sit down. And I'll tell you about it. Because Sophie—or Suing Sophie, as she's known on the Pacific—is my big worry now!"

We took seats, Roger Pelton sitting back in the high pew-backed chair he generally occupied, Doris snuggling up on a footstool close to my chair, her hands on my knee. We didn't have to conceal our affection from Roger Pelton. As a prospective son-in-law, I had passed all the tests!

"Well," I began, "I didn't relish coming back with that chattering world-tourist crowd on the *Robert Dollar* that was next due out of Manila. And if I hung over till the next boat, the *Pacifica,* due in Manila from Hong Kong, I would be as long getting home as if I went right away on the freighter *American Marine* that was just scheduled to leave. So I booked on it. I like being on water—as both of you well know."

"Yes," Doris pouted up at me from her stool, "but who's this wondrous creature—this Sophie?"

"Sophie," I said gravely, "was a tall plain woman about forty-five years of age, who wore a starched collar and a shirtwaist, stiff tweed skirt and jacket, and her hair in a topknot. She was—and is!—a missionary in the Philippine Islands—an independent one—doesn't work out from any church—has money of her own.

"Though not a bad traveling companion at all, Sophie wasn't," I added. "No, not a bad traveling companion at all!"

I paused. "Well," I went on, "it seems she comes back here to the States on a three-month rest every year—has relatives down around Oklahoma City, Northern Texas, and Arkansas. Always returns to the USA by the *American Marine.* Doesn't like the—well—flibberti-gibbets she encounters on regular vessels.

"The first night aboard," I continued, "the captain came to me. To my cabin. He was sort of troubled. 'Mr. Calthorpe,' he said, 'I want to ask a favor of you. Don't divulge to Miss Sophie Kratzenschneider-wumpel any details of where you live—or who you work for. Or who your friends are.'

"'Why—on earth?' I asked him.

"He stroked his chin uneasily. 'Well—she's known as "Suing Sophie." She invariably falls in love with a male passenger—if we've got one, that is—by or before we get to the end of our journey; and by Gad, sir, she's she's sued six of my past passengers now, for breach of promise! Rather, five of the six were regular passengers; the sixth was my chief purser on that particular trip.'

"'Do—do they propose?' I asked him.

"'No,' he said. 'But I suppose the moon makes 'em a little too friendly like. Or else it touches her someway. Or again, maybe she's just trying to catch herself a man. A woman alienist that came across with me once, when Sophie was aboard too, told me Sophie was a bit touched—but not dangerous. I think myself it's a racket of hers—for whatever they settle for—oh, yes, she's made a number of men pony up to keep from being written up in the papers all over the United States—she contributes to her mission in the Islands. So *you* watch *your* step. She's a heller for suing men!'

"So I watched my step," I told both Doris and Roger Pelton. "Though I couldn't see much necessity of it. Sophie Kratzenschneiderwumpel was a really entertaining and bright woman. And we sat on deck many a day, and many nights, talking about many topics. But I never told her anything concrete about myself, though—other than that I lived in Chicago. And was a salesman. And she didn't ask.

"I noticed," I now told them both, "that the last night aboard ship she seemed a little bit sentimental. Poor Sophie! You know, I feel sorry—"

"Ne' mind pitying other wimmen," said Doris sternly. "Go on with this confession."

"Well, little jealous cat," I told her, "I noticed that Sophie acted a little skittish. And she said to me, curiously: 'I—I don't know what to say, Mr. Calthorpe, about your proposition. I like you immensely—but I have my work.' Then I knew that the old psychosis—or racket—or whatever it was—was getting in its work. Boy—oh boy—and was I glad I had kept my trap shut about myself!

"We parted friendly enough at the pier," I went on. "I told her to write me care of General Delivery at Chicago until I got located. And she gave me some address in the South. Which I subsequently threw away. And as her taxicab started to drive off towards her depot, she leaned out the window.

"'My answer, darling,' she said, 'is "yes." I will be your wife!' And off she went."

"Why—Clay Calthorpe!" began Doris. "Did you—"

"Wait, my sweet," I told her. "Remember, I've never asked anybody to be my wife but you, ever."

She smiled up at me, a little uneasily; so I hurried on with the story so that she could see how ridiculous the whole affair was.

"Well," I stated, "when I got aboard the train for Chicago, right after buying myself a bag to put my traveling essentials in instead of a battered-up suitcase plastered with labels, I nearly had heart disease. In fact, I was several hours out from 'Frisco when I got the shock—that I *did* get. I was looking in my pocket for my notebook. A little slender pebbled-leather affair, with maps in it, and alphabetically indexed. One that has your name in it, Mr. Pelton—and your address here on Diversey—entered from way back when I first came up here to the house, at your request, to see you about coming into the sales end of your business. And the correct name and new Austin Avenue address of the company too. Probably you recall my putting that down that night. But it doesn't matter. The book also has the name and address of John Barr—you've both heard me speak of John Barr, I'm sure—that friend of mine who's somewhat older than myself. And Mrs. Winterbotham-Higginsbottom's name and address, just as I entered it when I first saw that upstairs room of hers that I liked so much. And it has a number of other names and addresses, put in as I first encountered them." I paused again. "And as I hunted all over my clothes for that fool notebook, I suddenly remembered where I'd had it last. Sophie and I had had a discussion, that last night aboard ship, about the actual location of some South Sea Island where she'd converted some cannibal chief who had accepted the Jewish Faith, to Christianity. I was certain she had located the island wrong, even if she had been there. And I told her I had a small notebook around somewhere in my things that had some microscopic maps in it. And I went to my stateroom and got it. And last thing I know she had the notebook in her hand—open at the map of Borneo and the South Seas. And we were talking about some brand-new topic. The Fourth Dimension, I think it was."

"Oh-oh!" commented Doris. "And you forgot and went off to bed without it—and she put the notebook in her purse. And omitted to give it back to you next day. And she has it now?"

"Exactly," I admitted. "And if you don't want your future hubby sued for breach of promise by a poor woman who has, so far as I can figure it out, wheels in her head—bless her soul—good scout, Sophie, outside of that confounded suing habit of hers—with my picture and hers, and yours too, in all likelihood, in all the newspapers—then you just be sure, if and when you get any inquiries about me from her general direction, that you don't even know me." I turned to Roger Pelton. "Will you back me up on that, Mr. Pelton?"

"Oh, sure, Clay. Sure. You don't even work for us, in case she tries to line you up through the factory or office. Kindest thing we can do, in her case, is just to cut off all leads to you. And I'll fix it with Filkins, the butler—it's his night off—and Marie, the maid, too. Don't worry. Sophie Kratzen—and so-forth—will just surmise, if she inquires about you, that the notebook she has isn't something of yours personally at all—that it's just something you found in your stateroom. Sure it hasn't your name in it, though?"

"Yes. Absolutely sure. My name isn't in it. And my telephone, as you both know, is an unlisted number, and can't be gotten from the phone company by hook nor crook, bribery, threats, coercion or wire-pulling. But the book has in it the names of all the rest of you folks all right, all right. And there's the rub!"

"Well, you just tip off such other persons as are in it—though watch out that you don't overlook some salient one—and we'll cleverly put a stop to all possible suing. Poor creature. Will she call up? Or what?"

"God knows," I said. "She may call up Long Distance from Oklahoma City. Or somewhere like that. Or she may get hold of a lawyer down there—the captain told me she's hired lawyers before—who will try to get a line on me for her."

"Say, Clay Calthorpe," put in Doris. "Did—did you make love to that woman?"

"Listen, sweetness," I told her, "anybody who would make love to poor Suing Sophie when he had a Doris Pelton back home would be as minus brains as an editorial writer on the *Chicago Tribune*. In short, he would have 'scathered wits'—as a certain plainclothesman here in Chicago calls them."

"Scathered wits?" echoed Roger Pelton amusedly. And then began to look distraught again.

"Yes," I said. "Scathered wits! Which reminds me: First of all now, I got in last night—instead of tonight. I didn't lie over at 'Frisco for the twenty-four hours my wire said I was going to."

"Well, well, Clay," was all Pelton said. "And we thought tonight was your first night back in Chicago."

"And where have you been keeping yourself, sir?" Doris chided me. "Who's the woming?"

"I've been sleeping," I told her. "Fifteen hours—on fifteen grains of multiplonal!"

"Clay Calthorpe! Have you become a drug fiend as well as a philanderer?"

I smiled.

"Folks," I said, "my taking that multiplonal was because I had an adventure. The durndest adventure you ever heard. It couldn't have happened anywhere except in Chicago. Do you want to hear it?"

"Sure thing, Clay," urged Roger Pelton. "Let's hear it."

"Well," I commenced, "it was this way. When I walked west from the Union Station at Randolph and Michigan last night about 7 o'clock, I boarded a Broadway car under the big Marshall Field timepiece. I chucked my black bag under the seat I sat down in. Under myself, in short. And when I got up at Burton Place and Clark Street, some twenty minutes later, to leave the car, I reached under myself, grabbed—and got a bag."

"Your bag, you mean," corrected Doris.

"Not exactly. For it seems that at Chicago Avenue we reversed the car, the controllers, the trolley poles, the backs of the seats, the passengers, and the conductor's brains all at the same time! For this Teutonic supergenius in hyper-geometry had the gall—or supreme ignorance—to reach down in back of my seat and shift two similar bags that he saw underneath it—he thought, you see, that myself and the man I was riding next to had got 'ge-shifted,' as he terms it, with respect to those two bags, or that the bags had gotten 'ge-shifted' relative to us. Neither of which was the case, of course. So the bag I took out from under the seat was the other man's. And the bag that got left—and which at the time I knew nothing about—was my own, which fortunately had in it seven or eight of my cards, bearing the address of the Essex, strapped together with a rubber band." I paused a second. "And so as I say, I blissfully drew forth the other man's bag. But he was busy reading and wasn't paying any particular attention to things about him, though probably the outcome wouldn't have been any different if he had been."

"Did he afterward get in touch with you?" asked Doris. "Through those cards?"

"I was afterward gotten in touch with—yes," I replied unsmilingly. Which was about the best way I could answer *that* question, at this juncture of my narrative. I paused a second. Then went on.

"Well, to go back once more to the time of the exchange of bags, I jumped off the car and hurried on toward Dearborn Parkway. And believe it or not—as Ripley says—but a chap on the car who'd been eying me rather generously all the way, followed me clear to the steps of the Essex and stopped me long enough to get a match with which he looked me well over after 'twas lighted. But I reached my room with no further delay, and finally found an old key that would unlock the bag, which I found wasn't mine when I went to open it with my own regular key.

"But here," I continued, "is the funny part about the adventure

—and let me advise you that thus far you've heard only the first portion of it. The chap that followed me was a Chinaman—"

"A Chinaman?" echoed Roger Pelton and Doris together, almost in the same breath.

"Yes," I asserted, watching the expression of utter wonderment on Doris's delicate face. "And the bag contained a skull in which was driven a round metal plate, that read—"

But Doris had risen suddenly to her feet. She was staring at the high-backed chair in which her father was sitting.

"Quick—Clay!" she cried. "A glass of water. Father has fainted!"

CHAPTER VI

JOHN BARR

I have never been able to boast of having many close friends, the reason being, very likely, that from the time I was left alone in the world at the age of sixteen, I've been too busy earning my living to cultivate them. But, like every well-established rule, my condition of relative friendlessness had its exception.

That exception was John Barr.

For five years we had been as chums—almost brothers, one might say. And this, in spite of the fact that he was old enough, nearly, to be my father. My age was twenty-nine; his was forty-nine. Like myself, he was a bachelor. But while my condition of bachelorhood, however, appeared to be one that was soon to be terminated, his, on the contrary, seemed to be established for life—a part of his very nature.

In appearance he was a big, broad-shouldered man, with a face which was by no means devoid of the charm that seems to appeal to womankind. He wore a brown Vandyke beard, which he kept always neatly trimmed; and a mustache, also as precisely and neatly trimmed as the beard which seemed a very integral part of it. Yet no dandy, in any respect, was John Barr, for he dressed always in dark blue or black suits, with ties and other accessories utterly subdued in tone; and, strangely, the man's individuality was actually heightened by such quiet garb—and not lessened! As for his tastes, they seemed to be nearly identical with mine in everything. We roasted

51

the same best sellers, liked the same plays, went to the same wrestling matches. He manufactured, as I say—though on an extremely tiny scale—what was known to the trade as the "Barr-Bag"—an efficient overnight bag of unusually up-to-date lines, and extremely honestly made to every last one of its hand-drawn stitches and hand-driven rivets. And when I say tiny scale, I mean just that, for John Barr had the soul of a craftsman—and not of a Ford automobile factory; and his bags were turned out in a small attic shop over on Fulton Street, provided with a sloping skylight whose north light showed in advance any falsities in the hue of the leather going into them, and his whole output was created by but two expert leather workers working ever under his appraising eye. He was the rest of his shop crew—of his entire company, in fact, for he functioned as salesman as well as sales manager, and advertising manager as well as stenographer, scorning, in the latter matter, such things as type-written communications, and writing all his correspondence by hand on heavy de luxe grey-toned linen paper headed "BARR-BAG"— THE STUDIO WHERE IT IS CREATED. And he obtained such orders as he did obtain either through direct correspondence with leather-goods stores all over the country, or, as was most often the case, their writing in to him for prices because customers had asked for "Barr-Bag." He had brought up his little pseudo-artistic business to a point where it now earned a fairish income for himself, yet he lived the quietest of lives.

The circumstances under which we met were unusual, to say the least. Three years ago I had started in the employ of Roger Pelton. And to familiarize myself with his field, I had begun as a city sales-man. One of his biggest customers, a Greek who ran a downtown Eat-Shop under a French name, and who simply couldn't see Greek confectionery, one day paid me some $450 on his bill, taking my receipt for it as a representative of the Pelton Company, for a tea-reader in one of the many tea-reading lunchrooms about the Loop had told him his place would get held up that afternoon. The place didn't get held up—for the tea-reader must have misread the leaves—and neither did I, for that matter. I just lost the $450—to a pickpocket on a Madison Street car whose own tea-reader must have told him to try, at such and such an hour, the left hip pocket of the man on the third left strap in such-and-such a car. Which man was myself. And all I had to remind myself of that wad was the memory of the jostling that slick-looking beggar had given me.

I didn't have a cent to my name to make it up to the Pelton offices. Moreover, Roger Pelton had seen on my desk, the previous week, a copy of *Colliers Eye,* the paper which gives all the racing information. It wasn't my copy—one of the clerks had dropped it there. And though I disclaimed ownership of it, I could see that he wasn't sure that I wasn't playing the races. He was death on gambling—so all the employees said.

I thought things over. Here I was, in line for a good sales-managership—from which I might get bounced before it even began to develop with me. The cheapest thing to do, so far as I could see, was to go borrow the money—and pay it in. And pipe down on any stories about losing it, which wouldn't probably be believed at all.

But—$450! I I didn't have a chance. Every loan shark in town, when he learned I had worked only two weeks for this firm, and had no collateral whatsoever, turned me down.

I placed a blind advertisement in the Chicago Tribune stating that I was a young man in financial straits that were not of my own making, who wished to borrow a considerable sum of money on my salary—and against huge prospects. Among the many answers I received, most of which were form replies sent by the very loan sharks who had already turned me down, was a kindly letter from one "John Barr," asking me to call at his rooms at 251 East Superior Street, which were on the North Side, just on the western fringe of "Streeterville." I did so. I found him such a pleasant—and at the same time sympathetic and understanding—individual that I told him the whole story. With the result that he financed me through the crisis—loaned me the money with no security but my note—not even a salary assignment—which note I was a good year in redeeming. And not even 6 per cent interest on said note would he ever accept! A year afterward, I fell sick with typhoid fever. And after just paying up an old moral debt connected with my father's last illness. Again John Barr—to my rescue with money for hospital bills, doctors, nurses, medicine, and what not. "Don't annoy your employer," he had said, "by trying to borrow from him on your salary. For he'll respect you more if he thinks you've got a nest egg." That was John Barr's theory—and so he insisted on financing my illness. But he provided far more than the mere details of medical attention, for I didn't know Doris Pelton then, and many dreary hours I would have spent if it had not been for John Barr at my bedside reading to me—talking to me—or else cheering me through my convalescence.

So much for the friendship existing between John Barr and myself. It has lasted all these years—and I have no doubt whatever but that it will endure until one or the other of us passes—across! Wherever "across" may be!

After I left Doris's home—from which I made a hasty adieu after we brought her father out of his faint, and got him to bed and called their family doctor—puzzled beyond all description at his sudden illness—collapse—whatever it was—I at once made my way southward to East Superior Street, where shortly I was ascending the high wooden steps of No. 251, the tall new skyscrapers of Streeterville just to the east giving a glimpse between themselves of the moonlit lake beyond. My coming must have been expected by John Barr, for, when the lace-aproned servant girl which No. 251 boasted appeared, she stepped aside with the remark:

"Go right on up, sir. Mr. Barr said he was expecting you to call tonight."

As I had anticipated, he was waiting for me in the doorway of his two-room suite on the second floor. "Come in, Clay," he said cheerily, "and tell your obedient servant all about it. Did you tie up all the Julu berries in the Philippine Islands? I got your wire all right from Salt Lake City, and dropped in on you last night; but you were out—so I got tired of waiting—and came back home. For I'm supposed to get plenty of sleep and rest in preparation for a certain little forthcoming op—er, never mind! Did you know I'd been over to your diggings?"

"Yes," I told him, seizing his outstretched hand. "Mrs. Winterbotham-H told me you had. And about the Julu berries, I have them all tied up to the thousandth generation of the berries now hanging on the vines. But I didn't come up to talk about Julu berries. I came up to—well—ask your wise opinion about a curious little adventure I've had. And a further aftermath of it. Up at the Peltons' tonight."

"Come in," he said.

I entered his big commodious room, with its antique furniture, its highboy, and its polished brass andirons fronting the fireplace which, in spite of the steam radiators in the rooms, he actually sometimes used on winter evenings; and he closed the door. I dropped into a comfortable woven-reed chair, and he into an oak one.

"Fire away," he said smilingly.

"Well," I began. "But—say—didn't I just hear you say something—rather—start to say something—about an operation? Or—or did I get something all wrong?"

He gazed at me with the quizzically painful expression of a man who hated, like everything, the least solicitude—at least on the part of his friends—about his own well-being; of a man who had inadvertently let slip something of which he would far preferred to have said nothing.

"We-e-ell—yes," he admitted reluctantly. "I guess you heard right!"

"Why—you alarm me, old chap. What's—what's it about?"

"Nothing at all," he hastened to assure me. "Just a throat operation. And something, moreover, that can be done right in the doctor's office—and will be. Either tomorrow morning at 11 a.m. Or the next day at 2 p.m. in the afternoon. Depending on when my doctor gets back from some Medical Conference going on at Minneapolis. And lets me know by phone that he's ready for me. It'll be done by 'suspended laryngoscopy'—at least that's what the specialist calls it. It's a manner in which, for the operator, is thrown into his direct view the patient's entire pharynx, larynx and the upper end of his esophagus—if you know what them things is! I can't say that I do."

"But what's—what's the trouble, John?"

"Nothing now. So we want to avoid it later. Remember that curious rasping cough I had? Well, it was due, as appears now, to a tumorous growth on—on the right side of my throat. Yes, several inches below the tonsils. Yes, that's right—around where the windpipe comes in! An angioma, the specialist calls the growth. It's benign—not malign, for he clipped out a piece and had it under the microscope. Also, right across the way from it—in the same neck of the woods, you might say!—I'm a symmetrical sort of a culprit, it seems!—I've a nodule. A no-account, good-for-nothing nodule— that doesn't even rank as a laryngeal tumor. But—well—I'm getting on towards the cancer age, you know—no, boy, they're not cancer— really!—and the specialist says the thing to do is to chop 'em out so that they never can get that way. One must keep one's throat in trim, you know, to sing the necessary paeans to the Republican Party— once it gets back again into the White House!" He dropped his bantering tone. "Anyway, he's going to chop the angioma out—under cocaine or some kind of local anesthetic, and looking down in this periscope all the while!—and, while he's down there, he's going to take the nodule off 'tother side at the same time. Sort of—fall housecleaning! 'Twon't hurt a bit. And won't endanger me. So don't look so grave. To tell you the truth—knowing all the fuss you'd make over me—it had been my original intention to have the doctor's girl secretary ring you up over there at the Essex on the downstairs hall phone—for I seem to have mislaid your personal phone number again—ring you up, as I say, twenty-four hours after the operation was past, over and done with, and tell you briefly of the facts."

"Well," I replied, "I'm sure glad it's nothing but what you say it is. And as to my personal phone number—here 'tis again: Delaware 6622. And, moreover, if this gal sec'tary had done this, she would have learned from Mrs. Winterbotham-H that Mrs. Winterbotham-H didn't even know me—and that I don't even live there."

"That—that you don't even live there?" he echoed puzzledly. "But—you do. Why—how—"

And so, dismissing things surgical for the moment, in view of the fact that they were not so grave as I had at first imagined, I told him about Suing Sophie. Disgruntledly. He surveyed me dryly. And there was a twinkle in his eye.

"Well, confound it, Clay, what do you want to seduce virtuous Christian ladies aboard ocean vessels for?"

"Seduce her?" I exclaimed bitterly. "Why I never even squeezed her hand. She's known, I tell you, as Suing Sophie—she sues 'em right and left."

"Must be a psychosis," he commented gravely. And dropped his persiflage. "And you say my name's in your alphabetical notebook too? Then she'll maybe be trying to get a line on you—through me?"

"Yes, and confound it, John, if you so much as let out a peep—"

"Cease thy fears," he said. "I won't know you any more than the next Republican President will know a Democratic job-holder the day after election!"

"Then that's that," I said, a bit relievedly. "We'll come back, before I go out of here tonight, to this—this matter of your operation. And how soon I can call on you. And in the meantime—well—I was about to tell you about my adventure."

"Proceed—do," he ordered me, untroubledly.

"Well, it begins first," I told him after a brief pause, "with a very fine and de luxe bag, made of genuine leather, known as the Barr-Bag."

"I know the bag well," he declared solemnly. "For I make it!"

"Yes, and man alive—if you knew the sales campaign I put up for you in 'Frisco—you'd book me up to receive a weekly commission for life."

"How so?"

"Well, when I got off the ship I didn't want to lug the monstrosity of a suitcase I had, aboard a Pullman. It was ancient enough when I took it West, and now, coming back, it was plastered with labels to call the attention of all the world to its being one of Noah's original suitcases. So I checked it for the time being. And went into a leather-goods store. The first such store I found. And told 'em I wanted a handbag—overnight bag. They showed me plenty—but no, a Barr-Bag is what I must have! The finest bag in the world—and the only one a decent man would carry. And I walked out on 'em."

"Attaboy, Clay! And then what?"

"Then I went on up the same business street—and into another leather-goods store. And the same thing all over again. Man, but I was loyal to you and your bag. I could have bought a dozen different kinds. But I was out to keep the business in the 'fambly'! So—no Barr-Bag. And on I went. This time to a big department store. Shadduck's, I think it was.

"Here, in the leather-goods and travelers' sundries department I bowwowed and belly-ached so loud about the virtues of the Barr-Bag that all the clerks, for a hundred feet around, stopped to listen. And they found one—up on a shelf somewhere. And I bought it. And thus began my adventure."

"And likewise," put in John Barr, "begins my regret that all this didn't happen in Chicago—instead of 'Frisco. For one thing, because said Barr-Bag would have cost you nothing. And for the other thing, that I've since improved it a bit. For it has now incorporated within it the Billy Bulger Bulge—which, though simple as the devil, costs me sixty-six cents per bag in royalties."

"And what does the Billy Bulger Bulge do?"

"Holds the bag rigidly open to any point you pull it out to. It—but do you remember that leather pocket-like affair inside the bag?"

I nodded.

"Well, keep a mirror stuck in there, pull the opposite side of the bag halfway open—stick it on a shelf—and you have a shaving mirror. It's a far more handy contraption, the bulge is, than it sounds—and so the old Barr-Bag is no more."

"I see. Well what is the Billy Bulger Bulge—and who is Billy Bulger who made the bulge?"

"He doesn't make the bulge! We make it. And pay him for the privilege. Billy Bulger is just a mechanic up in Michigan. He patented his bulge—and we, and all other bag-makers, from now on pay him royalties. It's just what its name is: a bulge, or convexity, shaped like a sine curve, which we stamp into the flange of the outermost of the two pieces of metal framework which form the jaws of the bag. At each end—over the pivot-hinge. And there's a sort of round teat, also, on the flange of the innermost jaw. Same place. We stamp both the bulge and the teat into the respective pieces with dies. You can see the bulge from outside the bag—it looks more artistic than like a defect—but you don't see the teat. As the bag is opened, the very convex teat travels along the sine curve representing the concave side of the Billy Bulger Bulge, with constantly increasing pressure against the edge of the curve, so that the more open the bag is made and the more it consequently tends to fly shut—the less it can close. Yet if you depress the hinges with your thumbs, just as you do any bag—you release the pressure instantly and the bag flies shut."

"Well, old man," I said chidingly, "since you've now incorporated in the Barr-Bag the Billy Bulger Bulge—why in the devil don't you incorporate in it also a lock that can't be opened?"

He looked puzzled. "Don't you know," he queried, "that we never put intricate locks on bags of any kind? That people lose their keys so frequently that we have to make locks simple enough that they can dig up another key?"

"I see," I said, as a new angle of the bag-making industry made itself known to me for the first time.

"Have you lost your key?" he asked. "Here—" And he pulled out a ring of keys from his pocket, and started to work off from it a key with a brightly polished flat nickeled head. "Here, son, is a master key that unlocks every one of the twenty-eight combinations of tumbler mechanisms in the simple Fornheimer lock that appears on all Barr-Bags. I give it to you—as one of the perquisites of friendship."

I waved it back before he had it detached. "Thanks—but I lost the whole Barr-Bag! And have no further use of keys for same."

He ran the master key back to its companion keys. And looked at me helplessly.

"Well now, what—or is that the adventure? That you bought one of my bags—of the type that from now on will be archaic—and that you lost it again?"

"Gosh no!" I told him. "That's just the beginning."

With which, leaning back in his comfortable woven-reed arm-chair, I told him the whole of the tale from beginning to end, not omitting to recite for him all the data that was inscribed on that round circular plate driven into the clean round hole in the skull. I felt, I confess, a little too sheepish to tell him that I had been ill-bred enough to sequester not only the fragments of the carbon-copy letter that had helped to stuff the skull and hold the bullet therein, simply for the reason that at the time I had done that sneaking bit of pettifoggery I hadn't any justification whatsoever for prying into another man's personal affairs. And John Barr himself being a gentleman, if ever there was one!—well—I did, some-how, want to hold on to all of his respect. But I did tell him, at least, of how I raked the pieces of paper out; and, as best as I could remember, of the puzzling statements: "his heart is whole, and mine"—"He's gone"—"Every hour is filled with fear for me"—etc.—which showed up on some of the fragments. He heard me through, eyes wide, chin in hand.

"Well, Clay, such an adventure as that could happen only in Chicago, the town where life invariably outdoes drama. Mrs. Winterbotham-Higginsbottom did tell me the initial part of it—namely, that a Chinese footpad, with long black mustaches and resembling exactly Fu Manchu, and carrying a long knife in his hand, and walking in felt slippers, tried to sneak up on you last night presumably to knife you in the back, but that you escaped him by turning quickly in at her place. I knew the lady's tendency to dramatize quite ordinary incidents, and so figured that some laun-dryman just asked you for the time, or that some Chinese panhan-dler followed you to beg you for a nickel. But now that the real facts come out as between the two versions—well—A Chinaman who quotes the Bible—a minister transporting a dead man's skull—the skull stuffed with paper containing—well—such sentiments as you've described, plus a bullet!—and—but you were a real thor-oughbred, Clay, just as I always found you to be, to put 'em all back in the skull, and—or did you?"

Thoroughbred! Clay Calthorpe—a real thoroughbred!

Ouch!

"Yes," I muttered. "Stuffed 'em all back in—no, didn't even put 'em together—stuffed 'em in—bullet too—hrmph!"

"And lost the whole shebang," he commented. He ruminated a moment. "But man, that should have all been in the papers this morning? Which it wasn't, I'm sure—for I read the *Herald-Examiner* pretty thoroughly. No, there wasn't the least mention of you—and your experience. How—how come, do you suppose?"

"Well," I told him, a bit glad to change the subject from that of my being a 24-carat thoroughbred, "I didn't spill to the desk sergeant at the Police Station about what was in the bag. I was trying to be decent, you see, to the Reverend Duncan Craig—and here, by golly, the Reverend didn't even exist! So I naturally had to keep shut up about it afterward, to the plainclothesman who went back to 1870 Lake Shore Drive with me. As for the Chinky hold-up man— yes—that would have made a story all in itself—but the desk sergeant had some kind of a grouch on last night against the leg-men covering East Chicago Avenue, all of whom, when I came in, were down at the corner swilling beer—and so they missed out. For which I'm just as glad. And now what's your theory about it all?"

He thought deeply for a long minute.

"Theories on a thing like that are damned hard to create. Like yourself, I believe it was the Chinaman who decoyed you over there to that deserted house, and not a white confederate—for you say he asked you for that match in a more or less disguised voice. Funny, though, that the heathen should know how to quote the Bible. A sort of ecclesiastical tangle, all in all. And it—but you say that your employer, Roger Pelton, fainted dead away when you got to the point in your story where you opened the bag?"

"I'll say! He just passed out pronto. We called their doctor, and I got out, after asking Doris to ring me up only in case there were something serious."

He shook his head slowly from side to side.

"It's a puzzler all right, all right. But I'm very much inclined to doubt, Clay, whether this man Pelton is likely to have anything to say when he recovers his composure by a night's rest in bed. I'll bet you a half a dozen Barr-Bags, all equipped with the new Billy Bulger Bulge, that he'll just claim he was overworked—tired. But I will tell you, Clay, exactly what I would do, if I were you."

"What?"

"As follows. I would—" But John Barr stopped speaking as a knock came on the door of his rooms.

He stepped to the door and opened it.

The same servant girl with the lace apron, who had let me in, stood there. "'Scuse me, Mister Barr, but a Mr. Jake Chudders—yes, Chudders—is on the downstairs wire. Do you want me to say you're in—or out?"

"Chudders, you say? Oh yes—Chudders. No, just tell him I'm out, and—no, wait—never mind. I'll go down and talk to him. Have him hold the wire."

She left.

"The most indefatigable leather salesman in the Middle West," he said smiling. "If he ever just once got hold of the unlisted number of this phone in my rooms, he'd ring me not less than once a week, and probably at midnight at that, by Long Distance in the bargain, even if he was in Los Angeles, to talk me into buying some especially good hides. I couldn't keep him from getting hold of the number assigned to No. 251 E. Superior here—but I do keep him off my private phone. However, I am getting a bit low on leather—so I'll talk with him."

He rose. "However," he went on, "I'll give you something to entertain yourself with while I'm gone. It's a long narrative poem, in manuscript form, by a Chicago poetess named Abigail Sprigge. Deeply profound—as well as deeply moving! How it comes to be in my hands, I'll tell you when I get back. I—"

"Listen, John," I said faintly, "you—you know what I think about poetry. And poets to boot. Tell me all about it—and Abigail too, if you wish—but don't, for Crissakes, make me read the effusion. Have—have a heart!"

He grinned.

"I'm only kidding you, boy. Just because I do know how poetry bores you—and how you hate poetry writers. I held this out purposely to show you tonight—it's one of a number of submittances to Philodexter Maxellus's proposed new magazine—what?—haven't I ever told you about Philodexter?—well, anyway, read it. I held it out for you because, in my estimation, it's your kind of 'pome.' Just the length you can stand. And just the amount of poetical depth you like!"

I looked at him searchingly. I detected that I was catching a good-natured ribbing, in spite of his grin. He was opening the drawer of his study table, and withdrawing from it a folded, but evidently single, sheet of green-tinted paper.

"Be back in a couple of seconds," he said, handing me the sheet. "And will tell you all about Philodexter and his venture."

And he departed.

Disgruntledly, I opened up the poem. Whose length, according to J. B., was calibrated to my grasp of poetry! And whose depth was exactly that of my poetical appreciation!

And when I looked upon it, I winced. For I knew I had been deeply, deeply kidded this day!

It was but four typewritten lines. And very, very short lines, too. Alongside of which had been stamped, in red ink.

LETTER ACCOMPANYING: FILED

And in its entirety it ran:

POOR PICKINGS
by
ABIGAIL SPRIGGE

A burglar entered by mistake
A poetess's room one day.
And finding there was nothing else
To steal, he stole away.

But what I didn't know while I read the jingle—for jingle was all it was—was that within twelve hours—and helped as much as was possible by John Barr himself—I would be trying with all my might and main to get in touch with Abigail Sprigge. The finding of whom would solve not only many mysteries—but one or two problems in my life as well!

CHAPTER VII

ADVICE

I was still sitting with the poemlet on my knee when John Barr returned. And closed the door behind him.

"Well, indefatigability certainly pays," he commented. "For Chudders sold me! Twenty-seven complete hides. Of a new kind of leather!" He dropped down into his oak chair once more. "So now back to our conversation. But first—did you read Miss Sprigge's immortal work?"

"I did," I said. And added grumpily: "And thanks, John, for the compliment. Yes. The one you paid me just before you stepped out. And if you ask me—well—it's a damned good poem. Because it's got but four lines, and they're damned short! And it's further a good one, because it isn't all gooey with flowers, and springtime, and love, and what—the—"

"—hell!" he finished. "Well, I just thought I'd get a rise out of the anti-poetry hound," he added. "That's why I held it out. To show you tonight."

"Well," I queried, "who is Miss Sprigge? And who is Philodexter Maximum? Or Maximus? Or whatever his name is? And what's it all about—since I'm the goat?" He smiled. And took the poem from my fingers.

"Philodexter's a sort of rapidly growing business friend of mine. I met him sometime back when he came up to see us personally about a specially made Barr-Bag. He was, years ago. he says, business manager for *Poesy*—now many years defunct. He has a good bit of money today that he doesn't exactly need, and thinks the time is ripe—with certain circulation ideas he has—to start up another magazine. One dealing with Pegasus, that is! In fact, he's ready to launch it. And is going—at least so he says—to call it just *Verse*."

"It'll fail sure," I retorted. "All poetry is a drug on the market."

"I don't know," was John Barr's reply. "He's got a lot of good circulation ideas. For one thing, he's going to publish *Verse* in flexible cloth covers. Some new cheap process which actually gives cloth for not much more than the cost of paper stock. Which cloth covers will lead people who buy the publication once to keep on buying it—to build up an actual cloth-bound poetry library. A sort of—of forty-two-foot shelf, you might call it! Also, he isn't going to circulate it by mail. Which will give him an opportunity to work a lot of high-class prize offers—and contests—for purchasers of it—stunts that come almost too close to being lotteries to allow him second-class postal entry—or even mailing. Though they're all innocent enough, so far as I can see. Again, he's going to put it on the news-stands sealed—but at fifty cents the copy. In other words, make poetry lovers pay dearly for a small thirty-two-page magazine catering to them alone—and one which won't cost more than nine cents to produce. He says that those who like poetry and verse will pay the fifty cents without cavil; while those that don't—like yourself, Clay—couldn't be induced to carry such a magazine off, free gratis."

"Huzzah—and correct," I said.

He went on speaking.

"Also, amongst Philodexter's ideas is an ingenious one: to have no unsold copies. It isn't the sold copies, he says, that make a publishing game profitable; it's the unsold ones that break a publisher! Anyway, he's dividing the entire USA into a series of circular zones radiating out from Chicago. All copies of *Verse* will have to be returned by news-dealers complete. That is, not just covers, as with an ordinary magazine. They'll then have a new date-page tipped in—in place of the old one—and be shipped out again, to the next zone outermost. For instance, Clay, the returns from Zone 1 will be shipped out to Zone 2. The unsold copies of Zone 2 will be shipped out to Zone 3. Each set, of course, with a new date-page. So that, at one stage, there'll be five different editions of *Verse* on sale in the USA—all with the same date line."

"Damned brilliant idea," I grumbled. "For a fool poet."

"Oh—Philodexter's not a poet. He's a business man. Yes, the idea is good. All the ideas, in fact. Big profit per copy. No reading at the news-stands. And no copies—or practically none—unsold. Just those that suffer spoilage, and those which fail of sale in Zone 6. I think he'll make a go of it.

"Anyway, another of his ideas is to pay a flat rate of $10 for each piece of verse, serious or humorous, long or short—that is, regardless of whether it's as long as Vincent Benet's 'John Brown's Body,' or—"

"Or as short as Abigail's rhymelet?" I put in.

"That's right. A flat rate of $10 to—"

"Fat rate, you mean," I commented. "For I'm saying that's a damn tall rate—for poetry."

"Well, aside from your prejudices with regards to things Pegasian, Clay, it is—I believe—a high rate. But that's one of Philodexter's advanced ideas. Another one is that he doesn't intend to employ regular verse editors. He thinks their judgment is too— well—technical. He wants the stuff passed on by men in the street like you and me, who—"

"Leave me out," I grunted. "You like to read poetry, and have at least an appreciation of it."

"Be it so," he said. "But, to boil this story short, Philodexter ran his ads—ads for material, that is—in all the newspapers and author-and-writer magazines. To see whether he could get enough submit-tance of good stuff before starting *Verse*. And—"

"And his worries on that score have ceased?" I put in sardon-ically. "I'll bet he was swamped!"

"Right, Clay. He was. He just got inundated, with material, no less. That $10-per-verse—cash on acceptance—just set every poet, poetaster, and poeticule in America to poetizing!

"Anyway," John Barr went on, "he brought a whole armful of scripts over to me, while you were gone. And asked me to read the whole shebang. And rate those I thought were whimsical, clever, truly poetical—and so forth. I confess it made me feel a bit—well—jittery, as they used to say seven years ago—back in '33—to hold so many fates in the palm of my hand! But I plunged in on the reading of 'em."

"And I'll warrant," I put in derisively, "that after you'd read a couple of hundred—or thousand, whatever the case was—you got utterly deadened yourself."

"Pretty near, Clay. I—I got a bit anesthetic, anyway! However, I done my best! That is, all but Abigail's here. And sent the whole bunch back to him today—all marked up with different grades according to whether they seemed to me personally to be clever, bright, deep, profound, good—or plain bad. As for poor Abigail here, I—listen—do you really mean, Clay, you like her poem?"

"Yes, I do," I said stoutly. "It's—it's short, brief, and to the point. With no flubdubbery. Frank and honest. Poetess money no has got. Burglar no can steal nothing! That—that appeals to me. And because of its honesty—and simplicity—I—I call it one of the best poems I've ever read. A fact! I'm a man in the street, am I not? So if it scans all right—and rhymes correctly—for I'm no authority there, I say—mark her 100 per cent. "

"By gosh, Clay," he said, "I will! If you—of all persons in Chicago!—like her rhymelet—then it should have acceptance. And for getting her a break like that, the lady ought to take you out to dinner. For Philodexter, you see, thinks so much of my judgment that he says he's going to print everything—sad—humorous—touching—deep—shallow—long—short—or what have you, that I mark as acceptable. All right. Abigail gets a break—thanks to you."

He took the green sheet from me, and laying it on the arm of his chair uncorked his fountain pen. Rather appalled at the swiftness with which I myself had become a poetry editor, I watched him writing across the top of it in his big flowing handwriting: "O.K.—J. B.—100!" But I stuck to my guns, now that I had manned them.

I wasn't sure yet but that he was bluffing me out—trying to make me withdraw my snap verdict—but he reached coolly over in the drawer of his table and withdrew one of his John Barr stamped envelopes. "Be with you in a minute," he said. "And you can mail this back to Philodexter when you leave. Which will conclude, I think— and hope—my functioning as a poetry and verse editor."

He sealed it up and wrote rapidly on the envelope. And handed it to me. Proving that he wasn't bluffing, after all. It bore the name Philodexter Maxellus, and some number on Federal Street—a number in the 500s—all of which 500s were so-called Printingtown, grave of thousands of hopeful ventures in publishing.

"Now," I said, stowing it in my pocket, "since I've earned a dinner from Abigail—rather, Miss Sprigge—and given you—and friend Philodexter—an expert opinion of a man in the street—let's get serious again. And now what's your opinion—of my case?"

"Yes," he returned. "Let's get back to our muttons. Your case. About that skull—and all. Which I was just about to advise you on when Jake Chudders called me to the phone." He paused. "Well, Clay, did you ever hear of trephining a living human skull?"

"Yes, I have. That is, I've heard how surgeons chop and chisel a disc of bone out of a skull, in cases of brain tumor, and things like that, and stick in a piece of metal. But you know, John, this hole wasn't chopped nor chiseled out. It was actually drilled in by a drill press—had beveled edges—and everything."

"It did? Such a high degree of mechanical work like that is puzzling. Yet you know, Clay, surgical skill has gone a long ways in the last quarter-century. With some surgeons. While others stay right in the same ruts. If you could see the difference between the new laryngoscope that this specialist I'm with is to stick down in my throat— and the one he has there, in use just three years ago—why it's like a Lincoln-12 compared to—to a phaeton."

"What's a phaeton?"

"Something that was just passing out of existence when I was a boy. And here you don't know what it is, even from hearsay. Gad, but you make me feel old. Well, there's one in the Transportation

Museum in Grant Park. But we're talking about the skull. And not equipages. And I'm telling you what I would do. That skull may have been trephined, Clay. By some method or device—as ingenious as this laryngoscope. Has it occurred to you that the presence of that bullet hole directly underneath the plate suggests that an effort might have been made to fish out the bullet? Yes. From the brain. An effort, however, which didn't succeed—that is, it's my guess that it didn't. For had it succeeded, Clay, the bullet in all probability would have been thrown away. But the fact that the bullet was there, wadded snugly in with paper inside that skull, indicates—at least to me—that the operation didn't succeed. In fact, the circumstance of the bullet being packed within the skull itself—and in the way it was—suggests two things to me: first, that it was put in there so that it wouldn't get lost or mislaid. As can so easily happen with small articles. After all, if that bullet killed the owner of that skull—it belongs with the skull—and nowhere else. Second, the fact that the bullet wasn't just tossed inside the skull, and the skull corked up—well, that's an easy one to guess."

"Is it? Why was it?"

"I'd say that it is desired by someone to preserve the delicate microscopical ballistic markings on that bullet. Hence it was well wadded inside the skull to keep it from rattling and bouncing around—soft lead, you know, against hard bone!—and thus obliterating those markings—or any part of them."

I nodded. And spoke.

"As the Dutchman said, John, I think you 'got right'—on everything you've said."

"Well, it's all guesswork, of course. Guesswork based on logic—that's about all. It—"

"But who would have occasion to—" I put in, and broke off. "Why would they—" And broke off again. For I was asking John Barr for hypotheses—while back in my room I had a few bits of torn paper that might or might not—throw some light on both the questions I had started to ask.

He was speaking again.

"Well, Clay, I'll tell you what I'd do—if 'twas the last thing I ever did. And it's as follows: I'd call up my doctor tomorrow—and ask him if it's at all possible to trephine a skull as neatly as this one apparently was; moreover, I'd ask him if there's any connection, with brain surgery, of the name M. Prior that you say was on that plate. For surgeons have been known, you know, to record their names on reconstruction work done on patients. So as to maybe hear ultimately the final outcome of a case."

"Meaning—"

"Well, just to hear the outcome of it. I read of a New York surgeon who recorded his name on a difficult piece of jawbone reconstruction, and when the patient died four years later from necrosis, the surgeon was able to learn that that particular type of reconstruction made for trouble!" He paused, reflecting. "Only a surgeon pretty well known, though, could count on some later surgeon letting him know the sequel to some old operative procedure. That's why I'd inquire about the name Prior."

I thought deeply for a moment. Then spoke. "I can't get it altogether out of my head yet—considering the work on that thing—that it isn't a specimen from an anthropological collection of some sort—and that that hole was drilled through by an actual drill press, and the plate put in as a classifying marker. But on the other hand, the—beveled edges of that hole seemed to clamp that disc with a savagery as though to say that that disc must stay in there—and that air, microbes, and Rudy Vallee's crooning must keep out." I was silent. "I'll do it. For your suggestions are all to the rosy—and particularly the one as to the thing having been trephined to get that bullet out—and save a life."

"I think so too—that is, regarding the latter. To fish that bullet out from where it was lodged. Although the fishing, it seems, was poor!"

At this juncture I surprised myself by suddenly yawning so widely that my hand nearly proved not big enough to cover it. And I felt suddenly blotto in the upper story. That multiplonal!

"John," I said, rising suddenly, "I'm going home! That damned multiplonal is suddenly developing a second kick. That confounded Mick who got me to swallow it warned me about the second kick— but only after I'd gotten the stuff down. From what he said—and the way I feel—unless I start now, I'll wake up tomorrow morning in somebody's grass plot, snoring with my head in their flower bed. About all I've done in this town since I got here is sleep! Who on earth is Mayor of Chicago now? And now—once more—about your operation? This—this tumor excision? Or rather double tumor excision—call 'em angiomas, nodules, or what you will. Sure—sure there's no danger?"

"None," he asseverated firmly, rising as I did. "'Twill be done in the doctor's office—and over with, he says, in less than an hour. If done tomorrow morning, I may even go downtown later in the day and revise my literature on the Barr-Bag, so that it talks up the mechanical principle underlying the Billy Bulger Bulge. On the other hand, if the operation isn't done till 2 p.m. the next day— I'll guarantee to take in a night club with you that night."

"Oh, sure," I chided him. "Lots of fun—while your throat is all soaked with cocaine. And after that wears off—what? Ow-woo!"

"You worry more about my fool operation than I do," he chided me back. "I'm—I'm sorry I ever mentioned it! Forget it, do!"

"All right," I said. "I'll try, anyway."

Now we stood in the doorway of his room for a moment.

"And come see me again, boy," he said, a little sadly. "And let me know all you find out. I don't like continued stories—unless they're concluded! Drop in—any time. You know," he went on, and with a rather bitter note in his voice, "you'll be marrying your Doris before long now—and then—I suppose one more friend will pass out of my crabbed old life."

"Nertz," I said, and placed my hand on his shoulder. "You and Doris are the only two people in the world who count 1-2-3 with me. When she and I are married, our home is always going to be open to one John Barr. In fact, we're going to buy a special chair for you. Why, man, on the day I introduce the two of you to each other—I know you'll think each other is hunky-dory—A. No. 1—

the flea's knees! Good-bye and good luck."

With which I marched downstairs, mailed Miss Abigail Sprigge's rhymelet—the acceptance of which, it very much seemed, I had been the sole cause—at the corner mailbox, and made for my solitary room. Made it just in time, in fact. And did no jigsaw puzzles, either! For I was one-quarter asleep by the time I extricated myself from my trousers. One-half, by the time I dragged forth my pajama suit from under my pillow. Three-quarters by the time I got into the pajama trousers. Nip and tuck! Lights out—and my head on the pillow barely in time. For the second kick-back of that multiplonal was truly terrific. Were I poetic, like—well—like Abigail Sprigge, I might say it swept over me like the spray of Niagara over honeymooners: instead, I prefer to say it trampled over me like a drunken mule with elephants' feet grafted onto his ankles.

I woke up in the morning, at least; and not the next evening. Woke up, reflecting crabbedly that I had been in Chicago for about thirty-eight hours now, and hadn't even yet looked at a Chicago newspaper. But as I wound my head around, to see if any mail had come, which would at least prove it to be 9 a.m, I saw a dainty little letter stuck under the door of my room. The mail had come, all right—and a sudden chill of apprehension passed over me when I saw the color of that envelope: pink. It must be from Doris. And why was she writing? I climbed out of bed, retrieved it, sat back on the side of the bed, and opened it. It was from her. And was brief. She had written:

Clay Dearest:

Our marriage is all off. Father has aged ten years in a few hours—and refuses to let me know what has gone wrong. But one thing he does say—and that is this: that my marriage to you is now hopelessly barred—that I must give up all thoughts of it forever—that it can never be. Oh, Clay, darlin', what can be wrong? Come to see me at 7 o'clock, the evening of the day you get this. For, if I cannot marry you with Father's permission, I cannot marry you at all.

Doris.

Letter in hand, I sat on the edge of the bed, staring out of the window at the clouds that were floating by. But I did not see them; in fact, I saw nothing. I was thinking in the exact kind of words that Abigail Sprigge would use. My dream castle—had tumbled to pieces—in a single night!

CHAPTER VIII

JIGSAW!

Now I did, indeed, have "scathered wits"!

And the first thing I did after collecting them together sufficiently to finish dressing, was to place Doris's letter safely away in
my chiffonier, and step to my telephone, with its outgoing service.
For I had no intentions now of going to the plant; I held within me
a grim determination to run down this skull mystery even if it
should take me six months. For one thing was certain: I wasn't going
to stand by and lose Doris Pelton without a struggle of some kind.

But the first number I called was that of the plant. And of course
I got Elfrida, the switchboard girl.

"This is Clay Calthorpe, Elf. Yes, I got back all right. Put me on
the Old Man's wire, will you?"

"Sorry, Mr. Calthorpe, but Mr. Pelton's daughter phoned in this
morning at 8:30 to say that he was ill and wouldn't be down to the
office at all today."

"Hm."

"Yes. Which makes it bad. For the foreman wanted to ask him
a few questions. Because of the new night shift we're putting on."

"New night shift?" I queried.

"Yes. We'll run continuously now, at least in the taffy depart-
ments. Because of that Crispo-Taff always crystallizing when it's
pulled within either more or less than seventeen hours of the time

it's boiled up. In fact, Mr. Calthorpe, this is my last day on days—
I go off duty today at noon—then I come back on tonight. Anything
I can do for you?"

"No, I—wait. Listen, Elf. If you get any telephonic inquiries
about whether I work for the company, say no. Tell the parties calling that you've never heard of me. And instruct Harry, the correspondence clerk, to do the identical same thing with respect to
telegrams. Also fix it with the other switchboard girl. You can confirm this from Miss Pelton, if it sounds erratic."

"We-ell—whatever it sounds, Mr. Calthorpe, it doesn't sound—
well—erotic. However, we'll take care of it. But I won't bother to
confirm it yet from Miss Pelton, because she seemed very worried."

"Very well. See that you watch your step now, on divulging my
connection with the company. And that goes for night and day both.
If anyone of you all slip—it'll be just too bad!"

And I hung up.

If I had had my pebbled-leather notebook which Suing Sophie
now had, I could have called up my next party—Dr. George
McBean, in the Marshall Field Annex Building—without having to
look him up. But look him up in the phone directory I had to. And
got him. For thanks to that cursed multiplonal, it was already 10
o'clock in the morning. He was an opthalmologist and rhinologist
of high repute, who some time back had imposed a little calisthenic
work on one of my eye muscles which thought its life mission was
to pull its opposing muscle clear over to China. And one of the most
pleasant and kindly men I had ever encountered.

"Dr. McBean speaking," came his well-modulated voice.

"This is Clay Calthorpe, Dr. McBean," I told him.

"Oh—hello, Calthorpe. Eye not misbehaving, I hope?"

"No, Doctor. It looks wherever I direct it to look. No, I'm only
looking for information, and—and oh yes, here's more trouble.
Say—are you busy?"

"No, not right now. A patient who should be here on appointment has failed to come in. So go ahead."

So I told him about having been to the Philippines and about

Suing Sophie. I was beginning to effect the most expert condensation of the story by this time. A few more narrations of it, and I knew I would be able to synopsize it in ten words.

"And so, Doctor," I finished, "I hate to even ask you—but if you get any inquiry about whether I was ever one of your patients, do you mind telling a white lie to the effect that you never had me for such?"

"Yes," he said frankly. "I do mind. But I can take care of that problem. I've a new office assistant who answers all correspondence and phone calls. She has access to my entire case-history files. So I'll just remove your card. Yes. The minute you hang up. And I'll take it home with me. And thus, if she's asked by any inquirer whether you've ever been one of my patients, she'll quite naturally report that there's no such person on the Doctor's books!"

"Oh fine!" was all I said. "And now I'd like to know if—but I say, Doctor, has that patient shown up yet?"

"Quit worrying! That right internus of yours will tighten up—and your eye will be turning in in another minute. What is it you want, Calthorpe? I'll be glad to give it to you—if you'll only tell me."

"Thanks, Doctor McBean. Well this is all I want to know: How, in general, have skulls been trephined? In the past, that is?"

"By whom? The Egyptians? They did it with a hammer and a bronze chisel, and a rock with which to knock the patient unconscious first."

"Well, no, Doctor, not quite so far back as the Egyptians. Say—up to and around maybe 1914? Or even to date?"

"We-e-ell—there are more different techniques, Calthorpe, for trephining a skull than there are colors that patients of mine who are poisoned on tobacco can't discern! Once upon a time, of course, the surgeons drilled a couple of holes about an inch apart, with a cranial drill—passed a threaded probe through the holes—then passed a so-called Gigli wire saw through, and sawed away from in—out. After which they bit out an actual hole with a Rongeur's forceps. But there have been dozens of ingenious instruments devised for cutting into the living skull, even to electric rotary saws which I imagine must take extremely skillful handling so as not to rip their way into the dura mater. The membrane that covers the brain, you know. And there's—but I say, Calthorpe—if you want to know all about trephining—or even trepanning, as it used to be called in its cruder aspects—I'd better put you into touch with somebody who actually does cranial surgery. I send many patients to various such specialists—when I find evidences, as I occasionally do, on the retinae that there is organic trouble inside—in the brain."

"Well, by gosh, Doctor—if you know a few specialists on that line of stuff—and I didn't even know that your field ever crossed the field of the brain surgeons—then maybe you'd have the complete lowdown on exactly what I want to know. Here it is: Has there ever been a great brain surgeon in the East—named Prior?"

"In the East? Why—man alive!—right here in Chicago. Dr. Max Prior."

"Whooey, Doctor! I believe I've got just what I want. Who is he?"

"Well, it's all set forth in *Who's Who*. But I can tell you briefly. He's the son of Major General Horace Prior, of the Union Forces in the Civil War, who right after the Civil War married a Minna Schlotterbeck—the *Who's Who* won't tell you this—but she was the beautiful daughter of the great German brewer of those days whose brewery was later sold to the Schlitz people, and became the nucleus for their present vast plant. Major and Mrs. Prior continued to reside, in Milwaukee, and their son Max studied medicine there, but came here to Chicago after he began to specialize in cranial surgery."

"Do you know him personally, Doctor McBean?"

"As well as one physician knows another. That is, I've sent him patients who wanted an exceedingly accurate diagnosis of what appeared to be brain tumors. Poor devils—most of them! They—but this Dr. Prior is a natural-born neurologist as well as surgeon. And one of the best in the country for localizing a tumor with exceeding accuracy. Some surgeons, you see, go into the skull at one point—and then have to forceps their way all over the map! Not so, usually, Max Prior. And in addition to diagnostic ability, he is one of the finest operators in the country on craniectomy. And he's probably used, in his day, every form of operative procedure found in the textbooks—and in the instrument catalogues to boot! Does this answer your query?"

"I'll say! Do you suppose a common bird like me could get in past Dr. Max Prior's seventy-seven office boys?"

"Office boys? You won't meet with any office boys! Dr. Prior is retired. Has been retired for years. He's about seventy years old, you see. But the most unassuming and kindly old gentleman that ever existed. He lives somewhere in Hyde Park, and is more interested in his gardening, I understand, than sawing holes in people's heads!"

"A thousand thanks, Doctor McBean. I'll get in touch with him right off."

"No you won't! Not if you depend on the Chicago telephone directory. You'll need a *Surgical Who's Who*. So wait a second. I've a new one here. Hold the wire." And I could almost see, with my mental eye, Dr. McBean pulling down from the rack above the little Chippendale desk in his consulting room, the book required.

"Yes," he was saying, an instant later. "Here's the address: 5323 Greenwood Avenue. Five—three—two—three. Yes. And tell him George McBean sends his regards."

"I will, Doctor. A thousand thanks, and good-b—"

"Wait—Calthorpe! I wouldn't descend on him before at least 11 a.m. For it says here: 'Consultation, with the profession only, 11 to noon, weekdays only.' Dr. McBean paused dryly. "the older we physicians get, Calthorpe, the more touchy we get—on what last vestiges of our professional days remain! Which is—er—our hour to be seen! Better put in a little while first, warning any more people— like myself—about your friend—er—Litigious Lucy. Or Suing Sophie, I believe you said her name was? Yes. About Dr. Prior, if you go before or after his particular hour to be seen, you may—"

"Strike a belligerent Dr. Prior? Yes, I'll adhere strictly to the letter of the law, Doctor McBean. And thanks again."

And now we said good-bye in earnest.

I had my information all right, all right.

But so because of Dr. McBean's injunction, and the fact that I might meet with a very testy old gentleman; and because, after all,

I had to eat; and, besides which, there was a little matter of a certain jig-saw puzzle now to be put together, as well as a few more people to be belatedly warned about Suing Sophie, I didn't rush out on the street and flag a taxicab. As I would mighty well like to have done. In fact, I got immediately down to business—and right off the bat!—and rang the other three names I knew to be in that pebbled notebook: Bailey Samelow, Joe Glozer, and Carl Link. And having rung them all at their offices or the places where they worked, I got them all. And warned them carefully about Sophie. And got their solemn assurances that they wouldn't know I had ever even existed— if any inquiries were made. Now I was ready either to eat—or to start the jig-saw puzzle. But starting the jig-saw puzzle, fortunately, proved to be a thing that could be done parallel with my eating of breakfast. For as I hung up after talking with Carl Link, I heard the clump-clump-clump of the oil mop on my door which proclaimed that Sandy MacDougall was swabbing the hardwood floor edges on the second-floor hall.

Where Sandy MacDougall had ever gotten the name Sandy MacDougall I do not know; nor never will know. I had heard it said that his black mother had read the famous Scotch number of *Ballyhoo* just before he was born; and if this were so, prenatal influence was proved. For Sandy MacDougall was an ignorant negro who could not read nor write—in fact, he had been officially proclaimed by two psychologists to be a moron, and Mrs. W-H always hid her faithful servitor in the basement for a few days whenever the usual moron-roundings-up took place, due to the newspapers using that conveniently short word in their headlines in lieu of the correct and longer words applying to the perpetrators of certain sex crimes. But moron though he was, Sandy MacDougall had won the $1000 jig-saw contest at the Coliseum, putting together a 5000-piece jig-saw puzzle in eight hours forty-one minutes and sixteen seconds quicker time than the nearest of forty-one other contestants. And proving thereby that it is an instinct for matching up edges—and not brains, that solve jig-saw puzzles. True, Sandy drank up his thousand dollars within a month after he won it—but that was neither here nor there.

I opened the door. It was he, his kinky-haired stocky coal-black head bobbing up and down as he massaged the floor.

"Morning, Sandy."

"Mo'nin', Mist' Caltho'pe. You back, huh?"

"Yes, Sandy, I'm back. Sandy, how's your jig-saw faculty this morning?"

"Huh? Ah ain' got no jig-saw fact'ry. But Ah is de champeen jig-sawer ob de wu'ld, Mist' Caltho'pe."

"Yes, I know you are. How'd you like to earn a dollar? Starting on one—while I eat?"

"Huh! Ah'd lak dat mo' bettah dan moppin'. I'se des' achin' fo' to do a little jig-sawin'."

"Come in here." He stood his oil mop in the corner and shuffled diffidently in.

I opened my chiffonier drawer and withdrew my rolled-up pillow slip. And dumped its contents out in a pile on the floor. Shaking it well, to get out the last piece. "See those pieces of paper?"

"Yessah. But dem ain' jig-saws—dem ain' got no pictuahs on 'em."

"No, but they got edges—and the great psychologists who analyzed you, Sandy, said that you worked solely from edges. And by intuition." I tossed them about with my foot. "See—some of them got writing on them."

"Yassuh. Typenwritin'."

"Correct. Sandy, while I'm downstairs bribing Corona to throw me together some ham and eggs—and to loan me Mrs. W-H's *Tribune*, I want you to pick out all the pieces that have writing on them. Yes, those. Then, if I'm not back upstairs yet, start putting them together. Sure—just like a jig-saw. That's right! Here—wait till I get you a sheet of paper." I reached in the proper drawer and withdrew one. Also a mucilage pot. "Paste them on here, Sandy, as you match them up. Yes, with this stickum-goo." I was safe on that, for I could cut them apart again, if they were matched hopelessly awry. "Get as far as you can—till I come upstairs again. Then we'll both work together."

"Yassuh. Ah'll git dat jig-saw undah way. Go 'haid an' eat."

"OK I will. And Sandy—"

"Whut?"

"If you even get so far as beginning the jig-saw, build it up so that the typenwritin'—as you call it—is on top?"

"On top? Yassah. On top."

And I left Sandy to wrestle with the problem. In most likelihood he would have a half hour's work just examining every piece for "typenwritin'."

Corona—Mrs. W-H's negro maid—did give me a cup of coffee, and did throw me together some ham and eggs. And lent me Mrs. W-H's *Tribune* to read while I waited. The *Tribune,* in its lost-and-found columns—which were all I was interested in—had nothing about any lost, nor found, bags. So I attacked the ham and eggs. And the coffee. Which had stood on the grounds since breakfast time, and was as strong as Zybysco's back muscles. With the tremendous surge of energy it gave me, I felt I could speedily advance whatever Sandy had accomplished.

Twenty minutes later I was tramping back upstairs.

Sandy was again mopping away methodically in the hall.

"What's—what's the matter, Sandy?" I said, aghast. "Did you run out on me?"

"Ain' run out on nobody, sah. All put togethah."

"All—put —together?" I stammered. "Why, Sandy—you didn't even have time to examine each piece of paper both sides to see—to see if it had typewriting on it?"

"Huh—didn' need to do all dat. Dem whut had typenwritin' on dem wuz kinda blue-white papah—whilst dem odders widout no typenwritin' was white-white papah. Des pluck 'em all out by de colah—lak mah Grandaddy he pick cotton."

Long live half-wittedness! It took a half-wit to see what I couldn't.

"But you say—you got them put together?"

"Oh—dat wuz easy—compahed to dat big thousum' dollah contest Ah winned."

"Ah—ah verra mooch doot yer wur—rd, Sandy," I said mockingly. "But—here's your dollar."

And I went in. Sure enough, on my window-sill, as I saw from the doorway, was a completely pasted-up sheet of paper. Pasted up, quite plainly, upon the sheet I had given Sandy. The mucilage stood back on my chiffonier.

Truly, it paid to hire experts!

I went over to the window-sill. And took up the put-together page. Which, though upside down as yet, I saw at the very first glance had been beautifully assembled, every serration of every edge seemingly fitting into its companion serration on the edge of some other piece. And I inverted it. And proceeded to read it.

And, reading it, found that I had the best clue yet toward the unraveling of what this confounded skull business was all about— that I had stumbled upon a source of illumination better, perhaps, than Dr. Prior might prove to be.

CHAPTER IX

THE ELUSIVE MISS SPRIGGE

For the scraps of carbon-imprinted paper—and, as I say, Sandy had put them together with marvelous exactitude—were no letter. They were a poem—and, I guess, a good one, for it impressed even me, the unimpressible one, by its lines. If not its intricate scheme of rhyming—indentation—and what not! A poem, by Abigail Sprigge! A sonnet—whatever that might be—and I'd heard somewhere that it was the most difficult poetical "animile" to give birth to.

It ran:

IF HIS LOVE DIES—SO MINE!
A SONNET
by
ABIGAIL SPRIGGE

He's gone: I would he had my wounded heart
That, by its aching beat, he might remember,
In these white days of Passion's dead December,
The love of Passion's June. I would the art
Of Cupid might rekindle with my fire
That heart of his, and light it through and through,
The flaming of my own heart to renew
Again, igniting all my first desire.

But his heart's whole, and mine is in my breast,
And every hour is filled with fear for me
Lest anguish, through each hour, become distress,
And then, by slow degrees, forgetfulness.
For every sun expires in the West,
And lo! a new moon shines above the sea.

I was certainly puzzled.

In what way was Abigail Sprigge, the poetess, connected with a case which might have cost me my death if that Chinaman had only struck a bit harder—or a bit closer to thinner bone?

Had she previously lived in the same room where that skull had later been stuffed—and packed in that bag—leaving behind her the paper, and carbon sheets, and the discarded carbon copy of her poem that was subsequently used? Or did she live in that same house— right today—and had she loaned a bit of spare paper to someone who had packed the skull? Or had she—oh, there were plenty of possible hypotheses—but, find where Abigail lived, and I would find who tore up all that paper—and packed the skull's interior so as to hold that precious bullet from rattling around, and, presumably, obliterating some of its microscopical ballistic marks.

There was, however, no address on the poem. But the carbon sheet might show more than the poem did.

I picked up a scrap of it.

And held it to the light.

Backwards.

It had been used but once—for the typewritten letters were etched clearly in it—and it showed the words:

of Passion's June
rekindle

That was part of this same poem. I picked up another carbon— sheet fragment. It also carried words of the same poem:

every sun
lo! a new

Carbon sheet, therefore, was but an identical replica of the poem. And, like the poem, could have no address.

But the problem was no problem now. In fact, it was all too easy!

I stepped over to my phone. And called up John Barr. Not at his quarters now, but at his bag-making "studio" on Fulton Street.

And got him.

"Hello, John," I said. "I won't hold you for a minute. All I want to know is—but say, shouldn't you be getting operated on now? Or in a little while?"

"I haven't had the call yet from my doctor," he told me. "He's to ring me a half hour or so before I'm to come over. I guess it won't be till tomorrow now. Although he may, at that, ring me any minute. But what can I do for you?"

"Well, John, I want to get the address of Abigail Sprigge."

"Abigail Spri—what on earth—why—are you starting a poetry magazine too?"

"No, John. I—I didn't like to tell you last night. I—I was ashamed—like the devil. But I—I kept all those scraps of paper that that skull was packed with. And replaced them with more paper. And just now I picked out the bunch that had carbon imprintations on them. And put them together. And they constituted a poem—a sonnet, whatever the devil that is!—by this Abigail Sprigge."

"Well—I'll be damned! What do you know about that? Sure, I'll get her address. Right away. But did you do anything on the surgeon business? The skull surgery angle, that is?"

"I'll say! I'm all set on that. For an interview, in a little while, with the very doctor—Max Prior—who has something, in some way, to do with the name on the plate in that skull."

"That's fine. I'd say with the two leads you've got now—this woman Sprigge, and the surgeon—the mystery is probably as good as solved. Well, stay where you are, and I'll ring you back—Dearborn 6622, didn't you say?—as soon as I call Philodexter. As you saw by that envelope last night—that is, if you mailed it!—his office is at 538 Federal Street. And I have his phone. And I know he's got all the scripts he's received tabulated and entered up. And all letters filed that have come in with them. And—but how was this particular script titled? The reason I ask is that, since you found remnants of only the carbon copy, Philodexter might have the original of it in his office now. For he's advertised pretty extensively for poetry, you know. And if he has the original, then that sort of doubles the strength of your lead to Miss Sprigge, I'd say."

"It was just titled," I told him, "'If His Love Dies—So Mine!'—followed by the words 'A Sonnet' and then by the words 'By Abigail Sprigge.' And its first line begins: 'He's gone: I would he had my wounded heart.' And—and, John, the thing was damned—well—pretty—er—pretty good."

"What—the—devil! Are you at last—getting an appreciation of poetry?"

"Well—maybe I am. Maybe I am. I don't know."

"Then the millennium has arrived! But hold the wire, and I'll call you ba—"

"Wait—you can't call me back on this phone. Incoming service is cut off. And I probably won't be able to get it restored till late today. I'll call you, say, in—"

"All right. Call me back in—say—two minutes. And keep ringing, in case you get a busy signal. I'll get Philo right off. And the first line, you say, runs 'He's gone: I would—'"

"'—he had my wounded heart.'" I finished.

"Okay, Clay. I'll call Philo pronto."

I hung up. And waited, tapping my foot. While the seconds merged into minutes, and the minutes added themselves up to at least three in number.

Then I impatiently rang him again.

And got him, as before.

"Bad luck, boy," were the first words he said.

"How so?" I asked.

"The letter accompanying that Abigail Sprigge verse I let you read last night has no address accompanying it, Philodexter says. He has the letter there all right. It's filed under 'Sprigge.' Short, and signed on the typewriter. The woman just says she wants the verse thrown into the wastebasket in case it isn't available. That she makes fair wages, and doesn't need the exceedingly few dollars that the verse might bring. Just would like to see it in print, and know that it merited publication."

"The devil! Does this Philodexter fellow know where the script was postmarked from?"

"Yes. He has the original mailing envelope. He filed it with the letter so that, if he did have occasion to use her verse, he wouldn't be eligible for a suit for not mailing her an acceptance first. The envelope's just postmarked from the downtown station, here at Chicago."

"Well—that's that, then! And since it wasn't on the verse itself—then I guess that settles me from following Miss Sprigge up."

"I guess it does, Clay. Philodexter has the verse itself there now—thanks to your mailing it back to him all right last night. And, since I put my OK on it—thanks to you, you unpoetical bozo!—he's stuck it in the accepted files. So, Clay, I guess that ends not only your chances for finding who helped to pack the inside of that skull, but to collect your dinner out of the $10 Miss Sprigge won't receive!" He paused. "True, Philodexter says he hasn't opened up the ton or so of stuff that came in this morning—but even if he did have the original copy of your 'If His Love Dies—So Mine!'—is that correct?—if the writer didn't send any clue to her whereabouts with the little verselet, she probably won't with the sonnet. However, when do you see your surgeon?"

"Right away, John. As soon as I hang up. In fact, I'll let you go now. So I can hop a cab and start out there. It's way on the South Side."

"All right. Good luck. And drop around when you get acclimated to the home town, and give me the lowdown."

And we hung up.

Now I did go out on the street. And flagged a taxicab. And ordered the driver to take me to 5323 Greenwood Avenue.

CHAPTER X

FINDING AND LOSING—A CLUE!

Twenty-five minutes later I was dismounting in front of the number which comprised my destination. Greenwood Avenue was a cool pleasant street, just like its name. And 5323 was a tiny vine-covered cottage with its number laid out in oyster shells on the front lawn.

In a large flower garden at the side of the house, a man of about seventy years of age, with snow-white hair, was digging. Rather, heaping dirt over some bulbs or roots in preparation for the coming snows of winter. He had a short, squarishly Teutonic white beard which showed the German that had come to him from his mother and his life in the city of Milwaukee. And silver-rimmed spectacles with rather thick lenses. His complexion was ruddy. A bony-looking active Negro woman, about thirty-five, with red glass ear-drops, was handing him a trowel. Noticing that I was standing fumbling for the latch of his gate, he came forward, the trowel in his hand, and looked inquiringly in my direction.

"I am looking for Dr. Max Prior," I ventured.

"I am Dr. Prior," he said simply. And there was the faintest sign of a German accent to his speech—although one so barely discernible that it could not have been depicted in writing, but which nevertheless betrayed that Minna Schlotterbeck had decreed what language was to be spoken in the Schlotterbeck-Prior menage!

"May I have a few words with you, Doctor, concerning a—a skull? Dr. McBean gave me your address."

"Oh, McBean? *Gott im Himmel*—McBean! I haven't seen him for years. Charming fellow. And he certainly used to find things with that retinoscope of his. Things in my field, that is. Yes, indeed. A skull, you say? Well, skulls, my dear boy, are something I've had a bit to do with in my day. Yes, indeed. Just follow me." And he nodded his head in the lengthwise direction of a small brick walk. "To my study inside there. Where we can talk undisturbed."

He led the way graciously into the house. I saw a brass-cornered suitcase on the bed in an open bedroom and the bony negro woman was now packing it. He threw open the door of a study. It held an extremely large safe, but obviously of an old-time make. The walls of the study were lined with books, and in one corner was a glass instrument rack containing a weird congeries of instruments, most of which were badly tarnished and whose surrounding glass walls were thick with dust. It bore silent testimony to the sad and unescapable fact that men have their great day—then fall from the procession.

He seated himself in a stiff chair near the safe, and only after I had taken a comfortable armchair which he insisted I occupy.

"And now what can I do for you, my lad?" He was so old that I evidently seemed like a boy to him: "If you'd come this time tomorrow, I would have been out of the city."

"I noted a suitcase—" I began.

"Yes. Miranda, my housekeeper, is packing it. I am visiting my mother's grave in Milwaukee. She and my father are buried there. I go up there every year at this time. I leave tonight."

"Well, Doctor," I began, "my name is Clay Calthorpe and as I said, I'm a friend of Dr. McBean's, if you want to call him up and verify it. And I've come to you to get some information which is exceedingly vital to me. It concerns a case of brain surgery."

"Yes. So I rather surmised, somehow. Well, I did brain surgery exclusively for some thirty years. But retired more than fifteen years ago, so that steadier hands could go on with work which is of so delicate a nature."

THE RIDDLE OF THE TRAVELING SKULL

I leaned forward.

"Doctor Prior, some day and two nights ago—it seems like an eternity now—I happened through a whole congeries of peculiar circumstances into which I won't endeavor to go, to see a skull carrying a silver plate on which appears your name. M. Prior. And the number 82. And an apparent date beneath that: 9-17-'14. That skull, Doctor, is connected in some obscure way with a girl that I love very dearly—and her father—and on account of the way the thing is mixed up in our affairs, she—she cannot marry me. More than these facts I wish you wouldn't ask me—but I came here in the hope that you would at least explain to me what that inscription means."

"Hm. No. 82?" he said. "Odd—though not odd—for nothing is truly odd—I received an inquiry of somewhat similar nature to yours over the phone about four days ago—by Long Distance from somewhere up in Northern Michigan. The party, who talked with a decided lower-class English accent, said he had gotten my phone number from the *Surgical Who's Who* of some local physician. And asked what was the name of any such patient I might ever have had, whose case might be recorded as No. 82. And who were all the closest relatives of record.

"Which information I gave. Even as he held the phone. FoR he said—now what was it he said?—yes, that he was an agent for Department 17, of the British Government. And anyway, there really is nothing about such things that have to be concealed."

"Department 17?" I said. "I never heard of it. Although that would be natural enough. Do you suppose he was—"

"Fabricating? Maybe he was. Department 17—British Government? That does sound ridiculous, does it not? And now comes to me another young fellow—an American—his own affairs mixed up with no less a case than Case No. 82!"

He was silent. Studying my face intently. And again he spoke.

"Life! What a tangle it is, isn't it? *Gott!* People—objects—all bound together—in all sorts of odd relationships! And so another case comes to light, after all these years? Well I'll give you the information you ask, for I wouldn't want a young chap like yourself to lose the one girl in the world for him—especially if anything I can render would help him out. And again—such information is not *verboten. Ach,* no! And I'll not ask you any questions, providing you'll promise, on my return from Milwaukee, to give me certain purely technical information I'll then require. If you have it, that is. Nothing personal. Is that a bargain?"

"Yes, Doctor Prior. I'll give you all I can give you. But I'm asking you to give me the works—from A to Izzard. Everything about this case. The cause of the operation. Everything. Because—well—there are queer factors involved."

"There must be. Well, I'll get my manuscript copy out first. So you can have it all."

He twirled the dial of his safe, and swung open the door. And brought forth a large book, well-bound, which appeared to be composed of typewritten sheets interspersed with photographs—or photostats—also bound in. And followed the production of that by bringing forth a small leatheroid filing-card box which looked as though it might contain a couple of hundred small three-by-five cards. He laid the box atop a near-by stand, and throwing off its lid revealed that it did indeed contain filing cards and nothing else. But he was holding up the book.

"Here it is," he said, smiling. "My great work: *Clinical Studies in Brain Surgery and Craniectomy—Et Sequelae.* But until I get more *Sequelae* than I have—I fear the book is not ready for publication!" He pointed in the safe, where stood a volume just like the one on his knee. "There is its companion volume, made from the carbon copies of these same pages, and from extra prints of these photographs, which until only recently was in the library of the Royal College of Physicians and Surgeons in Kensington Gardens, London."

I was champing at the bit for information, but thought it polite to venture some sort of conversation. So I asked him:

"And why, Doctor, have you it here—with the other—in Chicago?"

"Why?" He looked up. "Because I am filling in the two volumes—with such *Sequelae* as are now available. *Ach*! I am seventy years old, my son. Not much longer to go. No!"

And he turned back to his book. He riffled over the large pages rapidly. All typewritten. And containing pages a-plenty holding mounted photographs, or even, in some cases, unusually large glossy photographs trimmed down to page size. Photographs of human heads lying on operating tables, with their scalps drawn away like the rinds of oranges, and held in curious clamps. Brains— or what looked like such—hanging out of cracks in heads like spume. Shortly he beckoned me over. A large glossy photograph showed a round silver plate, held upright so as to face the camera, in the jaws of a slender forceps of some kind. Photographed as it had been, under a brilliant laboratory light, the letters and numbers etched on it seemed absolutely stereoscopic in their depths. On the camera film itself had been scratched, very crudely, but backward so that they came out correctly on the print itself, the words: POSITION I (Case 82) FOR INSERTION OF PLATE IN TREPHINE OPENING BEVELED WITH KRONJEDT BEVELER.

"Is this the inscription you saw on this skull you spoke of?" He indicated, however, not the caption of the photo, but the words on the round metal plate itself.

Which it was, of course. The same letters, etched identically. I nodded. Particularly as he slowly turned the photographic pages one by one, showing further pictures in evidently the same series, since they were lettered with the succeeding Greek numerals, of the same round plate, now held, by apparently some gummy application, on the ends of three short metal legs spreading out from the end of a short metal rod; then poised, by the help of this rod, in front of an open hole in what was plainly a human head, with its scalp drawn away. The cuff of a nurse's sleeve cut across the corner of this picture; so it had obviously been taken in the operating room. Then came a photograph of a surgical hammer of some sort in contact with the free end of the rod, apparently in the act of driving the plate squarely into the hole. This one was labeled IN SITU. Then there appeared a final photograph showing the same hammer being applied to the free end of a small blunt-ended stylus whose other end sat against the edge of the plate where it was now in contact with the bone; and this one was labeled: VI, FINAL TIGHTENING OF PLATE (Case 82).

I pointed at the plate.

"That is it, Doctor. And such a neat piece of work I never saw in my life. I—I thought that that hole had been drilled by a drill press—by a conical drill of some kind. How on earth do you achieve a hole like than on—on a living head?"

"How? Oh, simple. Did you think we chisel our way in? No, indeed! We have a rotary trephine saw—and have had for the last thirty-five years—which cuts a disk out as cleanly as a button. It might be likened to—well—a hollow steel cylinder, with fine teeth along one edge. And geared to a hand-motor quite naturally. And of course it has a trocar-shaped centering point in order to keep it from slipping. We lift the bone button out with a trepan-elevator—and there you are."

"Yes," I queried. "But—but how do you achieve the perfect bevel that you did—in this case?"

"So? So you noticed that, eh?" The old man turned one of the photographs and craning his head about regarded some typing along its edge. "Yes. This operation presented the use of the Kronjedt beveler, I see, really more than it did the case itself. This must be the one, all right, where Kronjedt asked me to use his tool on one of my cases and give him a little publicity in my book. It is a revolving cone—exceedingly truncated, of course, with finely milled edges—which will ream out the inside of a trephine opening. To the exact same bevel as a plate. Which can therefore be prepared beforehand. Poor Kronjedt! Dead these last twenty years. Of what use to invent anything? Well, I see I did my best for him. I have showed all the positions: the plate held in front of the aperture: the three-legged rod to drive it in; the tapping around the edge with the stylus to drive it tighter. And of what use for Kronjedt? Dead—and each surgeon keeping on with his own individual ways!"

He was now at the typewritten sheet beneath the photographs.

And I resumed my chair, content to wait, for I saw he was willing to tell me anything I wanted. He ran his eyes over the sheet. And over the next sheet following. Then he sat back:

"The author of the telephonic inquiry sent me was not interested in the details of Operation No. 82. Only the identity of the patient. And of such relatives as are on the record. Which I gave him. From the card-index box yonder. I did not bother to read up the case itself. For I had not read my nightly installment of Kant—and I must conserve my eyes. So now I read it—as I go along. For I take it you want everything, *nicht wahr?*" I nodded most vehemently. "Well," he went on, "to begin with, the data you give me is—at least in its form—such as is inscribed upon many, many trephine plates—of all shapes and sizes—I have inserted in human crania during my thirty years of specialized practice. That is, amongst a selected group of cases where it was desired—for some reason—to obtain a later history of the case. If possible! The data, in every instance, as you gather, contains first my name, as surgeon. Then the number amongst my recorded cases—that is, only as collated in this particular work. No. 82, in this instance. Then the figures representing the date of the operation. In this case, the 17th of September, 1914—twenty-six long years ago, not so? Yes. Nothing recondite in all that, is there? It was an idea of mine—but an idea not at all new in reconstructive surgery, and prosthesis, I assure you—to inscribe such trephine plates as I might have occasion to use in a certain number of properly selected cases, and to collate those cases in a book like this—*Clinical Studies*—so that when the patients eventually died of something—as they eventually must!—and some of their respective crania were exposed at autopsies, or by subsequent operations necessitated—then the data about how the patient died would be available. For you see we don't always know what eventually happens when we interfere with delicate brain tissue. No, indeed. Secondary growths sometime spring up, years after. And other queer *sequelae*. Again, it might be desirable—at least so I thought when I inaugurated *Clinical Studies*—to obtain details as to the tightness of the set-in plate in later years, so as to confirm or subvert the desirability of the particular trephining technique used—and any evidences of possible necrosis around the edge of the trephine opening. And so forth. All could be forwarded to me, as I hoped—or to certain medical executors with whom this work will be left when I pass away—and inserted within it as 'Sequelae.' In that way, and that way only, would we have something really worthwhile in all the vast amount of brain—surgery stuff written. It is *Sequelae*, my boy, that makes value—and not descriptions of mere operations.

"The uniqueness of this particular operation—which I see is titled 'Intradural Hemorrhage,' is not so particularly great; evidently I gave it such copious photographs as I did, for poor Kronjedt. Whose beveler I seldom bothered with. For why fit a plate so microscopically fine, when the human scalp ultimately covers the site completely? *Gott*, yes—why? But perhaps nevertheless you wish the description of the operation, eh?"

"All you can give me, Doctor Prior. I'm a—a sort of a thorough person—when I go after information."

"Very well. Operation No. 82 consisted of the removal of a piece of bone in order to relieve intra-cranial pressure resulting from intradural hemorrhage. The patient? Now let me see. My memory for names is not so good. Phillip Whimsey, I think I told that party who held me on the wire. Or Whomsey." He turned and riffled over his cards. "Yes. Phillip Walmsley. That is it. No. 82! Address—twenty-six years ago, that is!—the Harrison Hotel, 42 West Harrison Street, in case you—"

"Pardon me, Doctor," I put in, "but said hotel is a parking space now. One of these automatic self-parking spots. I had occasion a couple of years ago to trace down a creditor of the company I am with, who was supposed to be living there. The hotel was just being torn down. And it no longer exists now."

"So? Well everything passes, my son. Hotels as well as men. So much for that, then. Phillip Walmsley is the name, anyway."

He turned his attention back to his book again. He ran his finger slowly along the lines as he recounted what he found therein.

"The patient—P. W.!—I see, was by occupation a bank clerk.

Not employed. His age twenty-two. Hm. Yes. On account of losing
control of a motor-cycle which he was operating, he was thrown
head foremost from it. On Ashland Boulevard. On September 14,
1914. He was taken to the Alexian Brothers Hospital at once. When
I was called, I found him—let's see—yes—'unconscious, very irrita-
ble, and in pain.' There was—yes—ptosis of the left eye; the left
pupil, dilated and stable. The right arm, partly paralyzed. His res-
piration—yes, 'labored'; his pulse—'slow and irregular.'

"I see I made a diagnosis of intradural hemorrhage, for the case is
so labeled. And why not? And I see that on September 17, I resorted
to the operation of 'cerebral decompression.' By craniectomy. The
usual preparation, my lad. But you say you want everything, eh?
Very well. Let's see what was done here. And I wonder who wrote this
particular case up for me—" He turned momentarily to the next
page. "Oh, yes. L. L. That would be my assistant Dr. Lucien
Littlefield—*Gott*—and Littlefield killed three years later at the
Argonne. Everything passes. Now where am I? Yes—as to the
preparatory work done here. Um. Yes. Um. Um. Yes, the scalp was
first shaved and washed. *Naturlich!* The patient—um—well
wrapped in hot blankets—propped up to a sitting position to mini-
mize the intracranial pressure—um, yes—preliminary injection of
morphine—now did I by any chance use as an anesthetic the new—
no, ether was used solely. Um. Um. Semi-lunar incision in the scalp.
Twelve clamps. Bleeding well controlled.

"Now the bone-cutting operation. Well, you've heard how it's
done; so we won't rehearse that. Here it is, in graphic form. The
Pelaux rotary trephine. Cutter No. 5. It tells the story simply, does
it not? And—oh yes—here comes poor Kronjedt—the Kronjedt
No. 5 beveler for Cutter No. 5. Used right away while the Peloux
motor was at hand, and the patient in position. Do you know, by
Gott—I half believe I recall this operation after all. For the nurse had
very red hair. Ach—so red! *Gott*—what red hair! Now let me see.
Um. Um. A fairish increase in the cerebro-spinal fluid, caused by
irritation from the hemorrhage. Which was drawn away of course."

He looked up jovially.

"And that's all there was to the operation. You have seen yourself how the plate was ultimately put in. And if you would see how the scalp was ultimately drawn together—go watch your tailor at work."

I smiled, though not with the same joviality that the old man across from me displayed. "Yes, Doctor, I'm in a position to know that you put that plate well in. And drove it tightly in, to boot. But do give me more about this operation. You know I warned you I'm thoroughgoing."

"So I see. Well, we will look at the convalescence. Um. The following day the patient is reported as conscious. Um. Yes. A good convalescence—though he talks incessantly for the first week. A month later he is discharged. But wait—that doesn't end matters. Comes here his later reports at the hospital. They show a slight irregularity in the sense of smell. Beyond that nothing. Not even a headache. *Gott,* it is good to do something. For sometimes they die. And then I don't have them in this book. Well, that is all. Except—" He turned to his little card-index file, which was still open where he had corrected himself as to the name being Walmsley instead of Whimsey. "Except the small remaining information. The name of the one relative is—or was then—Reverend Peter G. Walmsley, care St. Ignatius' Church, Denver, Colorado. Brother. And a small code letter after it shows that he remitted for my fee. Ach—we doctors must live! And I saved his brother's life."

He put the lid back on the card file, and closed the book on his knee. "There is the whole story, my lad. And if I didn't like you— and that McBean sent you—I would not have spoken so freely. Will you stay to noon luncheon with me? *Sauerbratten unt*—and—noodles. My negress Miranda is the best German cook in Chicago! And a cold bottle of Schlitz apiece! My maternal grandfather, you know, concocted the present Schlitz beer formula."

I had been busy with my fountain pen as he had given me the latter name and address. And I put it away and looked up.

"Doctor Prior, you're too kind. But I'm out on a—a sort of warpath today. And you have packing to do. And things to take care of. So I'll run along. You've given me information that I never could have secured elsewhere. Although it's all more or less Greek to me. But the name of the patient—who is now dead, and the man who paid the fee, will serve my purpose as a starter."

"Tell me one thing," asked Doctor Prior. "How did that trephine plate fit today?" "So snug," I said, "that, as I told another man, Rudy Vallee's crooning couldn't get in."

"*Ach*—my operation on him was a huge success then! That man Vallee! With his soophing and his sighing. Now give me Lohengrin—played by an orchestra with forty violins. There is music that is music!" He conducted me to the door and bowed. "Don't forget now. To call on me again. When you are at ease in your own mind. Which you are not today. Me, my mind is full today too. Going to my mother's grave. Just to think—and I am older today than she was when she died. Ach, Immanuel Kant is right when he says space and time are but categories of our own sense perceptions. For she is still *meine Mutter*."

I stood in the doorway.

"When will you return, Doctor?"

"I don't know. Call Miranda in a few days. Hyde Park 4567."

"I will."

When I left the cottage of the kindly old German surgeon I walked rapidly toward 55th Street so that I could find a taxicab that would bring me back to the North Side again.

A clergyman in the case again!

The dead man's brother who had paid the fee twenty-six years before had been a clergyman. In Denver. And a Chicago clergyman had been carrying the dead man's skull. What a clerical mess it all was.

But as I reached a news-stand—which was there on Greenwood Avenue and 55th Street by virtue of the fact that Fifty-fifth Street was a car-line thoroughfare, my eyes opened as wide as dollars. For, strung across the top of a noonday *Chicago Despatch,* were two head-lines which read:

SAFE OF REVEREND PETER WALMSLEY, EPISCOPAL
RECTOR, KILLED IN TRAIN ACCIDENT, FOUND CRACKED!

STRANGE DISCOVERY BY OFFICIALS OF THE
C. AND W. A. RAILROAD

I flung down a nickel and grabbed up the paper. The story was
so new that there was as yet hardly anything to it. It was all on the
first page. The right-hand column. Indeed, only the upper third of
same. I caught a confused glimpse of a lot of other sub-headlines and
heads—Mexico—Chorus Girl Sues—Alderman Indicted—More
Currency Inflation—but they meant nothing to me as compared
with those two lines. And standing there on the curb read every
word of the story. Which ran:

> *Among the five persons killed in the C. and W. A. train wreck near Spotts*
> *Forks, Nebraska, last evening, was one whose only identification consisted*
> *of an empty envelope with a Northern Michigan postmark, being the*
> *inscription: "Rev. Peter Walmsley, Rectory, St. Anne's Church, Chicago."*
> *In the upper left-hand corner of the envelope was the hand-printed return*
> *card: "Return in five days to Milo Payne, Palmer House, Chicago." The*
> *railroad detectives investigating last night at the Rectory, which is at North*
> *LaSalle Avenue and Eugenie Street, finally succeeded in locating Mary*
> *Boggs, of 1651 North Clark Street, the scrubwoman who ordinarily comes*
> *daily to clean up the Rev. Peter Walmsley's quarters in the Rectory. She was*
> *able to render the information that the Rev. Mr. Walmsley had left Chicago*
> *night before last, unexpectedly, in response to an urgent telegram, in order to*
> *visit a sick sister residing in Hutchins' Springs, Nebraska, calling her over*
> *to the Rectory just before his departure to give her some final instructions as*
> *to deferring any further cleaning until the end of the week, when he expected*
> *to be back to preach his Sunday services.*
>
> *But on opening the Rectory, in order to obtain, if possible, a picture of*
> *the Reverend Walmsley to clinch the identification of the accident victim at*
> *Spotts Forks, Nebraska, the railroad detectives found the library in utter*
> *confusion. The window glass of a window on a small inner court, accessible*
> *through a narrow passageway from Eugenie Street, had been neatly removed*
> *by the ball-of-putty and glass-cutter method. Every drawer in the library*
> *had been pulled out, and its contents strewn helter-skelter about the floor.*

Last but not least, the door of a small old-fashioned Jenkins safe had been blown out, the library rug having been wrapped around it apparently to deaden the sound of the explosion.

The only thing of value that could have been in the safe, according to the scrubwoman's belief, was something which the Rev. Peter Walmsley had locked in there ten minutes before departing for the depot to take his train for Hutchins Springs, Nebraska. This was a black leather overnight bag. It was found, however, not far from the open safe, cut entirely open, the Reverend Walmsley's own amber-handled razor having been used to open it. Its contents, pulled out in a heap through the opening, seemed to comprise only collars, a tie, a pair of purple pajamas with yellow circles embroidered on them, a pair of military brushes—in fact, the usual traveler's odds and ends.

In the wastebasket was found the original telegram summoning the Reverend Walmsley out of town and in a small bronze incense urn on his desk were found the ashes of what appeared to be a half-dozen business cards, completely burned, and crushed with the end of a pencil. None of the burned fragments are decipherable.

The Chicago police, apprised of the findings, believe it to be just an ordinary robbery, accidentally uncovered by the train wreck investigation, and committed doubtlessly night before last, in view of the fact that neighbors around the church heard, around midnight that night, a muffled pop which they thought was an auto-tire blowing out. Some petty cracksman was trying, they say, to get his hands on the previous Sunday's church collection, which collections the Rector was in the habit of banking very irregularly. In this case, however, the cracksman failed, for the Rector's bank-deposit book and church collection record showed that the $102.51 collected the previous Sunday was banked next morning.

CHAPTER XI

A SHOCK

The moment I reached the end of that newspaper story, two things became plain to my fuddled mind.

First: That the clerical gentleman, alongside of whom I had sat on the night I rode home to the Essex, was no other person than this Reverend Peter Walmsley who had been killed in the railroad wreck near Spotts Forks, Nebraska. And who, strange to relate, had paid—though from Denver, Colorado—Dr. Max Prior's fee in the trephining operation of twenty-six years before. Dead! And that beautifully prevented my following that clue any further.

Second: That the overnight bag which had been found in his library, not far from the opened safe, was my own bag. Those purple pajamas! And I strongly suspected, too, that the stiff ashes of those cards found in the incense urn on his desk were those of the seven or eight such that had been in that bag. And all of which oblongs of cardboard had borne my name and the address and telephone number of the Essex.

And as I climbed into a cab which drew whiningly up in front of me, trying to piece together all these peculiar facts, I thanked my stars that those cards had all been burned, for, had they been found in the rooms of the Reverend Peter Walmsley, any explanations that I might have given to the Chicago police would have looked peculiar—to say the least!

But I was by no means at the end of the trail. The Reverend Peter Walmsley was dead—that avenue of search was closed. But an empty envelope, it seems, had been found on his person after the train accident. Which envelope carried, according to that newspaper story, a corner return card, reading "Return in five days to Milo Payne, Palmer House, Chicago." But it had not been mailed from Chicago! Its postmark—so said the news story—was of a place, not specified, in Northern Michigan—that very isolated and sparsely inhabited region attached to the tip of Wisconsin—yet not of Wisconsin at all; and not even touching Michigan, nor any other State, thanks to being cut off by Lake Michigan, Lake Huron, and Lake Superior. And it was from Northern Michigan that Dr. Prior had been called by Long Distance, a few days before, by an inquirer who masked his identity by claiming to be a member of the British Government's Department 17—what rot!—Department 17. Plainly, Milo Payne was the man who had called Dr. Prior, and who knew the circumstances, therefore, concerning the existence of this skull. And Milo Payne, therefore, was my own last only chance. When I located him, I could probably disentangle the whole affair—either through my own efforts—or with his assistance. And I could not help but feel that, if only the Reverend Peter Walmsley hadn't destroyed the letter which had been in that envelope, the police would not have come to the conclusion that they had met with an ordinary robbery!

I woke from all these reveries only because the cabby, looking back in the waiting cab at me, asked me with a grin:

"Where to, Mister? North—South—East—or West?"

"Oh—the Palmer House," I told him. And settled back on the cushions.

We were there, at busy Monroe and State Streets, in thirty minutes. A huge towering structure of red brick, the Palmer House, its vertical upper lines emphasizing its height. Three times torn down and three times rebuilt, it was said, each time bigger and greater. Once its lobby had been paved with silver dollars.

I paid off my driver and made my way into its big busy lobby. And to the registration desk.

"Milo Payne," I told the clerk. "P-A-Y-N-E."

He looked over a registry-card index in back of him. And evidently found nothing. Then he moved sidewise to a much larger registry-card index file. And opening a drawer, turned the cards, till he stopped at a certain one.

"Checked out," he said laconically. "Registered here day before yest—" He paused. He scratched his head. "Oh—Payne? Payne? Say, you'll have to see the manager on him. All inquiries referred to him."

"And he's—"

"201."

I rode, seemingly, a half-dozen floors, before I came to that one technically known as the second. And went down the corridor about forty feet till I came to 201. I opened the door and walked in. It was fitted up more like an office than a living-room. Although it was half and half of each. At a flat-top desk near the window sat a bald-headed man with gold-rimmed eyeglasses, shuffl5ing over some papers. He looked up.

"I'm trying to get some information," I told him, "as to the present address of a Mr. Milo Payne who registered here day before yesterday. Your clerk downstairs just suddenly remembered that all inquiries on him are referred to you."

"Police Department?" he inquired.

I looked down at him appraisingly. He looked easy to convince.

"Department 17, United States Government," I told him laconically.

"Oh? Yes. Yes. Of course—yes. USA? Well, the Detective Bureau called up a while ago, and said they expected to have a man over here later on to look into the matter of this chap Payne—something touching on the matter of another man killed in the West—railroad accident or something—I didn't quite grasp it—but the Detective Bureau man hasn't got here yet. But Federal investigators are just as important, say I, as local ones. And so—but do sit down—" He moved over a chair. "Here's the dope on it. Such little as we have."

He reached into the top drawer of his desk, and took from it what appeared to be a large photograph to the back of which, but face up, however, was clipped a typewritten report of some kind, and since he consulted the slip of paper as he talked, I could not see the photograph.

"I can't give you very much," he said. "This fellow Milo Payne registered with us at noontime, day before yesterday, from Rapid River, Michigan. He carried a suitcase and a bag. The clerk and bellboy say they remember him because he looked very much like Sherlock Holmes in the moving pictures. That is, only in the way he dressed. For he wore a checkered cap, with a long beak. Probably forty-five years old—more or less. And he wore a monocle. English, of course. Even dropped his 'h's,' the clerk tells me! At 6 o'clock the same clerk who registered him, and who was still on duty, remembers sending up to his room a fellow dressed like a parson. About forty-five minutes later the parson returned to the lobby—the clerk remembers seeing him too, and he was carrying a black bag, now; and he left the hotel; and this Milo Payne came straight downstairs and paid his bill and pulled out, grumbling that he was extremely disappointed in the Palmer House because of its not having the famous silver-dollar-paved lobby he'd heard about for so many years. What is it, dope peddling?"

"No," I told him. And that was all I did tell him. For Lord knows I didn't know myself. I spoke. "Well, of course the principal question—and the only one worth while to an investigator like myself—is this: did this Payne give any forwarding address for his mail?"

I leaned forward, my heart in my mouth. Was I to lose my last clue?

"Nope, none," replied the manager. "In fact, he pulled out so hastily, he even forgot to check up his personal things. The maid who cleaned up his room after he left turned over to our lost-and-found department this photograph which she found where it had tumbled off of the bureau and fallen behind. If you'll receipt for it, you can have it, but I'd rather hold on to it—in case there's nothing to this investigation—and he writes in for it."

He turned over the photograph to whose back had been

attached the small memo he had been consulting. And handed it to me. One look at it—and a sickening feeling swept over me. It showed the delicate, spirituelle face of a girl—a girl I knew well. But, even had I been in doubt concerning the identity of the original of the photograph, the words, written in India ink on the bottom, were enough:

> *"From Doris ——*
> *with all her love!"*

CHAPTER XII

A TELEPHONE CALL

Either as a detective I was a good sofa-pillow crocheter, or else I was playing in the identical luck of the piccolo player when the eccentric millionaire filled up the instruments of each member of the German band with $5 gold pieces. For I had reached the end of the trail again. Milo Payne, Sherlockholmsian long-beaked cap and monocle, gone; present address unknown. The Reverend Peter Walmsley dead, as a result of a train wreck. Abigail Sprigge, whose self—or else whose quarters—had at least provided part of the paper with which to stuff that bullet within the interior of that skull, not in the slightest way reachable. The scar-faced Chinaman—where? As John Barr had advised me, I would probably be wasting my mental energies to expect any information from Roger Pelton. And Doris, in her note to me, had claimed that she herself was all in the dark about the whole affair. I could have endured all that, perhaps, but to think that this Milo Payne had had in his possession a picture of Doris—and a picture, moreover, of which she had never given me a copy—and with all her love added to it—was disconcerting, to say the least. And like any man who is fearfully in love, I began to form all sorts of bizarre hypotheses connecting Doris's note with these other facts.

She had written me to tell me that our marriage had been called off by her father. It hardly seemed like his doing, for he had

111

maintained the most friendly attitude toward me up to the very moment he had fainted. And then, following my receipt of this very note, I had discovered through a blind set of clues that an individual named Milo Payne had had in his possession a photograph of the girl to whom I was engaged—and one taken while I was in the Philippines, were I to judge from the newness of its pose, and the cute manner in which she had put her blonde hair up in charming biscuits above her shell-like ears. An infatuation of some sort, all right. Maybe he had told her he was a British lord! But how deep an infatuation, that was the question. Was it so strong that she had jilted me—and used her father for an excuse? It was hard to believe, somehow.

But what in the devil was the connection between her inamoratus, this Milo Payne, and the Reverend Peter Walmsley whose safe door had been blown open while he was being whirled to his death in a railroad accident, nearly 900 miles or so from Chicago—judging from the time it took his train to reach the point—and who even while his safe was being blown open was not yet 150 miles out of Chicago?

And why had he been carrying the skull of his own brother, Phillip Walmsley, once a patient, in a quite ethical operation for a condition known as "intradural hemorrhage," of old Doctor Max Prior?

And the thought of that "intradural hemorrhage" business brought me, naturally, back to the matter of that much smaller hole in the skull—the one vertically beneath the trephine plate. And the bullet which had made that hole. When was *that* hole made?

And last but far from least, why had I gotten knocked senseless in the vestibule of a vacant Lake Shore Drive mansion—by a Chinky, of all persons? I was forced to give it up. My head, from having eaten nothing, was beginning to ache—and my spirits were sinking lower and lower.

So I gobbled up a lunch in a Thompson beanery on State Street, and went home. Under any other conditions, I think, I would have taken a cab and impulsively gone straight up to Doris's—now that

I had come to such a perfect and complete dead end in all of my investigations—but the finding of that photograph, and its affectionate inscription, had pretty well taken the heart out of me when it came to rushing to her. And so, since she had told me in her note—and rather specifically, too!—to come at 7 o'clock that night—7 o'clock it would be, I assured myself grimly, and not one minute to—nor one minute after!

I met Mrs. W-H in the hall when I got back to North Dearborn Parkway, and learned from her that, in my absence, she had ordered my service restored on my phone. Good old Higginsbottom! No wonder she kept all her paying guests. Always thinking of their convenience and comfort. I went up to my room, and lay down on my bed a while—to try to think things out.

Although my thinking was confined, at best, to but two resolutions. One was, of course, to see Doris at 7 o'clock—exactly as she had asked me to do; and the other was to lug the whole affair to John Barr, and plump it squarely down in his lap, *after* I should see her. For twice in my life he had been the means by which I had been helped through dire crises—and, having her fall in love with another man, and call off our marriage in the bargain because her father had—or at least presumably so!—gone off at half-cock thanks to my story about a fool skull for whose possession I myself had been knocked into dreamland, was certainly a crisis for me. True, regardless of what she might have to say, John would be as much in the dark as I, but on the basis of our ages, his wisdom and experience should—and, judging from such dealings as I had had with him thus far would be 49/29ths of my own!

But I wasn't destined to lie there and pass resolutions about what I was going to do. For my first taste of my restored incoming telephone service came to me. In short, the phone rang.

I clambered up off the bed, and answered it.

A sort of cackly, though not unkindly, voice addressed me.

"Am I speaking to Mr. Clay Calthorpe?"

It couldn't be any representative of Suing Sophie, because none such could obtain that private, unlisted number. So I answered freely.

"Yes. Who is this?"

"This is Philodexter Maxellus. But you don't know me. Your private number was given me by a mutual friend of ours, John Barr."

"Oh yes. Well, I know of you, Mr. Maxellus. For John Barr told me about your thinking of starting up a magazine—to be called *Verse*."

"Yes. That is correct. Well, he called me up this morning, about 10:30 or so, and told me you are trying to get on the track of a woman named Sprigge. Abigail Sprigge. Who my manuscript records show sent in a little rhyme—or jingle—entitled 'Poor Pickings.' And who also wrote one, Mr. Barr says, a sonnet—entitled: 'If His Love Dies—So Mine!'—with an opening line running something like 'He's gone: I would he had my wounded heart.' Is this all correct, Mr. Calthorpe?"

"Yes. That's right. Has that latter piece come in—with perhaps her return address this time on the envelope?"

"I'm sorry to say no. And every piece of mail or manuscript that has come in, up to the present moment, has now been opened up, and read—at least sufficiently so that it can be booked up. Or filed."

"I see. Well—my bad luck then, I guess. I just thought it might have come in. And with an address on it this time."

"No, it hasn't. And Mr. Barr emphasized that you were exceedingly anxious to get in direct touch with this particular author—or rather authoress. But—now—I wonder if you could run down to my office, Mr. Calthorpe? Now—today—I mean. My office is in Printingtown—538 Federal Street."

"Why—yes—sure I could. I—I—yes—I'll be right down. Right away."

"Thank you. I wish you would. I'll be here."

I hung up. Considerably mystified. He had nothing for me. And yet wanted, apparently, to show me something.

So out I went on the street again. And once more, as before—for this was assuredly my lucky day on taxicabs!—found a cab. And was in Federal Street in twelve minutes. A dark gloomy little narrow thoroughfare, with the most ancient archaic office buildings frowning down on either side of it—if they could even be called such. The dolorous clank of printing presses, concealed God knows where, sounded continuously. Printingtown! Hundreds of trade journals being put together back of those hundreds of fly-specked windows.

Number 538 was indisputably the oldest of all the buildings on Federal Street. A short flight of broad wooden steps leading up to a soapstone archway comprised its entrance. Inside, a flight of narrow wooden stairs, worn at the middle of their treads into virtual pits, wound upward alongside a sinuous polished banister. A single elevator shaft, enclosed in a wire netting, encompassed an elevator which, however, drowsed at the top of the building—where all such elevators in all such buildings invariably hide themselves. So, finding from the small bulletin board, that Maxellus was entered as being in No. 303, I walked up the steps instead of waiting the inevitable number of minutes it would take for that elevator to wheeze asthmatically down to terra firma.

No. 303 was just a big carpetless room, ascetically furnished indeed for an office—and about as suggestive of things poetical as the inside of a tomb. A whole row of secondhanded vertical filing cabinets were ranged along the right wall. And with open soap boxes, bearing some kind of classifying tickets tacked on their fronts, spaced here and there between the cabinets. The soap boxes, I observed, were filled, or partly filled, with mail or manuscripts. A gigantic stack of exceedingly small halftone or zinc cuts, neatly piled, however, for the metal faces of one layer were separated from the next stratum by sheets of newspapers, stood in one corner. They were probably tailpiece cuts, and bought, so I surmised, from defunct art and pseudo-poetical magazines at the standard used-cut rate of one cent per pound. And would each and every one, in due course, probably be used as the tail-decorations of new poems. If, as I reflected then, Philodexter Maxellus lasted that long! And from the huge number stacked up there, I would then and there have been willing to have gambled that a decorative cut could be found to match a poem on whales, or a poem on love. Or even a still more specific poem: concerning love—between whales! A huge calendar, at least five feet square, on the left wall showed that Pegasus, if he flew at all, would have to fly by strict schedule. Alongside of the calendar a sharp-faced middle-aged stenographer in funereal black dress pecked away at a typewriter. What an office! Still, I reflected, the new *Verse* was only in the process of being born now. And I did not of course know then what I was to know later: that Philodexter Maxellus was a shrewd publisher, and an instinctively good one; that he was to put over $10,000 into *Verse,* that he was to obtain a patent on his peculiarly ingenious system for distributing his returned unused copies to new zones; that he was to make *Verse* into a really successful and brilliant publication, one which was to be read by thousands of poetry lovers, and quoted more often than not; and that he was to sell it—with its patented distributing system, that is—to the *Saturday Evening Post* people for $50,000. Had I known all this, I would have had more respect, I daresay, than I did when I first walked into the offices of *Verse*.

Philodexter Maxellus—for I was to find shortly it was he—sat at a huge table by the windows. A table heaped with manuscripts. Some set off into little separate heaps. Others filed crisscross on each other like railroad ties, and in various other ways. He looked exceedingly tired, exceedingly irritated.

He was a little wizened old man. Dressed in as funereal black as his stenographer. In age, about sixty. With bushy grey hair. And he kept a massive cane right at the side of his chair. Either he was lame in one leg, or the cane was used to slay budding poets with.

He did not slay me, however, but rose and bowed friendlily.

"Sit down, Mr. Calthorpe. Or—or is it—Mr. Calthorpe?"

I glanced troubledly at that cane. And made haste to state my non-poetical status. "Yes, Mr. Maxellus. I'm Clay Calthorpe." And I took the comfortable armchair that sat next his table.

"I see," I ventured, while he settled back in his own chair, "that the poets are swamping you?"

"They are indeed," he replied. "Aided and abetted by their companions in crime—the poetesses! But I have found out exactly what I started out primarily to find out: namely, that I can start my magazine and not run short of good material. While my magazine's success is based on certain circulation ideas, I wish it nevertheless to be A. No. 1 in contents. In quality. And I have lots and lots of good things already packed away in my filing cabinets. And in a week I shall be sending out the happy acceptance slips. And also the checks for such items as will be going into type for Number 1, Volume 1!"

"But no acceptance slips—nor checks—to Miss Sprigge?" I commented.

"I'm afraid not," he answered. "Miss Sprigge seems quite willing to accept the aggrandizement of her ego that will come from publication of her wares. And does not consider the $10 we are paying—as worth bothering with.

"However," he went on, after a brief pause, "I wanted you to read one of these contributions."

"Is it by Miss Sprigge?"

"No."

"Oh—I see. That is, Mr. Maxellus, I don't see." For the first time I began to realize that maybe I was puzzling him more than he was me. And so I elucidated briefly: "My fishing around, Mr. Maxellus, to try and get hold of the address of Abigail Sprigge must all sound rather mysterious. But the fact merely is that Abigail Sprigge is tangled up with a very curious affair involving me. To the extent, that is, of a manuscript of hers being mixed up in the affair. That is, just the torn-up carbon copy of it. In fact, the very sonnet which John asked you, on my behalf, to look up; that is, as to the possibility of the original of it being in this place. And so, because of all this, Abigail Sprigge can throw a lot of light on the affair of which I speak—at least so I think—by telling me exactly how her effusion got into a certain skull—into matters. Yes—more perfectly put, she can pass me out a lead to the solution of this affair. I'm not starting a poetry magazine, Mr. Maxellus. Really. So don't get me wrong."

"I'm not worried," he said dryly. "Start all the poetry magazines you want. Starting one is nothing but a lot of grief. And takes a lot of money even to get under way. And circulation ideas too. And not a red penny back from the magazine distributors until you've put out at least about the equivalent of three complete issues. No, come on in. The water's fine. If you don't freeze to death!"

"Thanks—but I'll stick to confectionary. That's my game."

"So John told me." He took up a script. Or at least a typed page of some sort. "No, the script I want you to read isn't by your woman Sprigge. It—but first read it, please—if you will."

"But I still don't see—" I began.

"No," he put in, and with a slight hint of asperity now, "but I wouldn't have asked you to come 'way down here unless I thought there was something that you should give consideration to. However, read this script first. Take you but a minute. Then we'll go into why I did bring you down here."

So I took the typed page from his fingers. A poem, as I saw the minute I cast my eyes full upon it. Just another poem of the many thousands he'd evidently received.

And, still mystified, I read it.

Not knowing, as I did so, that with certain other data Philodexter Maxellus would give me in a few seconds, proof would be at hand that I had at last located Abigail Sprigge under her right name and address.

CHAPTER XIII

AT LAST—A LEAD!

The poem, with its two stanzas, its heading, and certain information, on its tail end, about its submitter, ran:

A POCKET EDITION

by

O. M. LEE

You are six feet two, my father; I am five feet one;
I, a disappointing daughter, when you wished a son;
But Life stole your face and manner, gave them both to me—
Made me your second self, for all the world to see;
Bade me set my little footprints lovingly in yours;
Made of you my sun and stars, the while my life endures;
Gave me to you for a wistful, little trailing ghost;
Made me know in every instinct what would stir you most.

All your special, strong temptations are my greatest ones
(There are risky traits for daughters that are safe for sons).
When I see, within your eyes, that worried Memory wakes,
Walk I very circumspectly then for both our sakes.
Sister Jane is cold and sinless, Sister Edith mild;
And they say our little brother is his mother's child;
But when evening finds me creeping, eager, to your breast,
I can guess without your telling why you love me best.

Submitted by (Miss) O. M. Lee,
No. 49, 3753 Gardendale Street,
Chicago, Ill.

"Well," I said, looking up from it, "it's—it's a kind of a good—that is, a sort of an interesting—a rather nice poem, I think. But—"

"Well, well—and thrice well!" was Philodexter Maxellus's reply, given to me with a dry smile. "John said you were undoubtedly the world's perfect example of the man who hated poetry."

"I believe I was," I returned, though still puzzled, "at least till—till I first encountered Abigail Sprigge's work—and then, of a sudden, I seemed to—" I broke off. "Yet—yet I don't just see—"

"Turn it over," Maxellus said, "and glance at the back."

I did so.

Lengthwise of the paper ran a number of typewritten lines. Lines bearing underneath themselves, in pencil, the peculiar U-shaped marks and dashes such as we used to call, in school, "scanning marks." And with, moreover, their words and syllables set off, by short vertical lines, also in pencil, into what I at least remembered were called "feet."

Lines, marks, set-offs, and all, ran:

> |If he|had sight|to pierce|the hu|man breast|
> |If his|could know|the ach|ing of|my heart|
> |I would|my heart|had wings|like yon|der swal|low
> |He's|gone: I would|he had|my wound|ed heart|

I read the whole thing. And looked up.

"Well," was all I could say, "I—I don't know yet what all this stuff is—but that bottom line, Mr. Maxellus, is the identical opening line of the carbon copy of Miss Sprigge's which has bobbed up in my affairs."

"I surmised that it would be," he said promptly, "judging from the title John asked me to look up. Yes," he continued, "when I turned this over, after reading it, and laid it face down so as to put a paper weight on it for, by Jove, I—I liked it myself—in fact,

I'm going to take it, although I'd like to have John's verdict on it, though, alas, he says he positively won't read another manuscript!—well, as I was going to say, when I laid it face down, and saw that the author had chanced to transcribe her poem on the back of a page used to work out the opening of another poem, I could not help but see, when my eyes fell on this last line, that there was a sort of a con-nection—a decided connection—between this last experimental line, and the title I was asked to look up. And that is why I called you down here. For John said you seemed exceedingly overwrought when you called him."

"I guess I was, all right," I agreed. "Everything, at least in cer-tain fields—for me, was up Sally's Alley then! And is more so than ever—now. That is, until you called me, and then—but exactly what," I queried, "are these four lines—with their marks—etc.?"

"Oh," he said, with a deprecatory little jerk of his head, "those lines, Mr. Calthorpe, show the complete evolution of a poem. Of the opening line, that is. The author, as you can see, has made four starts in an endeavor to get across, and right off—off the bat, as you might say—a certain theme—rather, to put a certain atmosphere into her poem at its very beginning—and three of her starts she considers n. g. But on the fourth one she has apparently caught—what she wants. Yes—" He shook his head. "—I have seen too many poets, back in days when I happened to be the business manager of *Poesy*—you see, I used to have to pay the critters off!—as I was going to say, I've seen too many poets—working on their cuffs, on the walls, working most anywhere—get completely launched once they secured their opening line, and dash off a whole poem. Seemed they just had to have that precious first line to—to—well—unlock 'em."

I gazed down at the script and spoke. "Well, all I can say is that Miss O. M. Lee's work is undoubtedly Abigail Sprigge's work. I—I should have guessed it, by gosh, from the fact alone that—that I rather liked it!" I paused. "But now if I could just compare the typing in—say—Abigail Sprigge's letter, on file here—with this—both front and back—to make absolutely dead-certain, then—but have you a reading glass?"

"No," he said. "But that's a good idea. I confess I never even thought of that. However, you can make use of one of the lenses in my good comfortable plus-sphere reading specs here. They are four diopters in strength." He handed me a curious little pair of silver-bowed spectacles which he took from his vest pocket. And turned to his stenographer. "Miss Dove, give us the letter on file from Abigail Sprigge. Yes, the letter Mr. Barr asked us to look up this morning."

Having looked it up once, she knew right where to go this time, and was over with it in her hand by the time I had the powerful spectacles unbowed and, holding one thick lens off at proper focal distance, was contemplating—highly magnified!—the typescript of the poem "A Pocket Edition." I found, with little or no trouble, barbs missing on the right-hand sides of all the capital I's; the small i's all broken across their middles; the loops of all the b's filled up with ink; and the "o" and the "u" invariably touching—almost interlinking—whenever the latter followed directly the former. That particular characteristic, I knew, indicated a pure idiosyncrasy of type-touch upon a machine built mechanically like the L. C. Smith.

I brought the spectacles lens now to bear on the experimental lines on the back. They contained the identical type imperfections. All of those imperfections, including the one due to idiosyncrasy of touch.

Now I brought it to bear on Abigail Sprigge's brief letter. Again, the identical type defects. All of them! Including the touch idiosyncrasy.

The proof was complete.

Abigail Sprigge was Miss O. M. Lee. Of Apartment No. 49, 3753 Gardendale Street.

With a deep sigh of satisfaction, I handed back Philodexter Maxellus his convex spectacles.

"Well, Mr. Maxellus," was all I could say, "this is certainly a break for me. Yes, they all tally. Miss Sprigge is Miss Lee. And I've found the fair lady! And boy, oh boy, how I do want to talk to her; to find in what places she's been living—who she's had dealings with—and all she can tell me along those lines." I was busy writing down Miss

O. M. Lee's full address as I spoke. I handed him back the poem. "Just why, Mr. Maxellus," I inquired, "do you suppose she submitted first under a pseudonym—with no return address—and then in the next script gave her actual name, and where she lives?"

"Quite easily answered," Maxellus replied with a smile. "For I've been mixed up with too many magazines in my day not to know the answer. The fact is, Mr. Calthorpe, it occurred to her— as it would have occurred to us—that anonymous contributions— or ones with pseudonyms—and no addresses—might be looked upon by us as 'lifted.' Plagiarisms, see? So she decided to play aboveboard on all subsequent ones so as not to nullify her chances of being printed."

"Which is luck for me," I returned. "For this fair grey-eyed lady of thirty summers and winters can throw illumination—at least, so I believe—on a matter that's balked me in absolutely every direction I've tried to trace it down."

He looked puzzled, but courteously so. And not at all worried. Evidently he feared no rivals in the troublesome business of starting a poetry magazine—much less the possible stealing of possible contributors thereto.

"You say," he commented, "this fair—this fair grey-eyed lady— of thirty summers and winters? I thought John told me you didn't actually know Miss Sprigge? Or Miss Lee—to use her right name?"

"No, I don't."

"Well—where—where do you get the description—'fair grey-eyed lady'?—and the 'thirty summers and winters'?—in connection with her? Rather, may I ask—just what do you picture her as looking like?" There was a quizzically amused tone to his voice.

"Well," was my confident answer, "from—from her poems, I guess. Three of which I've now seen. Yes, I make her to be—about as I've described. Large grey eyes. And light brown hair. Combed back in some peculiar way from her forehead. Long pendant earrings of jade—or amethyst. Thirty years old—hardly a year more nor less. A sort of solemn gaze—that looks right through one."

He smiled skeptically.

"She won't look like that at all, Mr. Calthorpe. I assure you of that. For I know a great deal about poets. And poetesses. From those days of mine with *Poesy*. Where I met hundreds. Poets never look like poets. They look like anything but! I remember that some of the most delicately beautiful things we used to get in turned out to be by an ice-man named Pat Kelly—with shoulders five feet broad. And some mighty unusual dramatic narrative poems dealing with the underworld just bristling with authentic gangsterese—we used them because we considered them to be practically true historical pictures of the stirring days of '33—the last days of Prohibition, you know—well, they turned out to be by a shrinking little violet of a chap named Percival deFleur. A fact!" He paused. "Yes, a fact, Mr. Calthorpe. And you'll find it to be the case here. Your Miss Lee—O. M.—Olivia Marion—Ottilie Margaret—Ora Mildred—or whatever the O. M. stands for—will be as different from your mental picture of her as day is from night."

"Well," I said, "you know a lot more about this rack—er—game than I do. So you may be right." I rose, gazing out of the window. For the clouds had suddenly cut off the afternoon sun—the day had become grey—and so had my soul. Doris! "I'm going to hop me into a cab right off—and find out for myself. What Sister Lee looks like. Mind, Mr. Maxellus, if I tell her I got her address from you?"

"Not at all," he assured me, turning back to his desk. "Everything's 100 per cent aboveboard where this office is concerned."

I went out of the little cramped building, but had to foot it a half block north to roaring Van Buren Street to catch a taxicab. For Federal Street was so confoundedly narrow that most of the modern Gargantuan cabs, I daresay, were too afraid of being wedged between its two curbstones and stuck there for a week or so.

I did not myself know where Gardendale Street might be, and, moreover, had never heard of it before. But I told the cabby where I wanted to go.

He struggled hard to keep his face from expressing huge satisfaction, supreme happiness. It was a masterful attempt—one of the best I have ever seen. But I caught the look back of the deferentially dignified look—and realized that Mr. Cabby knew he was in for a nice long profitable haul.

Nevertheless, I climbed in. For, after all, I had over $14 on me. And thus we started for Gardendale Street—and Miss Lee, one of whose verses, beyond all doubt and peradventure, had helped to stuff that skull!

CHAPTER XIV

NO. 49—3753 GARDENDALE STREET

I sat back, legs comfortably sprawled out, in the cab. While we rode and rode and rode. And the meter clicked and clicked and clicked. We seemed to be on Ogden Avenue—in fact were—and the circumstance of our being on a diagonal thoroughfare alone showed me that the cabby was trying to make my bill as small as reasonably possible. We continued to bowl southwest. Old buildings changed to newer ones, and the newer ones got lower in height. I drew up one knee between my two hands, and wondered what sort of a woman Miss Sprigge-Lee would prove to be—and what light she was going to be able to throw on who might have prepared that bag—and put that skull in it.

Once we passed a small and obviously new two-story building of orange brick—a printery, as could be seen from the Gordon presses in its first floor windows—a printery which from the huge gold and black sign along its eaves was devoted solely to printing hymnals, tracts, Sunday-school papers and missionary material. Which set me to thinking, for a change, upon Sophie. Poor Sophie! Whom I had "ditched" so completely at the docks in 'Frisco. Or, rather, gracefully permitted her to "ditch" me. Where, oh where, was Sophie today? Somewhere in the South, of course. From where never could she pick up my trail, thank the Lord, in spite of that pebbled leather notebook she had. Until in due course she would be

127

on her way back to the Philippines again—and falling in love with some other male ocean traveler. Poor Sophie! Lucky for me, I told myself, that I had gotten to my friends, and acquaintances, and business connections ahead of her.

And thus I mused—over the course of this long ride.

For indeed it seemed an interminable time for us to get to our destination. I knew almost for a certainty now that we were headed for Suburbia. Or at least Semi-Suburbia. In fact, we were almost out in the country now; at least, mathematically so, for there was more vacant land, by actual area, than houses, and such houses as there were were but bungalows or one-story cottages with garden patches. And finally I saw, by a very bright new blue-enameled street sign on Ogden Avenue—in fact, Ogden Avenue was now being called, I perceived, Ogden Road—that we had struck our objective: Gardendale Avenue. And I lurched as the cabby turned sharply leftward—southward, in short—and pursued Gardendale Avenue itself.

A street, Gardendale, as bleak as Ogden Road. Cottages. Now and then. Bungalows. Here and again. Gardens. Plenty. A subdivision laid out over to the west. Sewers being put in. And on we rode.

And now up ahead I saw bearing down on us a high cement-stuccoed wall. A wall at least twenty feet high, and which ran, apparently, not only along the street we were now on—but along the street at right angles to ours. In fact, the district was so sparsely built up that I could see that the wall spanned a full block east and west, and if it did the same north and south—which, indeed, it appeared to do—then it encompassed exactly one square block.

My first thought, naturally enough, was that we were coming to a prison! A prison with, of course, quarters for women as well as men. But there were no prisons around about Chicago. Besides which, as we continued to draw nearer, I saw no guards patrolling the top of the wall with rifles. Nor watchtowers at its corners. Prison it manifestly was not. Unless, perchance, it was a prison based on some brand new psychological theory to the effect that no self-respecting convict, male or female, would try to climb over a wall that he—or she—could burrow straight through with a tin spoon; for the wall, plainly, was made of frame fencing plastered with stucco. But prison, or reformatory—no! Upon which, I thought to myself, one of those dour institutions where girls who had had the misfortune to have lived in correct accordance with their physiological selves were sequestered under the guidance of strict nuns who were living out of tune with their own physiology. Except, however, that the usual red-brick convent was not towering down over the walls.

Then it struck me: an insane asylum! The cab was at a halt now. At the corner, where the north-south wall joined with the east-west wall. And at the same instant I knew my theory about the place being an insane asylum was also wrong. For insane asylums never have walls. And, almost at that moment, I knew the flimsily walled area for what it really was.

One of those cheap subdivision developments called Garden City—or Beachview Gardens (with the nearest Lake Michigan beach at least twelve miles to the east!) with small one-story bungalows laid around within it, and little toy garages with red-tiled roofs in back of each. A single combined driveway and entrance for all the natives to get in. Or to get out. Exclusive! The Joneses playing bridge every other Saturday night with the Smiths, and vice versa on the intermediate Saturday nights. The Robinsons' children borrowing the Chipperfields' children's red wagon. Mrs. Decker borrowing Mrs. Doofely's ten-ride ticket to run down to the city on the nearest railroad. All for one, and one for all.

But the cabby, still drawn up at the corner-angle of the stuccoed wall, was speaking. Apologetically.

"Mind, Mister, walking along this here sidewalk the rest of the way? To where you got to go? F'r I really shoulda come around from Pershing Road, to the south. Just lookit that bog! I been out this way before. I know this half block o' Gardendale Street—'tain't never been paved yet, y' see—and I been stuck in it, good—and proper! Jesus, what a bog! Wors'n last time. We'd be in axles deep. That's 'cause o' that rain we had night before last. Remember it?"

I remembered no rain. And reason enough. Considering that multiplonal. But I could see a bog all right. Even though it called

itself a street! A bog, a bottomless pit of muck that looked as though
it were just aching to envelop one taxicab and its occupant.

"Jest a hundred yards up the sidewalk," the cabby was explain-
ing patiently. "An' I'll wait here to take you back to the city."

"Wait at your own expense then," I cautioned him, climbing
out. And tendered him the amount of the meter reading—which
was $3.60—and a quarter tip. "For I'm in for a long, long talk with
the occupant of No. 49 in there." I nodded toward the stucco wall.

The cabby looked at me with such a hopelessly baffled expression, that I began to wonder if, at that, the place was a sanitarium.
He took my money, however, and shut off his meter. And he was still
staring helplessly at me—as I saw when I looked curiously back—
as I started up the narrow sidewalk. Sandwiched in, as it were,
between the wall and the bog.

A half block up, just as he had told me, I came to the one
entrance of Beachview Gardens—or whatever it called itself. A big
arched gateway, spanning a concrete driveway, across which were
swung two broad solid Gothic-like wooden doors. Not locked, however. For one swung free of the other by at least the amount of its
own latch-bolt. Commuters could push one or the other of the doors
inside—or drive straight in with their Fords and bunt them open.
There was an ornamental iron grillwork across the top of the
entrance carrying on it the number 3753 in tall graceful figures of
beautifully burnished copper. All this outside artistry, I knew, por-
tended $2500 bungalows inside—$50 down, and $30 a month for
life. I noted now, as the taxi-driver seemed to have known, that the
commuters could get into their village all right by coming from
Pershing Road instead of Ogden Road; for the bog-like street south
of the entrance was planked in that entire direction so that any sort
of vehicle could traverse it.

Peaceful, though, I had to admit. A good place to write. Far away
I heard the melancholy wail of a train whistle. And the October
wind, picking up suddenly in conformity with the leaden grey in the
sky, actually rustled audibly over the surrounding countryside.

The wall was, of course, too tall to show the squatty little bungalows inside. But there was a small sort of house actually peeping over the wall near the gate—a sort of one-room house, built undoubtedly on stilts—like a railroad flagman's place of vantage. It—or at least its windows—could look out both over the street, and inside over the tenants as well. In fact, a man, within it, was nailing up a cheap chromo of some kind on one wall. And as he turned, hammer in hand, I saw that he had a red bristle on his face, and was smoking a corncob pipe.

But I stared not so much at the bit of houselet peeping over the wall as I did at the black wooden sign, with gilt letters, nailed just above the top of its street-side windows. And which read:

RESTVALE CEMETERY

And at that moment the whole explanation of affairs dawned on me. With perfect completeness, complete clarity. The daughter—wife—cousin—of the cemetery overseer! Occupying the lower section of that house that peeped above the walls, and which I had first imagined was on stilts. The daughter—a poet. Or the wife! All exactly as Philodexter Maxellus had foreshadowed. It took graves, silence, leisure, death—to make the lady create poetry. And so that little one-roomed space rather, the quarters underneath it—was where all these Sprigge manuscripts were emanating? I gazed now with considerable increased interest towards the red-bristlefaced man who was still hammering at his cheap chromo.

However, I had work to do. Facts to ascertain. And entrance to that literary sanctum was to be attained only inside those gates—and not outside. And since the doors were not, as I say, locked, I just shoved the leftmost one open, and passed on in. It was, indeed, a cemetery, just one block square. No trees. And a bit desolate because of that. Or perhaps, instead, because it was far from filled up. Indeed it could not be very many years old, because the wooden grave-markers—the little wooden posts protruding from the turf all over the place—were staunch and unrotted. Painted black, with brilliant white numbers on their faces. There was quite a fair scattering of variously sized headstones to be seen; and a considerable number of graves, too, without such. Here and there, too, a granite or marble shaft, with pointed top, reared itself above the sod.

The little house, however, as I had initially surmised, was on stilts. And had no under quarters. A small flight of wooden steps, with a handrail, led up to its door. I was just about to ascend them, when the sun at last broke through a hole in those clouds which had been making the sky, all afternoon, so dun and greyish. And I stopped short. For the golden-yellow light which flooded through that rift in the clouds literally poured itself upon a pointed granite shaft of unusually wide dimensions, scarcely 30 feet from the entrance near where I stood; upon the carven side, rather, of the shaft, facing the very gateway.

Indeed, letters were chiseled so deeply on the shaft that some were readable from even that distance.

I paused, a foot in mid-air, with my hand on the rail. And instead of ascending those steps, I strode straight over to that shaft. The black grave-marker in front of which bore the bright white numerals "49." And, my lower jaw hanging open, I read the inscription carved upon that granite face.

Which inscription ran:

> Here lies the famous
> O MING LEE
> The Girl with Four Legs and Six Arms
> Known to the Profession
> as
> LEGGA, THE HUMAN SPIDER
> Born Canton, China   Died Canton, Ohio
> 1917–1937
> Erected by the Chinese of America.

CHAPTER XV

INFORMATION FROM A CABBY

Ipassed a hand weakly over my forehead.

No. 49.

3753 Gardendale Street.

And here was Miss Lee—Miss O. M. Lee!

Blankly, for I was still fuddled, I turned and read the words chiseled on a small gravestone, alabaster white, that seemingly marked a tiny new-born baby's grave.

They read:

```
          b. 1884 d. 1936
              Here lies
        GEN. TOM DOWLING
           18 inches high
         20 pounds in weight
       Rest in peace, General!
```

What the—

The red-bristle-faced man was coming down the steps of his aerie. I advanced to meet him. Skirting around a huge grave in which—so I concluded at once—a husband and wife must be buried side by side. Till I saw, as I rounded it; on a large but temporary wooden marker, resembling a huge shingle, crudely painted:

ROSCOE PARKER
He brought happiness and
cheer to the world, with
a heart that, for sheer
nobleness, conformed with
his 612 pounds of weight!
B. 1885 D. 1935

The red-bristle-faced man was now on me.

"Om lak to halp yu elf yu vassen findin' grey vat yu lokking for. Om Misder Hvralek, grevyard sopperintendunt."

"Lithuanian?" I asked shrewdly.

"Czecho-Slav," he replied modestly.

"No," I said, knowing exactly what I would be up against plowing through a lingo like that. "Just—just peeping in, that's all."

And turned disgruntledly away—only to turn back, half hopefully even yet. Of something.

"You got wife?" I asked him. "You got daughter? Mebbe?"

"Om no got waff. No got dutter. Me liv' alone. Up dere." He pointed up at his eyrie. "Yu no lokking at grevs," he commented shrewdly. "Yu Foller Brosh Salzman, heh?"

"No," I said. "I'm not a Fuller Brush Salesman. Just—just the Big Bad Wolf. In disguise."

And I wended my way out through the gates, along that narrow sidewalk north, and to that waiting cabby who seemed to have known all along what 3753 Gardendale Street was.

And he was still waiting, all right, drawn up at the corner just where I had left him.

"Say, brother," I queried, "did you know where you were taking me—when we started out?"

"Why sure—mister. Sure, I did. But I didn't say nothing. Natchelly. In case—well—you know? If people are going to see their dead 'uns—well—they don't like to be questioned none."

"How—how long has that place been there?" I asked. "And

just—just what the devil kind of a cemetery is it? Yes—you can take me back to the city now. In fact, take me to 1515 North Dearborn Parkway."

I climbed in. And he answered my two questions.

"Well, it's the cem'tery f'r circus an' carnival people. And been there about—I guess—four years now." He was turning the cab about in the width of the narrow crosswise street, but went on talking just the same. "Far more people goes out to see the place, though, out o' curiosity, than to see their dead 'uns. 'Specially since it got wrote up in the newspapers. They go out to read th' cur'ous tombstones. For they's one or two o' every kind o' person buried there. A midget or two—an'—an' a giant, to boot! An' a fire-eater—he's in the northeast corner—his tombstone says 'If Hell There Be, He Hath No Fear of It.' And there's a couple o' sword-swallowers. One of 'em's grave hasn't no stone nor nothing—but is set off, all around, with the swords he used in his act—all rusty now, o' course. And there's a fat man—and a fat lady, too, somew'eres. And the oldest tent-stake driver in the country—Jed Hopkins—forty years with Ringlings and Barnums—is in another corner. And there's two—no—three trapeze queens. They don't live long, y' know. They allus bust their necks! And there's a rubber-skinned man too. Oh—there's a little o' everything in that place, I guess." He had made a beautiful turn on the narrow cross-thoroughfare, and long before the end of his explanation he was pointed properly on Gardendale Street and bowling northward again. "They say," he went on, "that half o' th' people in circuses and carnivals 'd ruther be buried there than—than planted with their own folks. In fac', lots has been transferred there from older cem'teries. And—but say—you didn't know what the place was, eh? Did—did someone hang somethin' on you?"

"Well—in a way—yes—no—that is, I just wanted to check up on a certain party living there—that is—dying—that is, resting there. Which—which I did."

"Oh—oh, I see. Investigatin' some old life insurance claim, eh? Oh yes—I see. And—but you didn't know Restvale Cem'tery was jest for them kinda people?"

"I'll say I didn't!" Nor did I add that I hadn't even known that 3753 Gardendale Street was Restvale Cemetery. "How come," I asked, as we bowled rapidly past the second cross-street north of rapidly receding Restvale, "that you knew the place so well? By just the street number, that is?"

"Well," he explained, talking back at me through the open glass slide that separated us, "as I was tellin' you, it got wrote up in the *Chicago Daily News* about three weeks ago; and for at least ten days everybody who hadn't nothing to do nor no place to go was askin' to be took out there. Most every cab driver in Chicago, I guess, caught at least one fare that wanted to be took to 3753 Gardendale Street. Me, I've caught sev'ral."

"And," I said, "not one of you, I'll warrant, has ever told his fare how blamed far the place is? Eh?"

"The rules o' the company," he responded stiffly, "requires that we don't make no comments whatsoever about the places we're asked by people to take 'em to."

But I must have embarrassed him, as representative of his great brotherhood, for he hastened to change the subject.

"Didja maybe see," he asked, "while you was inside there, the big shaft erected to the famous O Ming Lee? Boy, but I'd a-liked to a-seen that dame in life! My father seen her once—when she was just a baby in arms in 'Frisco. Jesus, but ain't she got the prize posish in that cem'tery? Or didn'tcha notice? Still you couldn't a-failed to notice. I ain't ever took anybody outa there yet but that they didn't come out chatterin' about O Ming Lee. Her grave's the first thing you see when you go in—an' the last thing you see when you're goin' out an' take y'r last look back."

We had turned off by now on Ogden Road, and were bowling rapidly northeastward back to civilization.

"They say," he went on talking, "that the Chinks all over the world is awful proud that one o' their race was worth millions o' white people payin' to look at. Every Chink in the United States, they say, chipped in from two-bits to a dollar to bury this here—now—Spider-Girl."

With which final information he lapsed into silence, and paid attention to his driving. For we had now reached a less country-like stretch of Ogden Road, and, since Ogden Road had no stoplights, vehicles, at the most unexpected moments, cut airy-fairily across it from intersecting streets.

As for myself, I felt like a fool.

Like two fools, to be exact.

The bigger of which fools I had certainly been made. By Abigail Sprigge. Who just, for a change, planted a spurious name and address on her poetical manuscript. And I could easily see the rationale of her so doing. For the Post Office, in attempting to deliver a letter from any publisher there, would perforce, from its six standard rubber stamps giving the reasons for non-deliverability, have to use the stamp reading "DECEASED." For certainly the stampings "MOVED, LEFT NO ADDRESS," "REFUSED," "NO SUCH NUMBER," and the others as well would hardly cover the situation. And, applying the "DECEASED" stamp, the letter—in this case, the letter of acceptance from Maxellus would have gone back to the publisher—who by the stamping thereon would then at least know that "Miss O. M. Lee" was a genuine person, even though now apparently dead, and that he need have no fear of publishing any of her immortal work that he might have in his files. As for Abigail Sprigge—that, after all, was her real name—as much so as the "Miss O. M. Lee" was her business pseudonym. And as for her selection of O. M. Lee—that was simple enough, too. Abigail Sprigge had been one of the many thousands of persons who had seen the *Chicago Daily News* feature article—and I happened to know what the cab driver did not know; namely, that all the feature articles in the *News* were syndicated to at least a hundred newspapers all over the country—she had come out here on a tour of exploration—and, when subsequently confronted with the desirability, if not downright necessity, of setting forth an address on her contributions, had thought of Legga, the Spider Girl. Buried at Post No. 49!

That is, this was my hypothesis. Because, to be sure, I was oddly troubled. For the tangle, involving apparently a veritable hodgepodge of things, persons, and places, had about it all a peculiar consistency. A traveling human skull—as against a graveyard. A Chinese footpad—as against a dead Chinese girl circus freak. A rich confectionary manufacturer gone, apparently, loco in the coco—as against a poor poetess. For poetesses invariably were poor. All a muddle, yes. Yet all seemingly a web of some sort, too!

We wound up at last—it was nearly 4:30 o'clock when we did—at Mrs. W-H's place, and once more I found myself lying back on the same bed from which Philodexter Maxellus had called me nearly three hours before. No wiser than when I had started. And minus a lot of money.

And I told myself angrily that whenever I got to meet Abigail Sprigge someday—that is, in the next ten or twenty years—for I would make it my business to meet her—I would tell her that her grisly humor in selecting literary pseudonyms wasn't appreciated by myself.

That was the generous time limit I put to the chances of my meeting her. Ten or twenty years.

But, as a matter of fact, I was destined to confront the writer of those verses in very much less than ten years. In less than ten hours, to be exact!

And to find that—

Abigail Sprigge was Sophie Kratzenschneiderwumpel?

No! Not at all. Though I could not have been more surprised had such been the case!

CHAPTER XVI

DORIS SPEAKS

O nce more, the early darkness of late October completely dropped now over Chicago, I found myself in Doris Pelton's parlor, studying her intently. For under the rose-colored lamps, she looked exceedingly pale. Under her eyes were faint rings, which showed that her sleep the night before had been brief. It was 7 o'clock—the precise hour she had asked me to come. I was just about to speak, when Filkins the butler appeared in the doorway of the parlor. A man of slight stature, but of extremely dignified bearing, Filkins was, with a magnificent command of English for a servant.

"I shall leave now, Miss Pelton," he said, "to deliver that message for you on the South Side. And thank you—so much—for giving me the gratuity which you did! It was gracious of you, indeed." And he bowed. And left the house.

And she spoke, relative to it.

"I sent Filkins away, Clay. To be gone for at least two hours. Marie, too, I let off. For reasons."

I looked at her. And spoke.

"Doris hon'," I started in, "I—I don't know how exactly to begin. After your father fainted away last night, I did a quick fade-out. As you know. And this morning I received a note from you saying—well—that our marriage could never be. What was the meaning of that, sweetheart?"

But she was to have nothing to tell me, as it turned out to be, about giving her photograph to a certain Milo Payne. And as she talked I found myself reflecting for the first time that that photo had said, "with all my love"—but not "to Milo Payne"! I sat forward in my chair and listened.

"Clay," she said, "I don't know any more about all this than you do. Only that at 10 o'clock last night Father called me into his bedroom. He stroked my head, and told me that my marriage could never take place now. He seemed to want to tell me something, and yet, at the same time, he seemed to be struggling to hold it back. After I left him, I wrote you that note. And got it into the last collection at the corner mailbox.

"This morning," she went on, "the telephone rang. Someone asked for Father. A man. I insisted he wasn't feeling well, but he insisted that it was exceedingly vital that Father come to the phone. In fact, he said to tell Father that it was something relative to the 'Palmer House matter'—and leave it up to him. I delivered the message to Father. He went to the phone at once. He evidently knew the man, the minute he answered. He talked a while. That is, Clay, all the talking was on the other end. And when Father hung up, he insisted on dressing. And he called for his car. And he went away.

"He came back in about an hour. And retired to bed again. Whatever transpired had disturbed him dreadfully, for his face was more haggard and worn than ever. At times, in his dressing gown, he opened the door of his library, which as you know adjoins his bedroom, and came out and patted my head as he used to do when I was a little girl.

"At 4 o'clock this afternoon, the phone rang again. Filkins was away at the time, fortunately, and so I answered that call too. A man's voice asked for Father again. It—"

"The same voice?" I asked. "The same man who called earlier?"

"Oh no. No. A different one, Clay. Unquestionably different. This one was indisputably an Englishman. Judging from one or two phrases he used. But I—I would not call Father. I just told him Father was out. And would not be in till shortly after 7 o'clock tonight. And that he should call up at 7:30. He said very well, that he would—that it was a vital matter—that—and here were his very words: 'It concerns Mr. Pelton as much as life and death, strike me pink if it don't.'"

"A Britisher, all right," I commented. "Of a lower class. But go ahead, Doris."

"Well you see, Clay," she hurried on, glancing at the big hall clock outside the parlor, "I knew that I had asked you in my note last night to come at 7 tonight and I knew that you would. And I knew how exceedingly punctual you always are. And it was for that reason that I told him he would find Father in at 7:30 this evening but not before. He said he would call up again at that time. When I asked him his name, just before I hung up the receiver, he laughed awfully hard—so it seems to me—and replied: 'Milo Payne, Miss. Milo Payne.'"

"Oh—ho!" I said. "The jig-saw puzzle flies together."

"What do you mean, Clay? Flies together?"

"Nothing, I very much fear. But you go on, darlin'."

"Well, there's nothing more to tell. Father is locked in his library. Just as he has been all day. He doesn't even know you're here right now. For you know that big thick hand-carved oak door he has on that library—and the wonderful joinery it has? And so I want you, Clay dear, to answer the phone when this man calls up—if he does—for he may not, of course—and to impersonate Father—and to find out by some means or other what is the cause of all this. You'll—you'll do that for me, won't you, Clay?"

"A million times more than that, Doris," I told her hungrily. "If you think I intend to lose you, you're—you're mistaken, that's all. But my wits are well 'scathered,' I'm telling you. When I think of a lot of curious factors. Like photog—But now about my voice. It's a younger voice than your father's, remember?"

She took a silk handkerchief from the bosom of her short-sleeved green silk dress. And a rubber band.

"I thought, Clay," she ventured, "that if you doubled up this handkerchief, and laid it across the transmitter—and slipped this rubber band about the loose part of the handkerchief and the hard rubber part of the transmitter too, so as to hold it on there, it—it would sort of muffle your voice a bit like—like a bad connection."

"Yes, it undoubtedly would," I said. "And—"

But my words were interrupted by the sharp ringing of the gongs on the old-fashioned wall telephone in the outer hall.

Instantly, Doris rose to her feet, her hand on her heart. "It's only 7:20," she whispered excitedly. "But—but it must be he. Oh, Clay—it's—it's up to you. Do your part—if it is."

I tiptoed out into the hall. Slipped the doubled-up silk handkerchief across the transmitter, and the rubber band about the mouthpiece so that the handkerchief stayed tightly on. What an archaic instrument for a well-to-do candymaker! But lucky for me that people tended to cling to the accouterments of their earlier days.

I raised the receiver. And spoke.

"Roger Pelton talking," I said quietly. And lowered the pitch of my voice for general good measure.

My voice carried, evidently, through the two thicknesses of silk.

"Eh?" I heard a voice say. "Is this Roger Pelton talking?"

"Yes," I said, a little bit louder. "This is—Roger Pelton."

"Damn'd poor connection," the man on the other end sniffed. "But d' ye get me all right?"

"Perfectly," I replied.

"Good enough." He paused a second. "Well, Pelton, you don't know 'oo I am, o' course." He dropped that 'h' so plainly, I actually heard it click on the floor at his feet. "Payne's my nyme. Milo Payne. Just a nyme to you, sir. Just a nyme. But I'll make it brief. First, I want to tell you wot I've got. I got the skull o' Phil Walmsley. Did you get that bloomin' nyme? Phil Walmsley." He gave a sarcastic grunt. "Yuss—the skull o' Phil Walmsley himself—trephine openin', plate, bullet 'ole—" Another 'h' dropped a hundred feet. "—and bullet, too, Pelton. And you know w'ere the bloomin' gun is, wot myde that bullet 'ole. You carn't get it, carn you? Eh, wot?" He paused, but did not wait for a reply. "Well, Pelton, I rather fawncy, down't y' know, that you want that skull. Skull—'ole—

plyt—bullet 'ole—the works. If you down't, o' course—the Styte's Attorney 'ere will bloody well like to 'ave 'em." He paused. "Well, 'ow about it?"

"Yes," I said, knowing that an affirmative answer was expected.

"Ah, that's tarking! Strike me pink if it 'int. Now w'ere shall I git it to you, eh? Someplace we can meet. Now if we were in Lunnon, I'd s'y Russell Square. No, by Gord, I wouldn't. Russell Square would be locked up tight at this hour. Nice thing about your H'American parks. They down't close up all night. Now w'ere's a snug little park, Pelton, nice and snug—for two to talk—on a bench?"

"Well—where are you now?" I countered.

"Eh—wot's 'at? W'ere am I now, did you s'y? Ts, ts, ts! Now 'int that nice! Well, if 'twill make you 'appy—" Another 'h' gone to perdition. "—I might s'y as I'm in Mouquin's Frog Cafay on 'Uron Street near the lyke—just startin' on my demmy tass—while you're on Diversey Bullyvard w'y up north! Four miles between us—if you 'ave naughty thoughts!"

"Naughty thoughts?" I repeated, tightening the silk a little, but still holding as low a pitch as I could. "What's the matter with my sending a young friend of mine—a close confidential friend—down to Mouquin's—to talk things over with you?"

"Bit of a yumorist, 'in't yer? Wot is 'e—one o' these 'ere Chycago gunmen? And if 'e 'int, 'ow much can we talk over in a French cafay full o' blokes? Now where's a snug little park, I arsks you, for two to talk on a bench?"

"Well—Washington Square," I said.

"Eh—wot's that? I carn't get it. What the hell's th' matter with yer insterment?"

I stretched the silk tighter.

"Washington Square," I said. He got me better now evidently, for he no longer asked for any repetitions. "But come to think of it—it wouldn't do. They ripped out all the lights there three months ago, but couldn't get hold of the money to put the new ones back in. So there's not a light in the whole square. And none are even promised before next July 1st. So it won't do."

"Th' 'ell it won't; It jolly well will do, Pelton. W'ere is it?"

"Delaware Place—and North Clark Street."

"Dela—oh, I s'y—you mean a little square up in front of a liberry called th'—th' Newberry Liberry?"

"The same," I said.

"I know the plyce. I was in it tod'y—when I come out the liberry. A-lookin' up some old newspapers—a couple o' stories h'about a gun! Yes, a gun, Pelton. A gun wot you carn't get your 'ands on. Well, we're set, eh, wot? Suppose you come there tonight at—let's see. Yuss—11 o'clock. And I'll be on the fourteenth bench. Get that? Fourteen! Down the walk leadin' from Clark Street into the park. No, I'll be on the fourteenth bench up the walk from the—the h'entrance wot's at th' southh'east corner. On the right. With the skull—the sweet li'l skull!—in my possession. An' th' bullet, o' course. The 'ole works. You'll arrive. I'll deliver it all over to you. Nice, eh? Now shall I expect you, Pelton?"

"Yes," I returned, my thoughts in a whirl.

"Orl right. Now let's 'ear you repeat the plyce I'll be?"

"The fourteenth bench. From the southeast corner entrance. The right-hand side."

"Good. Oh—oh—strike me pink!—I done bin an' gone an' forgot somepin."

"Yes?" I repeated, parrotlike.

"The bloomin' price, Pelton. The bloomin' price! Skulls costs money, Pelton. So now f'r th' price. Four thousand guineas—'ere—come orf it, Milo!—talk to a H'American in H'American. Twenty thousand dollars, in round numbers. An' cash, o' course. You bank in the Madison Street D'y an' Night Bank, down't you? And you know 'ow you ryte in Dunn and Bradstreets. If I know—you know. Eh, wot? Oh, you can get th' bloomin' cash orl right. So that's fixed. So twenty thousand it is, Pelton. Cash. Well?"

He waited.

"Twenty thousand dollars," I commented, "for a skull—for a skull—it seems to me—"

He gave a short laugh.

"I'll be wytin', Pelton. You know bloody well you're gettin' a bargain. Strike my pink, if you down't. I'll be wytin'."

A sharp click followed.

Then silence.

He had hung up. I turned from the telephone, dumfounded at all I had heard over the wire, if not the last-named proposition. Then my mouth fell wide open, and I stood rooted to the spot.

The door to Roger Pelton's library stood wide open. He, himself, clad in his mauve dressing gown, stood in the doorway grimly watching me. And I knew without any doubt whatever that he had heard my final words over the telephone: "Twenty thousand dollars for a skull—" and that he was fully aware of the fact that I had impersonated him!

CHAPTER XVII

PELTON'S UNUSUAL STORY

For a moment my employer stared toward me, seemingly pondering over the question of whether he should speak or not. As for myself, I said nothing, since I had been caught squarely in the act of pretending that I was someone else. Finally he raised his hand and beckoned to me.

"Come, Clay. Into the library. I've something I want to tell you—something that may explain a good deal of what has happened in the last two days."

Wonderingly, I made my way past the door which he held open for me, and into the library, with its open shelves of books, its parchment-shaded lamps, and its leather chairs. There I dropped into an armchair which sat near the lamp. Without a word he closed the door and fumbled at the big brass key in its lock. I knew that now was the psychological moment that all—or at least part—of this was going to be cleared up. Providing I didn't sidetrack it. Or abort it. I could read it in his face. But at the same time there was something vital that must be done by me—and done now.

"Mr. Pelton, will you call Doris? No, I'll stay right here with you! I only want to talk to her a moment. Yes, in front of you. Call her just to the door—if you will."

He opened the door.

"Doris."

She came. She stood in the doorway. Her face showed that she was frightfully upset.

"Doris, honey," I said, without leaving my chair, "l want you to do something. Right now. This very minute. Call this number! Superior 4444. Yes—four 4's. You won't need to put that down! That's a private unlisted phone within the quarters of my friend you've heard me speak of off and on. John Barr. Tell him you're speaking for me; and that I want him to do something for me right off. But find out first though, dear, if he's had an operation—a purely minor affair—that he perhaps might have had this morning at 11 o'clock— but that he may have, instead, tomorrow at 2 in the afternoon. If he has had the operation—then the cocaine that was shot into him is just about wearing off—and he'll be in considerable pain; so don't pursue the matter further in that case. But if he hasn't had it, after all, ask him to grab his hat—dash around the block in front of Mouquin's French Cafe on Huron Street—take up a position there—and follow a man who's due to leave there most any minute now. The fellow is on his coffee now. He'll look like an Englishman, probably. Monocle maybe—I think. Plenty of cabs available outside of Mouquin's. He can get one to follow the chap. Now have you got it all, darling?"

What a little trump she was! She should have been a $100-a-week private secretary—instead of a manufacturer's daughter.

"Perfectly, Clay. I'll jump quick!"

And she was gone.

Roger Pelton turned the brass key in the door now. And came back wearily to a chair across from me. He sank into it like a mountain sliding into a chasm.

"Clay, a man's sins find him out—always and ever. They can't be escaped."

"So—so I've heard," I replied, in the absence of any definite ideas for conversation.

"Clay, I've called you in here tonight to explain why you can't marry Doris. And when I've finished, you won't want to marry her."

I half rose from my chair. "Why—Mr. Pelton—nothing could come between her and—"

"Wait," he said sadly. "You'll be—oh Clay—what was that I heard on the phone. Blackmail, of course? And not the State Attorney's office?"

"Yes. Blackmail. A hard party too—if you ask me. Twenty thousand."

"To begin with. Oh, I know blackmail. There's no end to it once it begins. Well, Doris gets the candy factory—and no blackmailers will get that—if I have to shoot myself. Which I probably shall."

"Don't think about that," I urged. "Tell me. There's something on your mind. And you'll never breathe till you get it off. I'm in the family. Good Lord, man—we're all together, you, Doris and I."

"Yes. That's why I'm talking—to you, Clay." He paused.

"Clay, I'll have to tell you a story first. And don't stop me. Let it come, come, come. Yes, a story. Go back, Clay, first, in your imagination. For twenty years. Twenty-one years, to be exact. Two men. Young. Or at least only in their late twenties—like you are today. And both in love with the same girl. Doris's mother. The old eternal triangle. That's all." He stopped, and his eyes grew radiant, then moist. He wiped them. "One of the two fellows, Clay, was named Phil Walmsley. And the other—you've guessed it. Roger Pelton.

"Phil—teller in the Berkeley State Bank. In Englewood. Yes, it's still operating. Myself, second assistant superintendent of the McWheely Sweetworks.

"I'm going to depict, presently, an ugly situation. Your feelings toward me, when I'm done, won't be the same. You'll—you'll despise me. But I've got to talk to someone, Clay, or go under—mentally. So I'll go ahead the best I can—and then—well, that's the terrible question for me—what then?"

He bit his lips, and then forged on.

"This is a sort of matter concerning love, Clay. Money too, though. Yes, money. For Phil and I, as I just told you, loved the same girl. See? But we didn't let it interfere with our friendship. A friendship that had come from boyhood on up—oh, maybe we were a little bitter underneath. Towards each other. You know—

"But we managed to take our vacation together every year.

Generally in some sort of canoeing trip. Or camping trip. Or both combined. I say, Clay, am I rambling?"

"I should say not. You're talking as—as straight as a die."

"That's—that's good. I felt like I—I was rambling. Where was I? Oh, yes. Phil and I. Our annual vacation trip. But the one I want to tell you about is—is the last one we two took together. The one of—of July 1919, of course. Yes. We'd lost out two years running, you see. For I'd been in an Army camp down in the South. No, I never even got across to France. And Phil—they wouldn't even take him into a camp. He was in what's known as Class V. Ruled out, when they found he'd had a certain kind of operation. I'll go into that soon. And maybe you've guessed. He did war work, however. And did more good, I guess, than I did.

"Well, when the war was over—and all of us were back in peace-time pursuits again, we decided to resume our vacation trips. And we went to the place we generally went. Did I tell you the date? July. 1919. We went to a lonely point in the woods of Northern Michigan. Seven or eight miles from the town of Rapid River. On Rapid River, in fact. And God—what a river, Clay! Two miles below where we camped was a point called Hell's Rapids. And rightly named, Clay. A mile and a half of rocks—all sticking out of the water—some queer kind of geological disturbance—with the sharpest of spines pointing upstream—they hadn't been eroded yet, you see, by the water which boiled past 'em at forty miles an hour. No boat had ever ridden Hell's Rapids. Much less any swimmer. No floating body, even, had ever gone through it, without being chopped to pieces on those sharp spines—battered into absolute unrecognizability by its passage over that fearful stretch of water and rocks. And if that wasn't enough—two miles below that, where the river suddenly widened out again—the Devil's Whirlpool! A great pool, a-half mile across the river, that went continuously 'round and 'round and 'round like—like a great roulette wheel. The water in the middle, Clay, was fourteen feet lower than that on the edge. Anything that ever sailed into that thing went majestically 'round and 'round—closer and closer to the center—then down—down—down—and God knows what then. Some said there were more of those queer geological spines on the bottom. That ground up anybody sucked down to them like—like meat in a hamburger grinder. Whatever passed through Hell's Rapids and down Devil's Whirlpool, Clay, was no longer body of beast nor human. It—it was pulp!

"We liked the region, though. Above the Rapids and the Whirlpool, that is. We generally camped at least two miles above them both. The trip we took this time—did I tell you the date?— 1919—July—it was just about like the other trips—except for the sequel. Yes, except for the sequel. We had the usual camping implements: axe, lanterns, sleeping bags—oh; it gets cold at night up there, you know, in Northern Michigan, even in summer—cooking utensils—I had a brand-new .32 rifle—and there's a story to that alone, Clay—and Phil had a .36, I believe. What does it matter? And we had a sixteen-foot canoe. Which we rented from an Indian.

"It was on our second day, of this particular trip, that we went in for our first swim. And put all our clothes—including our chamois-skin money belts—together in one pile on the shore. A half hour later we came out. And dressed. But in some way or other, we must have gotten each other's money belt. Ten minutes afterward, when I was off in the woods regaining the axe which we'd left there, I took occasion to look over my money. But instead of having one hundred and forty-five dollars in my belt, Clay, I found exactly twenty thousand dollars—all in five-hundred and thousand dollar bills. In a bare second, the whole explanation came to me. Phil must have been short in his accounts at the bank and was preparing to skip—together with more of the bank's funds. And—"

But at this juncture came a diffident tap at the door of the room. The door was so thick, however, that the tap barely sounded through. "Open it, Clay," Roger Pelton almost groaned. "Doris—I guess."

It was. She looked frightfully puzzled. But managed to smile a little.

"Clay," she said, "I got your friend John Barr all right. Right away. And he hadn't had the operation. Tomorrow at 2, it will be.

And he said he'd skip for that restaurant right away. And will follow this man. If he can identify him. And will phone back here to me the minute he has something to report. For I told him you were closeted with my father, and might be for a long while yet."

"Good, darlin'. Watch the phone, will you? And catch the report right off."

I closed the door. And returned to my chair.

"Well," I said, "you found that you had $20,000—that didn't belong to you. Go on, Mr. Pelton."

He passed a hand wearily over his forehead. And, as by a mighty effort, went on.

"We—we were working hard, during the hour right after we dressed from the swim, preparing to move our camp several miles up the river. For the current was a little too swift where we were. And as we loaded our things into the canoe, I could see by Phil's casual actions that he hadn't yet discovered the accidental exchange of our money belts.

"A quarter of an hour later, when we were paddling up the river—Phil sitting in the prow of the boat, and I sitting in the stern—my eye happened to fall on my loaded repeating rifle at my feet. And there's a story to that rifle, as I told you. I'll go into that later. It seems to me now, Clay, when I look back on it all, that a mad, insane impulse must have seized me. It came over me with a rush that if a bullet should be sent into the back of Phil's head, I would have twenty thousand dollars—as well as a clear field for the hand of the girl who later, in fact, became Doris's mother. Just one of those greenish-yellow bullets my rifle contained—yes, some kind of brass-alloyed lead they were cast from—and the whole outlook of my life would be changed for the better. It—it just came to me, I tell you, Clay, all in one picture: that his body would be carried rapidly downstream to Hell's Rapids—chopped and battered all to pieces in that stretch of hellish water—and then on to Devil's Whirlpool where what was left of him would be sucked down and ground up as badly as—as if his body had fallen into a crocodile pool in Florida. Horrible. Yes, I know. You bet I know! Well, hypnotized by the whole picture, I raised my rifle, took careful aim at the back of his head, and fired. Crack! It must have taken him squarely, Jim, for he tumbled like a log straight over the prow of the canoe, whirled around a moment in the current, face down, and then was swept downstream. Horror-stricken, I realized for the first time what I had really done. I—I couldn't look back at first. When I finally did, I saw his body—with its blue flannel shirt—bobbing up and down far down the stream; then, carried around a bend in the river, it disappeared.

I hove to, and drew in to the bank. And sat there in a daze all afternoon. Till the sun got low. And I knew by that time there wasn't enough of Phil Walmsley hanging together—or so, at least, I thought—to signify who or what he ever might have been. Then I shook myself out of it, and made my way on foot to the nearest house. And reported—what I had to report! My pal had just tumbled out of the canoe when we made a sharp swerve. I'd tried to paddle after him. And lost him. When I hit, nose in, on a gravel bank. Which gravel bank—fortunately for my story—actually was there in the river at that point.

The river was searched that night as far as Hell's Rapids. But no further. Beyond that, it wasn't a bit of use. And after swearing to the usual form for the coroner of the County next day, I returned home to Chicago. My story, as I've just described it to you, was accepted by everyone. Everybody knew we were like—like Damon and Pythias. Nobody but myself knew that he cared at all for the girl who later became Doris's mother. I wrote and told his brother in Denver all the facts. The facts, that is—as I made them up.

"But, Clay, at the end of the month, a client of the Berkeley State Bank who was a big race-track bookmaker—he carried a hundred thousand dollar checking account, and daily cashed enormous checks—sent back a $35,000 check, which he claimed he had never presented. Its signature hadn't been particularly over-examined by the bookkeeper, since it bore Phil's special stamp—signifying he had cashed it personally at the window—and that he knew the drawer personally by sight. And I guess you can see now, what happened?"

"I think so," I admitted. "Phil Walmsley had been about fifteen thousand short in his accounts—so he put in this check—fixed his accounts—pocketed the difference—and prepared to get out before the end of the month should come and the monthly statements should reach the client?"

Roger Pelton nodded gloomily.

"Exactly. A muddy story this, Clay. Murder and forgery. Forgery and murder." He paused. "The bank called me in again, of course. And I had to rehearse my story all over again. And fortunate for me in a sense—or they might have thought I'd helped him to get away—but they found in Phil's rooms a sort of cheap ledger with the names of a lot of horses, odds, all worked out—bets—which seemed to show that he'd lost the whole $35,000 on the races. They checked it back carefully, and it proved up in every detail. They didn't bother me any more. The—the inference was too obvious. The—the ponies had gotten it all!"

He paused again. "Well, I tried to blot out of my mind that I had murdered my friend. It kept coming back to me—naturally—but I managed always to forget in some way or other. Usually by hard work. And then, too, I had Doris's mother—my wife—and later, little Doris herself.

"Time went on, Clay. In due course I found opportunity to buy the decrepit old Sol Isenstein Candy and Snapperjack Works. All equipped. For twenty thousand cash down. I bought it. With—with that money I got off of Phil. I'd kept it in a safety box—waiting my big business chance. I pretended I had a backer who didn't want his name in it. And I made the candy works pay, too. You know. Look what it is today! It was four years after I bought it that Doris's mother died. Boy, boy, what a blow that was to me! I kind of think, Clay, I—I paid then and there for all I'd done. But maybe not. Maybe not!

"And now we come to present days. Roger Pelton. Respectable candy manufacturer. God!" He paused. "Several days ago I went over to the rectory of Peter Walmsley to see him in regard to his request that I give a minor position in the candy factory to a young fellow in his parish. He had come here to Chicago some years after his brother—er—died! And we'd sort of kept in touch all these years. Since we were linked by the same person. At any rate, he was out. So the woman who took care of his rooms asked me to wait in his study for a while. I did so. Finally, however, I became tired of the delay. And so I crossed over to his desk, took a blank sheet of paper, and commenced writing out an order on the foreman to put this young fellow to work. And peeping out from under a brass urn on his desk was a letter which, strange as it seemed to me, bore the postmark: 'Rapid River, Michigan.' God, Clay, you—you can't imagine the feeling that swept over me on seeing the name of that town near which I—I had put an end to Phil's life.

"Immediately I scented danger to myself. Instinct, nothing else! The study was deserted. So I quickly drew forth the letter. It was a long one, several pages. And what did it read? It proved to be from—"

Again came that diffident tapping that marked Doris herself at the library door.

"Open it, Clay, will you," Roger Pelton begged me.

I did. She stood there.

"Clay, your friend Mr. Barr just called back. He says to tell you that he got to that restaurant—or rather near enough to it, to see the man you spoke of leave—but not to be able to follow him. There was only one yellow cab, he says, in front of Mouquin's. This man took it. And that left Mr. Barr high and dry. He wasn't close enough even to identify—the features of the man, but says he wore a long-beaked checkered cap like—"

"Like Sherlock Holmes, yes. Now I wonder—"

"If it is the man? Well, Mr. Barr said to tell you he himself went right into Mouquin's. And that all the diners, except a couple of women, were gone."

"That's that, then. I'll rejoin you in a little—"

"He's still on the wire, Clay. He wants me to ask you if there's anything else he can do?"

"Tell him no, I—but wait." I turned to Roger Pelton. "Mr. Pelton, do you own a revolver?"

"No, Clay."

"Hm. Well, neither do I." I turned to Doris. "Doris, ask John Barr to send a messenger boy in the next couple of hours or so to this house—with a package containing his imported French Severignac eleven-shot revolver. And with eleven cartridges too. Tell him I've a sort of—of appointment to talk some curious things over in a Chicago park tonight, with an ugly customer."

"Surely, Clay. I'll tell him."

And she was gone.

I resumed my seat.

"So you read the letter postmarked Rapid River, Michigan?"

"Yes. And it was from some Englishman. Who signed himself Milo Payne. Hammered out on a typewriter. Crudely, as though he didn't know how to operate the machine except with two fingers. And sort of illiterate in the bargain. Or better—only half illiterate. He claimed he'd recently come into 400 guineas—an inheritance—and was using it to make a westward jaunt around the world. And incidentally stopping off at Vancouver, Canada, where he had a few days' business of some sort. The nature of which he didn't state. He said he was hunting and fishing a bit up in the North Woods—around Rapid River—had heard about the country up there—wanted to see it—and that while he'd been digging for worms he'd come across a skull buried in the bank of the river. Rather, a skull and jawbone together. At a bend, about a half mile below the Devil's Whirlpool. Get that, Clay! A bend—something built up by silt, you know. He said the skull had a surgical plate set in it—and a bullet hole below the plate. And a bullet right in it. A bullet, he said, made of some queer kind of lead that looked greenish in one light—and yellowish in another. He said a boy was with him when he dug it all up—a boy named Tommy Huckins. And that he'd cleaned up enough of the plate, with saliva alone, and friction, on the river bank itself, so that the boy and he were able to make out part of an inscription on it. And he said he realized right off that there was foul play of some sort—and so he'd had the boy clip off a piece of lead from the base of the bullet and retain it in an envelope so's the lad could identify the bullet in court later. If necessary. Well, he went on to say he took the skull to his hotel room, and cleaned it all up well with acids and solutions, and made the plate bright again so that it could be read entirely. He'd once worked in England, he said in his more or less illiterate way, for a surgeon, as a porter, and happened to know that inscriptions sometimes were put on different kinds of surgical reconstruction appliances by surgeons. He went on to say that he'd consulted some country doctor in the North Woods someplace—gotten hold, in the latter's *Surgical Who's Who,* of the phone number in Chicago of the surgeon whose name was on the plate. And had called him up, and found that the number on the plate represented an operation that had been paid for by a Peter G. Walmsley, a clergyman of Denver, Colorado. A brother of the patient, in fact. But that when he consulted a Denver telephone book in a country telegraph office, he couldn't find any such name; but on searching through a number of telephone books of different cities, he located one in Chicago. Undoubtedly the one, he said, considering it was a clergyman—and had the same middle initial. He said he expected to be in Chicago on—well—the day he specified, Clay, was day before yesterday; and would be at the world-famous Palmer House which he'd heard of ever since he'd been a boy—and wanted to see the lobby that was paved with silver dollars! And—and he said that if Peter Walmsley would come there at 6 o'clock in the evening, he would be glad to turn over the whole shebang to him, as well as the name of the boy who was a witness to its disinterment—as he himself, he said, was heading on on that trip around the world, and wouldn't be bally-well bothered—as he put it—with 'no legal actions.' He'd have it all ready for the Reverend, he told the latter, packed in a black bag he'd bought in Detroit—and since he didn't feel like using the bloomin' bag—as he put it—any more after what was in it—he wouldn't object to the Reverend just reimbursing him for the cost of it."

"A fellow that knows how to measure nickels and dimes," I commented. "Except that now he's using a larger yardstick! But go on, Mr. Pelton."

He did so, grimly, desperately.

"Well you see now, Clay, what I meant when I told you that a man's sins find him out, sooner or later? There, after twenty-one years, was the proof that Phil had been shot through the back of the head—and not merely drowned as I had reported. There, after twenty-one years, was—"

Doris tapped at the door again. With that timid tap of hers. Or else the door was so thick that a rap only sounded like a tap. And I answered it again. Her blue eyes were saucer-wide.

"Your—your friend, Clay," she said, a bit fearfully, "is sending over to you—at this address—I gave it to him—that revolver. But he says to tell you that he has no cartridges for it. And that none can be gotten now, this side of France. Because of their odd caliber. But he says you are welcome to it if it is of any utility to you for pulling a—"

"Bluff? Yes. Well, maybe it will be. It looks like a cannon, anyway. But I don't know. Is he on the wire now, dear? If he is—"

"No. I offered to call you—but he said not to bother you. That the gun would arrive here, wrapped up, by a messenger boy, in not less than an hour."

"Very well, hon'. Run along now—and busy yourself. Your father and I—have serious business."

And flashing her a signal with my eyes that she must not interrupt matters, I closed the door on her.

And went back to my chair.

"Yes," I said. "And now—after twenty years—bobbed up the proof that Phil Walmsley hadn't been drowned at all. How do you suppose that his head, and not his body—"

"No body, Clay," he interrupted me, "could ever ride Hell's Rapids—and the spines at the bottom of Devil's Whirlpool, too. But a head could. Yes. That head was torn from that body probably at the first smash against the first spines in Hell's Rapids. Razor-back Narrows, the first stretch of Hell's Rapids was called. After that it sailed through with the boiling waters with no further trouble—probably went clear to the bottom of the Devil's Whirlpool—came up again, a half mile away—and got washed up into shallow water. And covered with silt. And buried in a gradually increasing promontory. Which in time became a bend in the river.

"God, Clay, they had me! They had me, I tell you. They had me a dozen ways around. The *corpus delicti*! For Phil *had* been subjected to just such a trephining operation on his head back in—oh, I think it was 1914. Something like that, anyway. I do know that a numbered and dated plate had been wedged into some operative opening in his cranium, and the scalp drawn back and sutured over the place. I'd felt the hard lump into which Phil's scalp was bunched right there, often and enough. And the surgeon himself had told Phil he had taken the liberty of incorporating his particular case in a certain set of records; in fact, he asked Phil to report any further symptoms—or developments at the site of the operation—if there were any—during all the rest of Phil's life. Oh they had me, I tell you, Clay. The surgeon himself was alive. He was well known in his day. Dr. Max Prior. Only three months ago I read in the paper where he—he was returning from a trip abroad. And those records of his must be available. Don't you see? The *corpus delicti?*"

"Yes," I admitted. "That—that is bad. Damned bad! Yet even then—a lawyer—a clever criminal defense lawyer—"

"Could split a jury, Clay? Prove that Phil, after he was drowned, might have been shot by some hunter thinking his bobbing head was a duck? No, Clay. Not a chance." He shook his head. "Not a chance. For the bullet could be proved conclusively to have come out of my gun—a gun, that is, which I and I alone had, during a certain three days between the time it left the arms factory—and went into the Chicago Historical Society here. I told you there was a story to that gun. And there is."

CHAPTER XVIII

CONCERNING ICHABOD CHANG

I stared at Roger Pelton in the lamplight. Bit by bit I was beginning to realize that this man was caught like a worm on a hook—unless—unless—

I passed my own hand over my forehead.

"Tell me—about the gun," I said helplessly. And surveyed him troubledly—for after all, he was my father-in-law to be. He was desperately pale, his face seamed. His fingers, trying to tap nervously on the chair handle, actually trembled.

"Well you see, Clay, the rifle!—I shot him with—it was one of twelve special rifles that had been turned out by the Cormington Arms Company of Cormington, Connecticut, in commemoration of the production of their millionth firearm. And all of which were given—not sold—to friends of the president. Their barrels were made of steel fabricated from the very cannon that had fired the last charge of powder at Vicksburg. The stocks were hewed from a piece of wood from the bow of Commodore Perry's flagship on his first trip to Japan. The time he opened Japan to the world. The front sights—what you call, Clay, the 'bead'—were cut from the bone penholder of Edward Rutledge, the Charleston, South Carolina, lawyer who was the youngest signer of the Declaration of Independence—and were from the identical pen that had signed that paper. The pen, it seems, had gotten accidentally broken up in some Southern museum—and the Cormington Arms Company had gotten one of the slivers from which to cut these beads. Thus these unusual guns. My particular weapon was numbered 1,000,004. My father, you see, had once done Henson Ames, then the president of the Cormington Arms Company, a big favor. My father was dead, of course—but Ames wanted to sort of return the courtesy, and he sent me one of the guns. In fact, he sent me a couple of boxes of some new experimental type of .32 cartridges with it. A type of cartridge, however, that was discontinued after the first sample lots were sent out. I remember even today the odd hue of the leaden bullets in those cartridges. How their color shifted from green to yellow—and back to green again. According to the way the light fell on them. Some crystalline formation in the lead, of course, due to its—its being alloyed in some definite proportion with brass—or even perhaps with other elements. And—but it's about the gun itself I'm speaking now. I received it the day before I left on that camping trip. Reporters came up to the house—interviewed me—photographed the gun—wrote it up in all the Chicago papers. And God help me—when I came back from that cursed trip—and a delegation from the Chicago Historical Society here attended me—and asked me whether I would not consider giving such a historic firearm to their society—I—I gave it. God—yes. Deeded it over to them. I—I couldn't bear the sight of it. 'Specially after—after what I'd done with it! And it's been there ever since—twenty-one years now—first in the old building on Dearborn Avenue near Ohio Street—then later in the big new building in Lincoln Park. Under lock and key. And guard. And all that. In the very same case, in fact, with the revolver which killed Abraham Lincoln! Go back to the papers of twenty-one years ago. You'll see where my gift of it to the Society was written up in the papers. Just like my receipt of it from Henson Ames. Three days between those two stories."

"Bad," I said. "Ballistics! In your possession just a few days. And the dates all of record. You didn't know about the science of criminal ballistics—when you gave that gun over, did you?"

"How—how could I, Clay? Such a thing was never heard of

then. Why, I—I didn't even know that the cartridges with the greenish-yellow bullets in them, that Ames sent with the gun, were purely an experimental lot—until shortly afterward I got a form letter from the Cormington Arms Company saying they had been such—and that they had been discontinued as—as not being wholly satisfactory. But, getting back to the science of—of criminal ballistics itself—how could I have heard of it then? A brilliant young fellow in New York—named Calvin Goddard—Colonel Calvin Goddard—came to the front—oh, sometime in the middle '20s—with the startling news that—"

"Yes, I know," I said. "The news that every bullet in the world can be tied up absolutely and conclusively to the gun from which it has been fired. And regardless of whether that bullet is made of yellow-green lead, cheese, iron or—or nickel-cobalt! Tied up by the microscopic scratches on its base—and the rifling. And about ten other points, too: And Colonel Goddard himself head of our Scientific Crime Detection Laboratory at Northwestern-U today! Bad, all right." I paused. And then went on speaking. "And now the following situation presents itself: It can be proved that that bullet which Milo Payne and Tommy Tucker—or whoever he is—rattled out of that disinterred skull was fired from this gun in the Chicago Historical Society. And which gun was in your possession when your pal was—er—drowned. Yes, they've got you, Mr. Pelton. That is, a blackmailer has got you. But go on. We'll figure on him later."

"Well, Clay," he said desperately, "I—I had to get that skull—and that bullet. I had to—that's all. For your sake—my sake—Doris's sake. I knew absolutely that Peter Walmsley would have it in the hands of the State Attorney by the next day. A stern, righteous man that Peter Walmsley. And—and he'd always been a little suspicious that there was something wrong about that story concerning the—the death of his brother. I'm positive of that. He'd asked me at least twice where I obtained the money to go into business with. And asked me other peculiar questions now and then. I could read back of them. So I had to get that skull. And there—

there was no one I could confide in. Nor did I dare to shadow Peter Walmsley myself. He knew me far too well.

"And so—so that brings me to Ichabod. Ichabod Chang. He—"

"Chang? A Chinaman? The dirty little son of a—"

"Yes, Clay. I know! I know. I'm only glad he didn't kill you. But let me tell it. Please. Ichabod Chang is the son of the finest old Chinaman who ever lived. Old Dong Chang. He's dead now, of course. Dong Chang worked for my father as a gardener. For years. He brought Ichabod up as a boy should be brought up. Sent him to Sunday school—a Christian, old Dong Chang was. And Ichabod was a genius—he really was. A Biblical genius, anyway. He could reel off whole chapters of the Bible. Quote verses on any subject. Yet in spite of it, by the time he was sixteen he was in the reform school. Hobnobbing with crooks, when he got out. A safeblower at twenty. Hold-up man. Opium smuggler. Lord knows what else. The old man could do nothing with him. I guess Ichabod sort of sent the old man to an early grave. Ichabod, in fact, was in the penitentiary at Joliet by the time he was twenty-five years old.

"He got his discharge the other day. And came to me. Down at the plant. Said he intended to go straight. And could I put him in the factory. I said I'd see him again. But good God, Clay, a $20 bill lying on one of the stenographers' desks in the outer office was missing right after he went out through there. He just couldn't be honest, you see. And so I decided that Ichabod was out—so far as we were concerned.

"But now, in my desperate emergency, I thought of him. About the only person on earth I could ask to help me, on—on work like this. And I sent for him at once. At an address he'd left with me— the address of a Negro who he said knew where he was living. Which was with a Sicilian family—over on our North Side's Little Sicily. And Ichabod came. And I told him that on such and such a night—which, of course, was night before last—the pastor of St. Anne's Church, on Eugenie Street and LaSalle Avenue, would leave the Palmer House some time after 6 o'clock in the evening, with a package, or valise, or a bag. Most likely a bag. And I offered

Ichabod one thousand dollars if he secured that satchel bag—whatever it would prove to be—and delivered it to me. But I cautioned him that there must be no rough play. No killing. No maiming. I swear I did, Clay! True, I—I didn't care what he did—even to holding up Peter Walmsley at the door of the rectory—but I wasn't tacking any more—killings on my conscience. God, no! And in case you wonder why I took such chances with Ichabod—well, my father and I were both awfully good to Ichabod's father. And they say a Chinaman, no matter how bad he is, will not only never double-cross his own father—but won't do that to anyone who was good to his father.

"Oh, I felt that Ichabod with all his underworld experience—his resourcefulness—his desperation for money—would get that bag. I felt no apprehensions whatever. Particularly after his last words. As he left me. He said: 'Mister Pelton, I'll get that bag. Positively and absolutely! I'll get it. And so long as you don't hear from me by phone—everything's all okay—except that I might have to lay low for some reason or other!' And off the yellow beggar went, cocky and self-assured.

"Well," Roger Pelton went on, licking his dry lips, "I—I was so darned confident about Ichabod's abilities, and his loyalty to me, that I even went up North with Doris to a dinner party—on the night that Ichabod was to do—whatever he intended to do. Although I didn't eat much. God—no!

"Came next day. No news from Ichabod. However, no news, he'd told me, was good news. And that night came yourself. And hardly had you walked in on us—and told us first about this Suing Sophie, than you commenced to narrate a peculiar adventure you'd had. How you'd accidentally carried off another man's bag from a Broadway car; how you got it safely to your room—and do you remember interpolating a remark at this juncture that in your bag were your cards?"

"Assuredly," I admitted. "Even more, I said, in response to Doris's question at this particular juncture, when she asked me if the other man 'afterward got in touch with me' that—yes—I was 'afterward gotten in touch with.' I was being ironic, of course; and I had in mind the bird who knocked me cold."

"Yes. Well, you went back a ways in your story after you'd carried it up a short bit, and told us that the peculiar part of your yarn was that the fellow who followed you to the steps of your rooming-house was a Chinaman—and that the satchel you had contained a skull. With a metal plate in it. God a-Mighty, Clay—the bottom of the world fell right out from under my feet at that moment. My nerves—they just cracked. Everything went dark on me. And when I recovered from the bad fainting spell I'd had, I knew that any and all plans of Ichabod's for securing that bag had been defeated hopelessly on account of those circumstances you'd recounted: the reversal of that street car—the stupid conductor—you remember?

"All night long I found myself unable to sleep. For, don't forget, you yourself had said your cards were in the other bag; and that you had 'been gotten in touch with.' Naturally, I believed the rightful owner of the other bag had gotten to you long since—and had reexchanged satchels. And that it would be only a matter of hours at most before a couple of detectives from the State Attorney's office would be up here at the house. With a capias for my arrest. As for Ichabod, I just figured that he was too sheepish even to call up; that he knew he'd messed everything. For I figured that he must have glimpsed that interchange of satchels from behind you and the Reverend Walmsley—or thought he did—and that he decided to follow you—but that you circumvented him by popping unexpectedly up the stairs of the Essex before he could—could pull anything. And so now, as I figured it, you and—and the Reverend Walmsley had gotten to each other on the phone. And either you'd gone over to Walmsley's in a cab. Or he in one over to your place—and probably with a couple of sturdy deacons, if you'd told him about being followed. And the skull was now in the Reverend's old safe. Again and again, Clay, the thought recurred to me: Will they electrocute me in Illinois—or will they give me life at hard labor in Michigan? And my poor little girl, I thought. She'll have to suffer too. For who will marry the daughter of a convicted murderer? Even Clay Calthorpe will drop her pronto. You see, Clay, I hadn't heard the rest of the story: How Ichabod had tricked you into losing that bag. Although it's as well, I guess, that I didn't. Considering that he himself subsequently lost it—or got tricked out of it somehow.

"For this morning he rang me. He told me to come to the place where he was living. And—and he'd give me the whole low-down on affairs.

"I went there. It was a terrible rat-hole of a place. On Townsend Street. Not far from the notorious Death Corner. He had a dingy room. Down in a basement. With the family of some Sicilian he'd met in a Federal penitentiary. Where both were serving a year or so for opium and morphine peddling. Some pretty hard men were living there, too. A one-eyed Negro. An Armenian. Riffraff. But I wasn't molested. He took me into his room. And gave me the facts. He told me how he'd followed the Reverend Walmsley from the Palmer House, not trying to resort to any desperate measures downtown on account of the lights and the crowds of people. In fact, he—he'd intended to—to stick the Reverend up on dark Eugenie Street, right after the two of them would get off the Broadway car and the Reverend would walk west towards the Rectory. He told me, too, about that shift of the car—its direction, that is—and the trolley pole—the seat backs—every thing—and that there'd been some kind of a mix-up of two bags—oh, he wasn't dead sure right at that moment, he said—but he'd seen the conductor bend over back of the Reverend Walmsley and the man next him, and adjust two bags—all he was sure of, Clay, he said, was that a chap riding next to Walmsley pulled out from under himself—at Burton Place—a bag exactly like the one that was being carried by the man that he—Ichabod—was following. The thing was so—so casual and open, he said, that—that he didn't look on it as a sneak-thief job; but he *did* surmise that a mix-up might have taken place—again, maybe not! —but he figured that unless he hopped onto the job at this juncture and hopped quick—everything might get beautifully messed up. So off he went. Followed the fellow. Yourself. To where you lived. Got a good look at him. And at the number of the place.

"Then he went over to Clark Street, and ate himself some dinner in a restaurant to give the Reverend Walmsley time to get home, put his bag away, and light his pipe. After which he went into a drug store. And rang the Reverend. Actually rang him, Clay. Says he was going to tell him that he was a native Chinese missionary just passing through Chicago, and that he had a personal message for him from the Episcopal Archbishop of Shanghai. And believe me, Clay, Ichabod would have outspouted the Reverend Walmsley if it had come to a mere matter of quoting the Bible over the phone. And then—then he was going to call on him. And if he couldn't snitch— that's what he called it—snitch the bag—he was going—to stick the Reverend up, right in the latter's study. Desperate, Ichabod was. I see it now. But, Clay, a domestic answered the phone. Told him that the Reverend Walmsley had just been called by a very urgent telegram to Western Nebraska—had left, in fact—and would be gone three days. And that, in fact, there would be no one at the Rectory until he returned.

"Well, Ichabod says he knew the bag would have been put some-where in the study pending the Reverend's return. So he—he breezed over eastward. And along Lake Shore Drive. And located a vacant house, that looked as though it might not be vacant. And made a note of its number. And—"

"Why?" I put in abruptly. "Oh, I know how he used that house. But did he fores—"

"Yes. He foresaw. That the bag he might get from the Reverend's rooms might be the wrong one. In which case he was going to ring you there at 1515 Dearborn Parkway—even though he didn't know your name. And decoy you over. He—"

"Yes," I put in, "and right there is where Ichabod tripped him-self up—and you—and me—and Doris all of us. For he himself was followed. And that house whose number he wrote down—probably standing out under the very street light when he did so—that house he was so, solicitous about—was watched. By a man who is now blackmailing you. And will continue to do so till you're bled white. And—but you finish your story first."

He looked at me helplessly.

"Yes, Clay I—I will. Well, Ichabod's subsequent narrative seems to show, really, what—what a desperate fellow he is. I—I never realized it, I tell you. He went back to Little Sicily. Got a safeblowing outfit from some crook he knew over there. Stuff, he says, Clay, that a man can carry right in his pockets. Putty—wedges—nitroglycerine. I—I never realized how simple those things are. To those, that is, who know all about how to use them. Well anyway, Ichabod beat time till midnight. And then he entered the Reverend Walmsley's rectory. At about that hour. It was easy, he said. A window on a dark interior court. Nothing looking down on it but church windows. He got in with no trouble. And pulled out every drawer in the library. No sign of a satchel. So he—he blew the safe. He said it was an old one. Just popped right open. And in it was the bag. Where the Reverend had put it—on getting back there and finding the telegram calling him away. But he wanted to make sure there was something in it that I must want. And he cut it open. With a razor he found there. And found that it was full of traveler's paraphernalia. He says the minute he saw purple pajamas in it, with yellow embroidered circles on them, he knew that it must be your bag. Because— well—as he puts it, Clay, you look like just such a fellow!"

"Damn his filthy, lousy little Mongolian hide," I said. "If I ever—"

"Hush, Clay! You can't do that. Let me finish this." Roger Pelton paused, helplessly. "Well, he went through the bag—thorough little devil he is—and discovered your cards. And now had your name as well as your location. He says he called you up on the telephone right there in the study. God—what nerve that little yellow devil has. I'd—I'd have been all of a sweat. Not him, though. Well, he told me he pretended to be another clergyman and requested you to—"

"Yes, I well know the rest of the story," I put in. "He decoyed me over there to 1870 Lake Shore Drive—beat it over there ahead of me—he was only three blocks away when he emerged from that rectory study—knocked me out—and got away with the bag. Only—"

"Yes," Roger Pelton put in. "That's just—just what he did,

Clay. Only he—he lost it again. That is, he says he did. And yet claims it isn't lost. But of course he's wrong. If a blackmailer is in the picture now."

"How does he claim he lost it?" I put in roughly. For I wasn't at all averse to the idea that a Chinaman might join forces with a Cockney to do blackmail, despite all the high-flung theories about father-friendships—and loyalties.

"Well, he says, Clay," Pelton averred, "that—that the minute he knocked you out inside the vestibule, he hurried down the front steps with the bag. But knew that at that hour of the night it wouldn't do for him to go through the streets—with that bag. Some police squad car would stop him, examine it, and the whole fat would be in the fire. Besides which, you might come to—flag a taxi—and he'd be on the police radio before he ever got over to Little Sicily. So—so he stalked diagonally across the Drive. And the stretch of parkway. And the bridle path. And into the gloom of the sloping stone esplanade that goes along the water's edge. Not even a pair of lovers in sight at this hour. And he trotted along the lake till he hit the Oak Street bathing beach. Here he was on the sand. And not on granite any longer. He found a spot. And buried the bag. More or less in the gloom—he says—for he worked only by the lights from the cornice of some big de-luxe apartment hotel over on the Drive. He says he groped around. Found a stake. And a piece of driftwood. Drove the stake down in the sand. Close to the bag. Till only three inches of it stuck out. That was to last him till morning. And he cleared away, with his foot, all the sand he'd disinterred.

"Then he struck out. By way of the darkest streets. And got back to Little Sicily. When he put on the old radio that was in his rat-hole, and shoved it far below the dial—he heard a police call going out for him.

"He was afraid, he said, to venture out all next day. Even to go to a drug store and call me. But he felt the bag was as safe as anything. And he stayed put all that next night. But when sun-up came, he took a chance and—and beat it over to the Oak Street beach. And what a beach—so he says! Crackerjack boxes—fragments of lunch—

a whole party of kids must have been there the day before. Holes dug all over the beach. Broken tin shovels. And one big hole, he says, right about where he thinks he buried the bag. But he isn't sure yet, that the top of his stake didn't just get drifted over with sand. It was windy the previous day. And in that case—as he says—the bag is still there. He wants me to get hold of a couple of children as—as a sort of a blind—and go over there myself tomorrow—and dig, dig, dig. And keep scraping around with my feet and hands for the top of that stake. But I'm convinced the big hole he found is the site of the disinterment of the bag. For—"

"Yes, you're right, Mr. Pelton," I put in gloomily. "It won't be any use now to dig. The little whelp is outwitted."

"You—you don't mean outwitted, though, Clay? You just mean that some child found the satchel—took it home to his father—and that his father has unearthed enough facts to—yet how could such a man get them? Hm? But you say they're demanding $20,000?"

"Listen," I asked. "Is the Reverend Walmsley—or was he—when he was still alive—for he's dead now from a train wreck—a communicative man?"

"Yes. Very. And Doris told me late this afternoon that she read in the paper about his having died. But about his being communicative. Yes. He would talk at great length about private matters—to anybody."

"All right. I have the whole thing. As clear as daylight. First, the Reverend Walms—but wait. One more point. Does Doris know any of the young men in his parish?"

"Yes. He invited her over there while you were gone."

"I see. And she fell for one of 'em. Fell hard! Even gave him a picture of herself. Love and ever'thing written on it. But when she hears what a rat he was—for he turned around and gave it to his pastor—probably to rub it into the old boy that the dames he was presenting around there were easy—well—she'll fall out of love seventeen times faster than she fell in. But I'll not ask her a damned thing about it yet. For the laddy-buck she fell for has cooked his goose. The dirty little churchgoing ras—"

"Oh, Clay—calm yourself. Girls do have occasional heart-flutters about other men. She really loves only you."

"All right. I can forgive. But I was telling you I had the whole lay-out of this affair now as clear as daylight. And I have. And 'out-witted' is the word. So far as that stinking little Chink goes. Now I'll tell you just what has happened: First, Milo Payne himself is the man who's now making the initial nick in you for twenty thousand simoleons. Which is only the starter. Peter Walmsley shot off his mouth to Milo Payne the other evening at the Palmer House, enough so that the latter knew that the thing he was letting go out of there was the pivot of a big murder case—a case against a rich man. The doddering old—oh, I suppose I should remember that de mortuis nil nisi bones—but the Reverend even took Doris's photograph to the Palmer House to show Payne what 'quality folks' you people were. And incidentally left it there. As Payne himself later did. But imagine how Payne regretted letting the thing—you know—skull and bullet—go out of there. He checked right out, like a house afire, the minute the Reverend Walmsley left; probably dropped his suitcase off at the corner in a Cabbagio Chain Cigar store—flung the bloomin' clark four shillin's, blarst my 'ide!—and picked up the Reverend Walmsley's trail before the latter even boarded the Broadway car. You know yourself that you sometimes have to wait ten minutes for a Broadway car there on State Street. He may have been on the very car. I can't say. I didn't watch everybody. If he was, he wasn't wearing his checked Sherlock Holmes cap. For I'm sure I'd have noticed that! Maybe he flagged a taxi, to tail the car. By God—I'll bet that's what he did. All right. If he rode alongside that street car—or in it—he must have seen by the number of times that that Chink looked back at the Reverend's seat—for remember, before the reversal of the car, the Chink was wadded in up ahead of us—that the Chink was following Walmsley. Whoops! Big money must be operating in back of this case! Somebody trying to circumvent Walmsley. Well, when he saw me get off—with the bag—rather, a bag—or a bag like the one he'd bought in Detroit and given to the Reverend Walmsley—or sold him, the nickel-squeezing bastard—and Chinky after me, he paid off his cab and up Burton Place—in our rear. After that, apparently, he followed Chinky. That is, to the Clark Street eating house. Then the drug store. Then east to the Drive. Saw him fix on a house. An apparently empty house. And set down the number of it, outside. Realized that a game of some sorts was going to be played there. I don't know whether he sat down, then and there, on a bench 'way over in the dark parkway across from Number 1870 or whether he tried to keep up with Chinky and ultimately lost him—and had to come back to Lake Shore Drive again to re-pick up the trail, or what. All I know is that he was across the Drive from No. 1870 in the dark parkway, at 1 in the morning, smoking a dry cigar—a cigar with no light on it, if you get my meaning—when Chinky secreted himself in the vestibule of No. 1870. And I came. And Chinky came out. Bag in hand. And headed diagonally across the Drive. And along the granite esplanade. Milo Payne keeping up with him—in his rear—either on the bridle path or in the parkway. Knew Chinky was going to secrete the bag. Saw him do it, in fact, by kneeling down in the shrubbery around the edge of the Oak Street beach—and I hope every dog in Chicago has irrigated that shrubbery within the last week!

"And there you are! When Chinky blew away from the dark beach, Milo Payne went over. Kicked around. In the gloom. Found the dampish sand. That had been dug up. And the stake. And then politely dug up the satchel. Dusted it off. Went to a hotel. On the Near North Side. Got a room. And now in addition to all the info he got from the Reverend Peter Walmsley, he has the skull. Skull, plate, bullet-hole, bullet. The whole thing.

"No, I don't know where he lives. I nearly found out tonight. But the cards were stacked against me. My friend John Barr—no, don't worry—he doesn't know anything about all this, and he'll not know, I give you my word—he tried to connect with him for me. As you heard, from Doris's report. But John failed. As you also heard. So that's that! But it doesn't matter. For Payne is ready to meet you now. Tonight. Washington Square. He asks a little matter of

$20,000. For which he'll deliver the skull. But what he'll deliver, of course, will—or would—be only a dummy package containing—nothing. He might even go so far as to have you stuck up for any money you might bring and—but no, I guess not. He's a stranger, and has no gunmen connections in Chicago. Well, all I know is that he's now embarked on a lifetime of ease, traveling back and forth between Chicago and London, or maybe settling down here entirely. The world tour—on 400 guineas—is all off!"

"Well, do you think it's at all possible, Clay, that maybe he is playing for just $20,000—and that that will satisfy him?"

"No. I don't. He's a hard customer. I can tell it. He's looked you up. Called the plant and wangled—as an Englishman says—out of the bookkeeper, the place we bank. Knows it's a day-and-night bank. He's found your rating. Hell, man, he's studied the whole lay-out. He doesn't intend to deliver that evidence until he has your whole business. Maybe then—l don't know. Even though a Londoner—he's a Cockney, to be precise—he can see that your 'styte's attorney'—as he calls him—can send you to the chair."

Roger Pelton covered his face with his hands. "Oh—Clay, what—what must you think of me?"

"Buck up," I said. "I'm not lecturing you, Mr. Pelton. I'm too much in love with Doris. And what's done—is done. Though I feel like hell—to tell you the frank truth. But what you did twenty years ago isn't what you'd do today. People change, as well as styles in dogs. And I know those sudden impulses—that seize us all. At times. We're all savages at heart. I only want now to save your life. And Doris's mental well-being. And to save that candy factory, as well, for her. And not stand by, and see you—and her—bled white from now 'till forever. And that, Mr. Pelton, means for you—San Do Mar!"

CHAPTER XIX

SAN DO MAR

R oger Pelton stared at me.

"You—you mean," he said slowly, "that I should go—to San Do Mar? That little republic? That used to be—"

"Yes," I repeated sternly. "That little triangle of land that used to be the western tip of Honduras. And which is now the Republic of San Do Mar. And recognized as such by the League of Nations."

"But—but why?" he asked helplessly. "Why—"

"Why me no whys, as Shakespeare said," I put in irritably. For, in truth, my composure was undermined by the ugliness of the whole situation, entangling as it did Doris—as well as myself. Though I could not help but marvel, as I spoke to Roger Pelton, how these last few minutes had changed the whole tenor of the master-and-man relationship which had formerly existed between us. "No," I went on, "it's you—for San Do Mar, Mr. Pelton. Because it's the one place we can park you that'll give us a chance to drive a real bargain with this Payne. Or his mob—in case he gets efficient, and gathers together a blackmailing outfit. For no one, as you know, can be extradited from San Do Mar on any crime in the calendar. Whether it's a matter of just a theft of $100 out of a National Tea Company store till—or murder—yes, I know that word hurts— you're safe in San Do Mar for the rest of your natural life. Sure," I went on, "there'll be extradition laws passed eventually. Some day.

But they won't be retroactive. No law ever can be retroactive. And such laws won't apply to anybody who has safely made San Do Mar—and gotten ensconced there. So the man who settles in San Do Mar has played the first trump card in any blackmail game against him."

"How—how do you mean, Clay? I'm all in your hands now."

"Well," I said—and a little less harshly, "I mean just this. Milo Payne will play a blackmail game as long as he believes that he can dangle the Illinois electric chair in front of your eyes—or hard labor for life in Michigan. Once he can't do that—once that the only thing he can hand you is mere exposure—he'll come to terms. Terms maybe on a par with that $20,000 he asks for as a starter tonight—or maybe double. In any event, it'll be checkmate: You there—doubtlessly wanting damned hard to come home: I here, running the factory for you, and sending the income down to you.

"But," I said, "it'll be a damned enraged Cockney if Payne gets so much as the slightest inkling that you're even heading for San Do Mar. Because that knocks his scheme sky-high. And he may suspect you're loping for it. 'Specially when I stall him tonight. Which I'm going to do. For I'm going to Washington Square, Mr. Pelton. Not you. Me. Yes. And I'm going to pull a stall. The first stall won't be so hard—no. The Day and Night Bank—stopped paying out big sums—at night—because Chicago—so full of gunmen—and receiving only deposits now—at night. Etcetera and so forth and boohoohoo! That'll be my story. The pith of which is that we couldn't raise the coin. Not tonight, that is. It's the later stalls tomorrow and thereafter—that will take more—well—finesse. And—how! I'll figure them out later. But all the time I'll bull him into thinking we intend to pay. That we want to pay. Oh so bad! But in the meantime you'll be hopping for New Orleans. No, I don't mean tomorrow. I mean right tonight! On the Southern Airways. Whose plane for New Orleans leaves at 12 midnight. And you can roost there in New Orleans just long enough to get a highball from me. No, no, I don't mean a drink. I mean a report. As to what's the next thing to do. Which will have to be one of three things. The first of which would consist of taking a fast United Fruit Company liner to Honduras—fast, yes, except that on such a boat you have to go the long way 'round—roundabout, that is, by way of Havana, Cuba. But once in Honduras you could get into San Do Mar by train. And without even a passport, thanks to the present traveling arrangements between Uncle Sam and Central America. The second possible thing you would do is—but have you still got your Mexican passport from your last year's trip down below the border—on the matter of looking into the cactus-sugar situation?" He nodded vehemently, though the gesture he made with his hand toward his desk was feeble. "Then the second of those three possible moves," I said, "is that you will board a slow New Orleans–Gulf of Campeche freighter across the narrowest part of the Gulf of Mexico to Campeche—yes, in the southern tip of Mexico—and crawl by rail and stagecoach across that neck of Mexico into Guatemala—across Guatemala, the same way—and thence into San Do Mar.

"In short, we've got to get you clear to San Do Mar by stalling. Once you're in there, you're safe on first. We hold aces."

"But—but suppose this man finds," said Pelton fearfully, "by repeatedly trying to get to me personally, that—that I'm not in town?"

"We've got to prevent that," was my answer. "He'll smell a rat. And maybe spring the works. Now—let's see." I thought hard for a minute. "I've got it! Filkins! Filkins is about your age. He's got a very dignified cast of features. And speaks the best of English. And remember—this Payne has never seen you. Now what you'll do is to put Filkins into your smoking jacket and your dressing gown, your library and your clothes—and to every stranger who comes here on any pretext whatsoever, to discuss the candy business or getting a job, or what have you—Filkins is Roger Pelton."

"But—but why couldn't I, Clay, just take the bull by the horns? And have you tell this man Payne that I've started, by air or steamer, for San Do Mar. And that he can—"

"Yes, I know," I said, "—or get off the pot!" I shook my head. "Christamighty no, Mr. Pelton. The jig is all up if you ever did that. The little countries all surrounding San Do Mar are jealous as hell of the new republic. And if Payne gets cuckoo with rage and springs the works—and the State's Attorney wires down to Central America to stop Mr. Roger Pelton, Esquire—well—do you know what will happen?"

"Wu-wu-wu—well—what?"

"San Do Mar is entirely surrounded by territory of other Central American nations. Guatemala on the west and north. San Salvador on the south. Honduras proper on the east; and British Honduras on the north. Trains, buses or stagecoaches going into San Do Mar from all sides would be searched. You'd be picked off. Boat lines—on both oceans—would be watched, and you wouldn't even get your feet on Honduras, Guatemala, San Salvador or Nicaragua, let alone traveling over them. Gad, Mr. Pelton, those little jealous countries would give their eye teeth to prevent San Do Mar, their new little-sister banana republic, from receiving another prosperous guest. Able to spend money—for you'd have the candy factory income—and make her more prosperous than ever. I read all about the condition in the *Literary Regurgitation*.

"No," I went on, "the only absconders, murderers, forgers, thieves, income-tax violators—criminals of all kinds who enjoy asylum in San Do Mar—if you can use the word 'enjoy'!—made the place *before* the facts were out that they were wanted. They were lost indeed had they not. So I'm telling you we've got to sneak you down there—while this Cockney bastard still believes you to be in Chicago—trying to raise the first 20,000 bucks."

He was silently reflective.

"Yes, I—I guess you're right, Clay. God—what a fate! But I earned it. Yes, I earned it. But—but what was that third possible move?"

I didn't answer him on that, as yet. So he asked a further fearful question.

"Do—do you really think you can successfully hold this man off until I—I—"

"Well," was my dubious answer, "I'll have to stall as never a man stalled before. As a matter of fact, Filkins is my big ace in the hole. Filkins is the man who can convince any stranger that you're right here in Chicago and on the ground. 'Specially if Doris should walk into the room and address him as 'Papa.'"

"What—what shall we tell Doris?"

"Nothing," I said. "We'll tell her it's something serious. And that we can say no more. Doris is a good kid. She knows when not to ask questions."

"Is there no other place—without extradition laws?"

"None! San Do Mar's the last such spot on the face of the earth. And it won't last long. Although for them as gets there now—it's safety. Furthermore, if that Cockney son of a—well—you know what I mean—goes loco finally, and springs the works, instead of making a deal with us, you'll—well—you'll have to stay on there in San Do Mar. For the rest of your life. With the others who've made it."

"God!" was all he said. "Stay on! Thinking, thinking, thinking—of things that have come back to me tonight so horribly! And with you—and all my Chicago friends—and Doris—knowing."

"Well," I admitted, "for one who hates bananas as you do—I won't deny it'll be a tough exile! And furthermore," I added, quite frankly, "speaking for myself, I wish I didn't know. About the whole thing. I tell you that! But what's done is done. Now where will you stay when you get to New Orleans? So I can send you that highball to move on fast—or to come home. For, coming home is—well—that third possible move."

He stared at me uncomprehendingly. Then seemed to grasp the significance of my words.

"Oh—you think, Clay—you think that maybe—"

I nodded. "Only—maybe. Only—at best. That this English fool may actually think that 4000 guineas is equal to all the money in the Bank of England. That it's a ten-strike like nothing else, so strike the blighter pink! And that if he gets it, he can set himself up in a shop in Lunnon—or a little eating-place—and quit the black-mailing business. To tell you the truth, I don't think it at all. I only 'ope it, like the h'ass that I am. Excuse me. I meant I h'only hope h'it like the ass that I h'am. Well, never mind. It's just the slightest possibility. And I don't want you heading further south like a scrooey swallow with his beak full of the first north wind—if this thing *does* get settled."

He was silent a moment. Then he spoke.

"Clay, I'm getting terribly nervous. I'll—I'll—take the midnight plane that you speak of. And I'll be there in New Orleans tomorrow morning, as you want me to be. But—but—by God, Clay, I'm—I'm afraid to leave an address with you—Doris—anyone. With this Cockney likely to go—to go wild. Suppose you let something slip—in pulling the wool over his eyes? And suppose he jettisons all his personal avarice and—and hands what he's got to the State's Attorney? Takes it right up—to Willeber's house? And Willeber puts me on all the police wires in the country? I'll—I'll be hamstrung for fair. With all the police of all the cities in America looking for me."

"Well, what's your suggestion then?"

"Well—my suggestion—is this, Clay. I—but first, have—have you a friend—whom you can trust implicitly? How is this fellow you speak of so often—this John Barr?"

"I could trust him with my very life."

"What does he look like?"

"Rather distinguished. A man of about forty-nine. With pointed beard. And closely, neatly trimmed mustache. To match. Dresses in dark clothes. Looks like—like a scholar. And he's a gentleman. For he'd never ask a question about anything we'd request him to do."

"Would—would he give you a little of his time?"

"Sure—yes. He's not tied to any time clock. He has—yes—an operation scheduled for tomorrow afternoon at 2 o'clock. A double-excision—of a couple of things that call themselves tumors. But the operation can be deferred, I know, for the growths aren't, either of 'em, cancerous—and hence doubling their volume every 48 hours. So the operation can be deferred all right."

"Well then, Clay, this is my suggestion. If you're really anxious to—to help me. I'll be there in New Orleans. As arranged. But under another name. And at no place that even you yourself can know. Some private rooming-house. Over in the French section. I don't even know myself yet. And if this fellow Payne does prove to be slippery—about handing over the—the goods—you know?—and obdurate on the money question—and we have to embark on this long stalling process—then you send this chap Barr down there. To New Orleans. My expense, in every way, of course. With instructions that he shall stand on—on—say—the northeast corner of—of Canal and Bourbon Streets. At 12 noon each day—and 6 o'clock at night. Wearing a—a bright red tie and—and—carrying—say—my Sunday walking stick—the one of redwood with the nickeled head. Yes. That's a busy corner. Hundreds of people passing there every hour. And I'll be passing that corner too. On foot. Or on street cars. Or in a cab. Or maybe only watching it from a hotel window in the vicinity. And if I see him standing there—then I'll know that I'm to head on to Central America—and head fast. But what—what do you think of that idea?"

"It's worthy of the sesquicentennial anniversary number of Nick Carter—that is, in the five-cent edition," I told him. "But the whole affair here is no less than Nick Carter in the dime edition. So it's all in keeping. And your suggestion is all right—if it eases your mind a bit from the specter of your being arrested. So consider it ratified here and now. Canal and Bourbon—northeast corner, 12 noon and 6 o'clock each day. Except—make that a blue tie, for John. And not a red one! For there's such a thing as asking too much of a man, you know! Yes. All right. We're all set on that. I'll get John to defer his operation. He'll do it for me. But you—you're in a nervous state, all right, Mr. Pelton. Do you think you can go through with it—can you book yourself clear to San Do Mar—in confidence that I'm skillfully holding the fort for you up here in Chicago?"

He pondered. "Yes, I—I am in a nervous state. I know it. And once I'm 900 miles or so from my home town, I'll—I'll be in a worse state than ever. I'm even likely to head back to—to Canada—instead of giving the police a chance to pull me off of some United Fruit Company liner."

"No," I said sharply. "You're done for—if you do that. Canada is as much of a refuge for you as—as a Wisconsin lumber camp is for a lost virgin. You stay right down in New Orleans until you get some news from me. And if John, with the description of him I've given you, stands on that corner, you head for Central America—and that way only. But if I come down there and stand on that corner, it means I've won! So don't blow the town in a blue funk—until at least one of us comes down. And, incidentally, if it's John Barr who has to come down—because of my having to stay here to play ball with that Cockney—I'll not take him into my confidence as to what it's exactly about. Except that it's a matter of almost life and death. And being a gentleman, he's one person who won't demand to know, either."

Roger Pelton seemed a tiny bit relieved.

Then suddenly he grew thoughtfully, strainedly silent again. And spoke.

"Clay?"

"What?"

"Have you stopped to think, Clay, what it might mean—our putting Filkins into my shoes here—to make this Cockney think I'm right in town?"

"No—except that I think it's a damned good idea even if I did invent it myself."

"Clay," he said slowly, "I—I don't think this Cockney wangled, as you call it, that information out of our bookkeeper. You know? About our banking in the Day-and-Night Bank? For George Duff is one tight-mouthed man. Nobody could get that information out of him—on the phone. No stranger. Why, Clay, George would be sure to think it was a gangster plot to hold up our payroll messenger some day—on his way back to the plant from the bank."

"Well, that's George all right," I admitted grudgingly. "He would reason falsely—for Chicago gangsters wouldn't even stoop to making phone calls to our bookkeeper. They have their own annual subscription to Dunn and Bradstreets—and they undoubtedly have us ticketed up completely right today in the Gangsters' Clearance

House—and we ought to begin now—we will, once you're in San Do Mar—ahem!—and use the Brinks Armored Express Car delivery. But, getting back to this Cockney, a stranger in Chicago from Lunnon. He got the information all right. Not from Peter Walmsley, I imagine, for the Reverend wouldn't know about our business affairs. And certainly the Cockney didn't get the information by flirting with any of our factory girls. For they don't know anything about our banking. Considering they get only envelopes with money in them. In fact, the Cockney has your rating—and he seems to know all he needs to know about you. But where—where do you think he might have got—all he has got?"

Pelton was thoughtfully silent again.

"I think," he returned, "that he got it—from somebody—in this house!"

My mouth opened up.

"Filkins?"

"Who else? Certainly not Doris. Certainly not Marie."

"But—but good Lord—Filkins—"

"No, Clay," he said, anticipating the very question I was going to ask, "I know very little about him, really. In spite of the fact that he works for me. And has worked for me, now, for nearly eight months. He's an Englishman—that you can tell right off. His references were quite ordinary. He told me personally that he once had been an actor—in and about the English provinces. I think—yes—he even said he had once done a turn of some kind in vaudeville in—in the music halls of London. Or maybe he said Liverpool. But that must have been long ago, Clay, for he's undoubtedly come down in the world. A long, long ways, too, for—well—he's quite a well-educated fellow, as you can see. And Clay, it—it would be ironic, indeed, if we put Filkins here—in my clothes—to make the Cockney think I was living right on here in Chicago—and it was Filkins all the time that the Cockney—was getting information out of."

"But," I expostulated. And repeated, "But, Filkins—hm!—Englishman? Yes. Hm."

I was silent, thinking. Then I spoke.

"Listen, Mr. Pelton, Doris sent Filkins away tonight. To be gone for a couple of hours. And I wonder if I could look over his room?"

"Yes, Clay. Doris will show you."

"Oke! Hold the fort here for a minute while I do."

I went out of the library. And into the parlor, where Doris sat, strained and worried, under the lamp.

"Hon', I want to go over Filkins' room. Quick. Before he comes back."

She asked no questions. A good trooper she was—in spite of the fact that she had been handing out her pictures, with love inscribed on them, to other fellows. I could almost have forgiven her, then and there. But, for the present, I had too much to do—to waste time forgiving people. She led the way down into the basement. To a little room, whose high window looked out on the dark lawn, its sill almost on a level with the grass itself. The steam pipes on the ceiling branded it as the standard servant's room. There was a simple rug on the floor. A single bed. A narrow chiffonier. A table with a drawer in it. All in all, the room was spotlessly clean. And exceedingly ascetic.

Ascetic, that is, did one omit consideration of the one alien note in it—a low steamer-size trunk underneath the table, with tarnished verdigris-encrusted brass-bound corners, and the almost obliterated, but still readable, words: "THE GREAT SIMON—THEATRE," painted on its side facing us. Its brass hasp-lock stood vertically upward, showing that it was not even fastened against the world. Probably it contained Filkins' winter flannels.

Yet what struck me, chiefly, was not the trunk—since Filkins apparently made no bones of his having once been something or other in the British histrionic and vaudeville world of long ago. But the typewriter! On the table. That is, presumably a typewriter, for I had, of course, to assume its presence by the fact that the typical rubber-cover shrouding it would not stand up by itself.

Odd—Filkins having a typewriter. Of course—it was all right. But—

Well, we would have to get to the bottom of all this. For if we did, by the least chance, have two blackmailers—or one, helped at least from within this house, we'd never outwit the Cockney.

I took hold of the handle of the drawer of the table, but my attention was seized by a business letter—headed "Lake Street Typewriter Exchange"—hanging face outward from a small spindle on the wall across the table. I leaned over and read it. It was addressed to Filkins—Courtenay Westlake Filkins—what a name!—at that address; it was brief, and ran:

> Dear Sir:
> We regret that Machine No. 999,806, in your possession the past month, has proven unsatisfactory. We take pleasure in sending out a machine of another make, but on the same terms, and trust that you will like that one better.
> Very truly yours,
> LAKE STREET TYPEWRITER EXCHANGE
> per L.

Just why had Machine No. 999,806 proven unsatisfactory, I wondered? And what kind had they sent him? It all had little or no bearing on matters—true—but I decided to be thorough. And so pulled off the cover of the machine instead of bothering with the drawer of the table.

Protruding from the platen of the machine was a sheet of paper. An uncompleted sheet, that is. Typed in purple ink—the same, I saw, as the ribbon now in the machine. I leaned over it and read the sheet—that is, what there was of it.

And, finishing it, knew that all that remained now to be done was to try to hurriedly figure out exactly how the devil much Filkins knew—and whether Doris and I could hold him fast and tight—and incommunicado!—over the few days it might take to chase Roger Pelton to San Do Mar.

For it was plain that I had found no less a person than "Abigail Sprigge"!

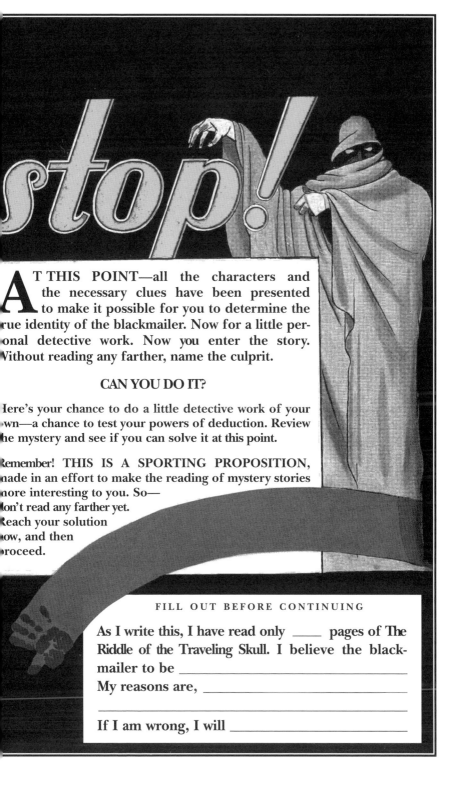

AT THIS POINT—all the characters and the necessary clues have been presented to make it possible for you to determine the true identity of the blackmailer. Now for a little personal detective work. Now you enter the story. Without reading any farther, name the culprit.

CAN YOU DO IT?

Here's your chance to do a little detective work of your own—a chance to test your powers of deduction. Review the mystery and see if you can solve it at this point.

Remember! THIS IS A SPORTING PROPOSITION, made in an effort to make the reading of mystery stories more interesting to you. So—
don't read any farther yet.
Reach your solution
now, and then
proceed.

FILL OUT BEFORE CONTINUING

As I write this, I have read only _____ pages of The Riddle of the Traveling Skull. I believe the blackmailer to be _____

My reasons are, _____
_____

If I am wrong, I will _____

Consider a membership in the

Harry Stephen Keeler Society

Since its inception in 1997, the group has grown to some seventy-five members in half a dozen countries. Its organ is *Keeler News,* appearing five times each year and featuring articles, letters, reviews, and a vigorous emporium of Keeler's many books. The *News* has produced fifty issues; all, back to the first, are available. On CD-ROM ($5), the full run comes with the Keeler Dust Jacket Vault, a compendium of original cover artwork. Mail payments to Richard Polt, 4745 Winston Road, Cincinnati, OH 45232—or consult the internet:

http://staff.xu.edu/~polt/keeler/index.html.

 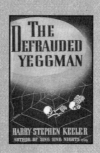 

CHAPTER XX

FILKINS THE POET!

Yes, it was plain that I had "Abigail Sprigge"!

For the sheet of paper contained a poem. Completed, too, although the subsidiary information—intended solely for editors and publishers—at the bottom had been interrupted in the typing. Perhaps by Doris's sending Filkins out on the very trumped-up errand on which he was now engaged. Or by one of the many other interruptions incident to butlering.

And, as usual, as with all of the confounded Spriggian work, I liked the elegiac. Or eligiambus. Or whatever things doleful in verse are called. The unfinished typescript ran:

RELATIVE!

The sun was brighter, the air was cleaner,
The skies were bluer
When I was young;
The task was lighter, the grass was greener
And love was truer,
More sweetly sung!

The maids were fairer, the men were braver,
The sages wiser
In days of old;
Now joys are rarer, and cares are graver,

189

> *And life a miser*
> *Who hoards his gold!*
>
> Submitted by Abigail—

Thus and there the typed page ended.

"This is all I want to know," I told Doris gravely. And rolled the sheet back under the platen where I had found it. And placed the rubber cover back over the machine.

She opened the door of the room silently, so that I could precede her back upstairs. But a vagrant thought came to me; and so I turned.

"Doris, my dear, I—I know you don't like this job—but serious things are afoot—in this house. Yes, Filkins is involved in another man's rascality—no, I don't know to what degree. But, hon, I want you to lock yourself inside this room here, and make a hasty turnover of the entire contents of that old trunk there. Probably it contains nothing but winter clothing, and so forth, but if you find anything whatever in it that a butler wouldn't ordinarily have—anything, hon!—well—bring it upstairs to the library pronto! In fact; hon, do the identical thing with those few chiffonier drawers—and the table drawer, yes—and that small closet there. Don't overlook the shelves. And report to me anything or everything that isn't according to Hoyle. Now I'm going back to your father. He's terribly nervous—as you know—and I don't want him alone. Not just now."

"Yes, Clay," she nodded obediently. "I'll do exactly what you ask me to do."

And, hearing the click of the key in the lock, I went back upstairs to the library. This time I left the door just slightly ajar, so that I myself could hear Filkins—if by any chance he should come in—and sidetrack him.

"Yes," I told Roger Pelton, once we were closeted together again, "Filkins is one of the gang—if we can call two a gang."

And I related to him, for the first time, how I had unpacked that fatal leaden slug, greenish in some lights, yellowish in others, from the brainpan of the skull—and repacked it back in again, worse luck!

And of how I had put together—or had put together for me by the moron negro, Sandy MacDougall—certain fragments of that paper packing, only to discover that I had the carbon copy of a poem by "Abigail Sprigge." Then I told him very briefly of Philodexter Maxellus' magazine—how "Abigail Sprigge" had already submitted there—how Maxellus had called me down there—and of how I had gone out on that wild-goose chase for "Miss O. M. Lee"—only to find that "Lee" was the pseudonym—and Sprigge the real name. Except that—well—I told him then the details of how I had just unearthed the fact that Filkins himself was the elusive "Abigail Sprigge."

He turned almost greenish-yellow himself at my very mention of that fatal bullet. And, after I had finished, seeing that I was finished, he shook his head, wearily, dazedly.

"Then—then your whole hypothesis, Clay," he said weakly, "about how the Cockney Milo Payne—got the skull back—from Peter Walmsley—falls through, doesn't it?"

I was thinking deeply in the meantime. My forehead was so corrugated, as I could sense by feeling alone, that an Eskimo's fur coat, sprinkled with nothing but Lux, could have been washed on it. At last I spoke.

"No," I said, "my hypothesis doesn't fall through at all. We merely add a bit to it now—that's all. And the adding is simple enough—with what we now know about Filkins."

I paused. To marshall together my premises as I elaborated my statement.

"Mr. Pelton, when Milo Payne came down to Chicago from the North Woods—he sensed he had something by which to blackmail *somebody*—if he could only get at the full facts. He hoped to pick up a lot from this Reverend Peter Walmsley. But he had no absolute assurance that he would pick up anything. See? But he didn't book up quarters in the Palmer House right away. No. He took quarters in some cheap rooming-house, most likely.

"What I think he did do was as follows: he went carefully over the back files of—say—the *Chicago Tribune,* in the Public Library— that is, from 1914—the time of this Phil Walmsley's operation in

Chicago, as given him over the Long Distance phone by Dr. Max Prior—and on up. Those things are all alphabetically indexed in the death columns, you know, and it takes only five minutes to cover a whole calendar month of deaths. He surmised that the fellow having once lived in Chicago remained thereafter a Chicagoan—probably knew, though he himself was from London, that history doesn't record a single instance of a Chicagoan with either brains or guts enough to get out of the town. Also, he surmised—and properly enough, too—that nobody, once of Chicago, would be permanently living up in that Godforsaken North Woods territory—that such a person as the man whose skull he had, had been somebody vacationing. On 'olid'y—as Payne would put it! And so, looking through the back files of the papers, he undoubtedly struck a death notice on Phil—'"

"Yes," Roger Pelton almost groaned, "there—there was one in—sometime in late July—of 1919."

"And there was a news story, no doubt, even if, but a small one, in the same issue—"

"Yes. A—a story of Phil's death—up there. By drowning. About five column inches. With a mention or two of me. A quotation, in fact. To the reporters."

"Ah," I said. "And there we have it! That gave him a clue to you: Roger Pelton.

"He found you," I continued, "in the phone book. Rode out here to Diversey Boulevard—to look your place over. To try and size up whether you had any money or not. And—lo and behold!—while he was out in front looking it over—who comes out of the front door but—"

"—but Filkins," Roger Pelton put in miserably.

"Exactly! And he knew Filkins. And Filkins knew him. No, I have no idea how or where they met back in old England. They could even be brothers. Half-brothers. Cousins. Boyhood chums. Connected in the British theatrical game Filkins tells you he once was part of. Or they could even have been servants in the same establishment in England.

"Filkins invited him in. And—but, I say—Filkins could do that, couldn't he? Without you and Doris knowing—"

"Oh, yes, Clay. Yes. Or even Marie. For Marie prefers to have the quarters in the attic—where she can have two entire rooms for herself. As—as for Doris and myself—neither of us are always here. Yes, Clay. Filkins could have asked him into his room there—by the front way—or, 'round the sidewalk—by the side door."

"Well, that's just what Filkins did," I told him. "I kind of sense, somehow, that Filkins had something on him. Enough so, perhaps, that when Payne started feeling him out about you—he himself felt Payne out as to what Payne had on you—and even made Payne come entirely clean with what he had. There was, I'm convinced, an interchange of information—perhaps some promises. And Filkins tossed in all he knew about you—your bank—your rating—the approximate size of the accounts you carry—the approximate volume of your business—everything—oh, Filkins picks up enough around here, serving at dinners you give to different officials in the plant. And other persons in the confectionary business, too. But enough for us to know that Filkins was now in the game.

"Now whether," I went on, "that bullet was packed in the skull right there in Filkins' room, so as to preserve its delicate ballistic markings, and with the result that a carbon copy of one of Filkins' 'Abigail Sprigge' poems got wadded in too, for general good measure—or whether Filkins, poem in pocket, was over at the other chap's room when the skull was packed—I can't guess. It really doesn't matter. What does matter is that the Abigail Sprigge poem got torn up, and wadded in. Which was the damnedest best thing, I'm telling you, Mr. Pelton, for you that ever happened. For otherwise we'd have dumped everything tonight in our proposed handling of this matter. We—"

"But—but, Clay—about the Palmer House? And Peter Walmsley—"

"Getting hold of the bag?" I said. "Simple enough now, Mr. Pelton, Filkins supplied all the information to Payne that he could. Being new on the job—he couldn't supply facts concerning things a

decade or two back. Like—for instance—your buying the old
Isenstein Snapperjack Works. Yes. And so Payne booked his room,
just the same, at the Palmer House—and filled his appointment
with Peter Walmsley, exactly as scheduled. To get more facts. I am
confident, Mr. Pelton, that there was no intention at any time of letting the Reverend actually get out of there with that bag—and the
skull it contained. To be sure—that had been promised him—in
that letter. But just to get him down there. The skull, even, was to
be shown to him. Anything—to get him to talk. I don't know
whether Payne's idea was to step to the clothes closet with the bag,
and to extract the skull out of it before turning it over to Rev.—just
as a gypsy fortune-telling woman does, you know, with her client's
money, knotted for good luck into the corner of a handkerchief—or
whether the Rev. was to be given a grand stall—just about the time
he was to go away. If the former, Payne muffed his stunt somehow—
and Rev. insisted on taking the bag. If the latter—well—maybe
Milo Payne scratched his chin—ventured that he believed, after all,
he'd put the thing into the hands of the State Attorney himself—
lest he be made h'accessory h'after the fact—I mean accessory after
the fact—and possibly after the preliminary stall he walked out of
the room a moment—and Peter Walmsley, not liking the chap's
looks nor ways—or possibly surmising that Payne was more interested in maybe doing some blackmailing than bringing about justice—just sashayed out, in Payne's temporary absence, with the bag.

"After which," I emphasized, "the story runs identically as I've
outlined it. Payne rushed out of the Palmer House, after the Rev.,
chucked his suitcase, already packed, at the corner cigar store, and
picked up Walmsley's trail. Followed him. Cab going alongside
street car. Or make your own selection! Then he naturally picked up
your Ichabod Chang's trail. And then the whole thing, thereafter,
just as I've outlined. Am I right—or am I right?"

"You're—you're right," he said.

He thought a moment. Slumped dejectedly in his chair.

"Clay?"

"What?"

"Do—do you—do you suppose—that—by any chance—Filkins—could be Milo Payne?"

At the first second of hearing his words, the idea in them had staggered me; but a second later I could see the utter fallacy of it.

"No, it's not possible," I said. "Considering that Filkins has been here in Chicago all the time. And Dr. Prior says he was called on the telephone, by his English inquirer—Payne—by Long Distance from Northern Michigan. Yes, I talked myself to Dr. Prior today. No, I wasn't snooping. Just—just investigating. Thanks to Doris telling me our marriage was up the creek! And be glad I did investigate. And—but Filkins has been here, I take it, all the time?"

"Y—yes, Clay. All the time."

"Well, that's that, then. Filkins is not Milo Pay——"

"Clay?"

But this time the utterance of my name did not come from Roger Pelton. It came from Doris, just outside the crack of the partly opened door.

"Yes, honey?" I called. "Through? Or do you need help?"

"No, Clay," came her words, trickling through the crack, "I've combed every drawer—every shelf—every square inch in that little room."

"Good! And anything—of interest?"

"Yes, Clay."

"What?"

She opened the door and came in part way. Even as I rose, and went the rest of the distance to meet her. On her face was hopeless bewilderment. And held out from herself, in her outstretched hand, was a grinning cloth and papier-mache doll. Probably four feet in height. Life size, in fact, only as to its enameled head. And which head held a hinged underjaw. A ventriloquist's talking dummy!

That in itself, perhaps, wasn't so all-surprising—considering the nearly obliterated words on that old theatrical trunk. But the dummy wore a little black velveteen suit sewn entirely over with hundreds, if not thousands, of pearl buttons.

It represented a London costermonger.

The Cockney of all Cockneys!

And Filkins—a ventriloquist!

And, of a sudden, a dozen things flew together lightning—like in my brain—and I realized that while Filkins, up to a day or so ago, could not possibly have been Milo Payne—that he could indeed be Milo Payne now. And, this being the case, where was the original Milo Payne? And where—

But what Doris was now silently holding forth to me with her other hand gave me the answer.

"Hanging—in his closet," was all she said. "And not his—for I've never seen it before in my life!"

It was a checkered Sherlockholmsian cap, with long beak and flaps buttoning back across the top. And when I took it from her, I found that it was damp—and clammy—and the smell of the fishy waters of Lake Michigan—as they always are in late October—radiated from it.

And I knew. Everything!

Somewhere, along the sloping granite walk that fringed the vast territory of newly made land at the foot of Diversey Parkway—and all the other streets both sides of Diversey—where Filkins and Payne had repaired to stroll—and talk in seclusion—about this now mutual blackmail scheme of theirs—that huge stretch of land, with its now vacant bird-shelters, its withered grass, its lugubrious trees, deserted absolutely in late October—Milo Payne's body was now floating, its belly distended with lake water like Professor Piccard's own stratosphere car. Shoved off the granite walk—into the deep water there—by the crafty hand of Filkins. Except that the characteristic cap, which its owner appeared invariably to wear, and of which he probably had two or three or even half a dozen, had been lifted out of the water where it had floated after he had been shoved in. By Filkins—so that the body, when ultimately found, would not be tied up, through the newspaper descriptions of it, with the strange and bizarre-looking Milo Payne who had lived at the Palmer House and elsewhere. And a 24-carat gilt-edge blackmail scheme, now 96 per cent under successful way, thereby ruined.

Indeed, I saw quite plainly that here was a second murder—which, like the first murder of years ago that had caused it to be brought about—could never be turned over to the police—by the combined family, Pelton-Calthorpe!

CHAPTER XXI

ROPES FOR FILKINS

My employer stared helplessly at his daughter.
I was already gazing into the damp cap. A small yellow silken label in it read:

KINGS ROAD HABERDASHERY
Chelsea, London

And underneath the printed portion of that label, but penciled in just in indelible pencil, was the added information:

The Holmescap
5 s each
19 s the half doz.

That was all. And I tossed the thing well across the room. For it smelled too fishy, and felt far too clammy, to be delectable handling.

And now I took the ventriloquial dummy from Doris. She must have had some of her fingers inserted, through the back of its body, in the very wire loops that worked the head, for, thanks to my clumsy disentanglement of it from her hand, it opened its mouth and winked one eye at me. It might as well have said, "Blimey, matey—'ave 'orf!" Disconcerting—to say the least.

"What else, Doris—in the trunk?"

"Just clothes, Clay—as you surmised. Nothing out of the way

in the whole room—I combed it thoroughly—except this cap—and I wouldn't have brought that—only it was wet, damp."

"You didn't, hon, er—find—er—a—er—skull?"

"Heavens no, Clay! I did find a rhyming dictionary."

Poet. Blackmailer. Murderer!

"Room all closed up now again? Lights out?"

"Yes, Clay."

"Then go back to the parlor. And, when Filkins returns, act as though nothing has happened."

I closed the door now, and locked it.

"Well," I said, holding up the costermonger effigy, "while your theory that Filkins was Milo Payne all the time was dead wrong, I realize now mighty well that Filkins is the bird who called up here today—and tonight—and did the Cockney talking. Which the other chap was in no position to do!"

He passed a hand weakly over his forehead. Things were coming too fast and furious for him.

"Filkins," I went on, "was out of the house—so Doris said—at the time 'Milo Payne' first called up here today. Again, he was out on an errand—when the Cockney voice talked with me on the wire. No, I didn't recognize it as Filkins—I had all I could do to interpret for myself the damned Cockneyisms. And Filkins probably used the voice he used to use with the dummy doll that sat on his other knee. Sure—all ventriloquists use two dummies. And they attain, by long practise and study, two voices different entirely from their own." I paused. "As for me, I don't know whether Filkins knew it was me—or not. I believe not. For I was talking through two complete thicknesses of silk handkerchief. Boy, oh boy, how Filkins must have blessed Doris for sending him out of the house—on a couple-hour special errand—around the very time he had arranged to call up!"

Roger Pelton still stared at me, dumbly, miserably.

"'The Great Simon,' it says on his trunk," I explained.

"And—where," he asked feebly, "do—do you think Filkins was—"

"Was talking from? From Mouquin's, just as he said he was. And

why not? For restaurants all have doublewalled telephone booths—
to keep the music out—in case they ever put in an orchestra. Yes,
Mouquin's. For remember, Mr. Pelton, John Barr—if you'll recall
Doris's report from him to me in here tonight—caught Filkins leaving Mouquin's and driving off in a cab—at least, a bird who was
wearing a long-beaked checkered Sherlockholmsian cap. This all
means, Mr. Pelton, that Filkins went from here tonight to Milo
Payne's quarters—brushed up a bit—put on one of Payne's nineteen-
shilling-the-half-dozen caps—then to Mouquin's—had a good dinner—and carried on the next notch of the blackmail scheme. He—"
I stopped. It seemed difficult now to convince him who only a while
ago had suggested the whole thing. But, quite plainly, he was more
or less dazed by the swift developments of the night. "Listen,"
I declared, "this thing comes together in my mind now in a way it
never has yet. For—get this! Mr. Pelton, neither Dr. Prior nor the
hotel clerk—through the manager, that is—said, out and out, that
Payne was a Cockney. True, they didn't say he wasn't, either. But
they'd have been bound—I think—to have made some mention of his
outlandish lingo—had the Payne they dealt with been the Payne
that's been talking to me. Yes. And I believe, Mr. Pelton, that Payne
is—rather, was—just a middle-class Englishman—but that he's now
been made into a Cockney—by the man now talking for him." I held
up that costermonger dummy significantly.

"But—but Clay," Pelton almost groaned, "why—why—just
why—would Filkins—do—the talking—the negotiating—for—
for this Britisher?"

I laughed grimly. As my eye fell on that damp fishy-smelling
cap across the room. And I reassembled the sinister picture now in
my mind.

"Because," I said, "Milo Payne is dead. Yes. This whole affair is
so much of a nickel novel already, that we might as well write the
finishing touch to it. That cap over there, Mr. Pelton, has been
fished out of Lake Michigan water—vintage of late October, 1940.
The only possible interpretation of Filkins having it is that he's
killed its wearer off—oh yes, yes—easy—walking along the Lake

Front together—foot of Diversey here where all the new-made land is—deserted this time of year—talking over this blackmail stuff—shoved Payne right off the granite walk. Except that he leaned down and fished out the latter's cap. And—well—if Filkins did all this—if he's canceled—Payne out of the equation then that would mean, since he knows where Payne lives—remember, he went out of here with a brown derby, and John caught him leaving Mouquin's with another long-beaked cap on—well, it would mean that he now has the blackmail assets himself!"

"In—in which case—"

"In which case he'll be absolutely forced to carry things through himself, from now on. And about Washington Square—well, I believe he saw enough today in this house to perceive that you had absolutely cracked up. That you couldn't get over, on hands and knees, to the corner now—let alone to Washington Square. Again—I'm certain he'd believe that the last person you'd ever send there to deal on that skull—would be your own prospective son-in-law! He would be certain that you'd send somebody—maybe Howard Crilly, your nephew on South Shore Drive—who never comes here, and hence has never seen him—or Jim Cronkers, your cousin in Evanston—the same situation, again—or somebody close in our confidence at the plant—but never, never me!"

He nodded unhappily.

"Y—yes—I guess I showed Filkins, all right, today that—that I had cracked up badly. And—yes—he would know I wouldn't send you. That—that I'd be afraid that, in some honeymoon tiff, you'd tell Doris some day. And he can see how I love that—that girl kid of mine." He paused. "What—what in heaven's name am I—are we to do, Clay? To find out—conclusively?"

"Well, quite regardless of whether Milo Payne is dead—or by some crazy quirk of Fate is still alive quite regardless of whether—*if* alive—he talks Cockney—or not—regardless of whether Filkins knows all—or knows only a small part—we'll do the same thing. The minute Filkins comes in, we'll have Doris send him in here. Then—but can you get hold of any rope? In a hurry, that is?"

"Rope—Clay? Oh—rope. Yes—yes. Rope? Yes—over in that closet there—is about a hundred feet. It's—it's that thin—b-but tough—Filipino rope—you know?—that was corded about that fibre box of dried Julu berries?—the first sample shipment we got, direct at the house here, from that old Revarantos. It's—it's still there."

"Good. Then I'll tell you to a 'T' what we're going to do! I'm going to have Doris send Filkins in here when he gets back. I'll lock the door on him. And by a little maneuvering—apparently friendly—I'm going to jerk his coat down back of his shoulders. And you're going to swing that rope about his upper arms and elbows as quick as one can say Jack Rob—in fact, go get it. And cut me off two extra lengths too. Yes—with the scissors there. About five feet each will do. I'm going to lay one of 'em around his neck. During which he'll talk no Cockney—I'm telling you!"

While he was getting the rope out of the closet, I stowed both the cap and the ventriloquial dummy back in the same repository. Then I went to the door and called to Doris. And told her to send Filkins in immediately he got back. She nodded assent, wide-eyed. I returned to my chair, and I saw that giving Roger Pelton something to do was the best possible thing I could have done for him. It took his mind off of his own fearful plight. The thin rope was coiled, but untied, at the side of his chair. Two five-foot pieces were cut off, lying diagonally across the coil.

My gaze wandered searchingly about the room. I stepped over to the mantel above the fireplace.

"What's this, Mr. Pelton?"

"Wh-h-y—just my little portable radio, Clay. You—you know?"

"Oh no, no, no—not that. This?" I held it up.

"Oh, that, Clay? That's—that's just a six-inch length of steel pipe. The plumber cut it yesterday, in order to move the gas grate further out from under the flue there. But he hasn't used it yet."

"Fine. That'll do me—till John sends me a real gun!"

I laid the two five-foot pieces of rope carefully across the handles of my chair, where, in fact, they would be behind my person as I sat down again.

And we resumed the conversation. Rather, I did.

"Now," I said, "since Filkins has taken over Milo Payne's identity on this blackmailing scheme—due to killing him off—which I tell you he has—'Milo Payne' won't be able to fill the appointment tonight—at Washington Square. *Nicht wahr?* That is, if we truss Filkins up here! In fact, his non-appearance there will be all the proof we need—to give Filkins the royal water-cure—such as he's never seen yet—and find out exactly where Payne's quarters are—and where, in them, that skull is being kept. On the other hand, if Payne, for some strange reason *is* alive— and is a Cockney—and is doing his own talking—and negotiating—well—he'll never be able to get in touch with his inside man in *this* house again! For we'll shove out a story to all inquirers—by phone or otherwise—that Brother Filkins quit us in a huff—packed his duds—and blew. And that we don't know his present address. And Filkins, damn his suave soul, will be down in the wine cellar for a few days—or a week—catching an alcoholic bouquet! And better that, Filkins will say, than being tried— for blackmail. "For," I added, "all we're trying to do—is to get the better of the blackmailer. And whether Filkins is blackmailer—or murderer—or both—we'll eventually have to let him go. We can't do a single thing legally to Filkins—even if we got back that skull—the skull of the man you murdered."

Roger Pelton shuddered visibly. At my allusion to the man he had murdered. So I took pity on him, and hastily changed the subject.

"Well now," I said, looking at my watch, "it's nine bells. So me—before Filkins returns—to the Day-and-Night Bank—with a check—to get twenty thousand smackers—to cover the chance that Milo Payne is alive and kicking—and the thousand-and-one'th chance that he might be sucker enough to close the deal for that sum. Have you that much money on deposit?"

He crossed the room sadly, and twirled the combination dial of his safe. Presently the iron door swung open. He inserted one hand and then withdrew it, holding a square packet of bills.

It's blood money, Clay," he groaned. "And I've had it locked in here for the last five years. Twenty $1000 bills! Exactly—exactly my share of poor Phil Walmsley's stealings from the Berkeley State Bank."

"I see," was all I said. And added: "But, if you're asking me, none of us all—you, Doris, or I—is ever going to be happy again. Not one of us. But let's get going. We've work to do. And I've an Englishman, whoever he is, to outbluff—outpoint—outguess—and outwit! And if there's anything shrewder than an Englishman— I have yet to see it. As for you, you'd better phone now to the air field—while Filkins is still out of the house—and make your reservations on that midnight plane for New Orleans. All subject, of course, to our getting the blighter nicely bound up, and—"

There was a loud—inordinately loud—rapping on the door.

"Whu—whu—who's there?" Pelton quavered. "D-d-doris?"

"No sir," came a polite, but very faint voice. "It's—it's Filkins."

"Get ready," I said in a low voice. And rose.

CHAPTER XXII

FAST WORK

I stood aside while Filkins, brown derby in hand, entered. His thin hair, parted in the middle, gleamed silvery in the lamplight. I closed the door behind him. And turned the key softly in the lock; fortunately, the well-oiled tumblers gave out not a single sound. My withdrawal of the key was equally noiseless. And I pocketed it.

He did not see all this action. He was facing Roger Pelton. And his back was to the door.

"You wished to see me, Mr. Pelton?"

"Y-y-yes, Filkins."

"If it's to take this old rope out, sir, you'll remember you told me—"

"Y-y-yes, Filkins. That's true. I did tell you to—to leave it be. However—" Pelton's voice trailed weakly off.

"You seem distraught, Mr. Pelton."

"I'm—I'm—not feeling—at all well. I wanted—a few words with you."

"Quite, sir. I'm at your service."

In the meantime I had come up casually behind Filkins. "'Scuse me, old man," I said, "but have you by any chance been waiting for a street car tonight—on the corner of Randolph and Clark Streets?"

He turned his face back at me, and his lower jaw fell wide open.

"How—how—how on earth, sir, did you ever—"

207

"Easy, Filkins. Some pigeon—or else a very large sparrow—has violated the old NRA code for birds. Yes, on your coat collar. The back of it. So I naturally surmised—the pigeons—in the eaves of the City Hall." I took up a piece of newspaper from a metal wastebasket standing near one wall. "Here—I'll get it off."

"Oh sir—don't mind. I'll take care of it—myself. Confound the bloomin' bird! No—don't mind."

"But I *do* mind! Here—stand quiet, old chap."

I rubbed away on his quite spotless coat collar. "Coming off," I said. "Mind unbuttoning your coat in front?—yes—fine!—let me pull this collar down a bit—OK—that's right—that's right—let your arms just hang that way—um—" Rub—rub—rub!

And then and there, that coat collar grabbed tight in my fist, I pulled suddenly down on it with a mighty jerk till the whole coat slid downward over Filkins' limp-hung arms. He turned to pull away, apparently suddenly sensing for the first time that that rope was laid out there for no good reason—for one Filkins.

But I had that six-inch piece of pipe up under his coattail—under the coat itself—its cold, round end pressed against the right side of the small of his back.

"Quiet, Filkins," I said. "Another jerk like that and I'll spatter your right kidney all over that gas grate."

He stopped struggling instantly. But turned his head partway around. And his face, chalk-white, was the picture of confoundment.

"Come on, Papa!" I snapped, to Pelton. "Shake a leg! With that rope!"

"Wha—wha—what are you trying—to do with me?" Filkins asked, staring at my prospective father-in-law whom I had just, for the first time in my life, called "Papa"—but talking, I guess, at me.

"Shut up—you," I ordered. "Or you'll have to filter your blood-stream through one kidney for the rest of your life."

And I bored into the region of that kidney with the pipe.

"Come on, damn it, Papa," I said. "Twist that rope around his shoulders. Wind it around and down!"

And now Roger Pelton, coming back to his senses, worked with the fury of desperation. He wound and wound, about Filkins' upper torso. And on down. Even encompassing in the tight convolutions of the rope the slipped-down coat. Down on past Filkins' waist he wound—to the latter's legs. The rope gave out at Filkins' knees, and he knotted its end savagely to the loop above.

Filkins looked like some strange mummy.

I shoved him over to the chair I had occupied, and forced him down into it.

His eyes were literally popping out of his head.

Now I brought his hands, which from the elbows down seemed to have escaped the wrappings, through the bars of the rear of the chair—and bound their wrists together with one of the extra five-foot pieces of rope.

Filkins seemed utterly, completely flabbergasted. While Roger Pelton, like a man with determination afire, was dragging forth the other cut section of rope.

He handed it to me.

I kneeled down, and with that length, bound Filkins' ankles together.

Now we had him, "hawg-tied"—as they say in Arkansas. And I stood erect, very much satisfied.

"Well, Filkins," I said, "we've got you! Just as you got Milo Payne. By quick thought—and quicker work."

"Milo Pay—" He began. "I say, sir—I say—listen—what—what are you trying to do with me?"

"Come, Filkins. Confess now. What were you to get—for giving information out of this house—to Milo Payne?"

"Who—who," he stammered faintly, "is—is this Milo Payne? And where does he—but I've never given information, sir—out of this house—to any—living soul."

"Come off it, Filk. We've got the goods on you, I tell you. Absolutely. You're Abigail Sprigge."

"Abigail Sprigge? Who—who is Abigail—Sprigge?"

"You know damn well, Filkins, who Abigail Sprigge is."

"I—I swear sir, I don't know. Who—who is she?"

"Oh come off it, Filkins," I retorted wearily. "I've searched your room. And found your poem."

"Oh—thank you, sir."

"Thank me? For what?"

"For calling it a poem."

"Well—what is it—if it isn't a poem?"

"Well—I—I thought—it might be doggerel. Though I was hoping it was er—poetical." Filkins looked down at his mummylike wrappings as though to assure himself that he was fast and put. Then up again.

"But—but—"

"Now listen, Filkins. I've read four of your recent poems, to date. And—"

"Four, sir? And recent? But you just couldn't have. For I've always destroyed all I've written. And besides—I haven't written but one— in the last four years—the one in my room. Sort of—sort of, sir, a little plaint that's been running poetically for years through my head. Since—since I started—to grow old."

I stared puzzledly at him. He must have been a good actor. In fact, in the long ago, he *had* been an actor. And so—

"So," I said, "the only specimen of your work extant—is this little—this little elegiambus that was sticking in your typewriter tonight?"

"Would you object, sir, if I corrected you—on your poetical classification? A true elegiambus, you know, is a verse of which the first half is a dactylic penthemimeris—and the second an iambic dimeter."

"Oh—I see! Now, with that out of our way, just how did you come, so all of a sudden, to write this particular verse?"

"Well, sir, I—I don't know yet why you have me tied up here. But I'll be glad to answer your question. I—I saw an ad in the news-paper—about a man who wanted lots of poetry—for a new magazine. The opportunity of a lifetime—he said—for those—who had an idea—to express—in—in poetry. So—so I tried my hand. I—I was going to send it in tonight."

"Oh—yeah? Then why in hell did you start to credit it to Abigail Sprigge?"

"Abigail Sprigge? I confess, sir, I don't quite get your allusions—to these different parties. I was going to credit this poem—to my dead mother—Abigail Leightenstone. She's—she's been coming back to me of late—in my dreams. And I thought, sir—it—it would be a nice tribute to her. For what poor poetical talents I have—have really come to me—from her. And she too busy in all those years—with us children—to express herself. As she wanted to do."

"A noble thought!" I said sarcastically. And added scornfully: "And B.S."

"B.S.?" He ruminated puzzledly. "I don't quite catch the significance of that, don't y' know. But, now, my mother—her name, sir, you can see today on a tombstone—in the little cemetery of St. Edmonds, Suffolk County, England."

"Oh—yeah? Well I used up eight good bucks today, in taxicab fare, chasing down just one gravestone—thanks to you!"

"Thanks—to me? Really, sir—you have the best of me."

I stared at him.

"By God, Filkins, I—I can't figure whether you're the world's worst damn liar—or the world's best actor. Or whether I've made an awful bull—of some kind. Of course, if I have—still, by God, I've too much on you. Yes, far too much! And so I—"

"Who—who, sir, if I may beg leave to interrupt, do you think—I am?"

"Well, I think you're the bird who killed Milo Payne?"

"Milo Payne?" He shook his head. "And there, sir, you are quite in error. If you'll pardon my flat statement."

I didn't quite get whether he was denying his killing of Payne—or denying actual acquaintanceship with the man. So I changed the form of my accusation.

"Well, let me put it then: that you're working with somebody—who at least called himself Milo Payne—to do Mr. Pelton some harm here. 'Fess up, now?"

But Filkins, tied fast in the chair, shook his head firmly.

"I've—I've never tried to do Mr. Pelton any harm in my life. Why—I wouldn't harm him. There's—there's some terrible mistake. Just because, apparently, I tried to write—a little poem."

I looked at Roger Pelton.

He looked at me.

I went to the closet. And came forth, holding the damp Sherlockholmsian cap in one hand—the ventriloquial costermonger figure in the other.

"Filkins, you were once in vaudeville—in Britain—as the Great Simon, were you not?"

"That is correct. Though not, alas, for very long, sir. 'Twas just a tour of the music halls—in the East End of London. The company I was in—the one playing a regular repertoire of plays—had failed in—in—yes—in a small town in—in Cornwall—in the south of England. Padstow—yes—that was its name. I was stony, don't y' know—no, stony means broke—and I had to 'op it—that is, hop it—back to Lunnon on a bally collier, threading its way along the north coast of the English channel. I knew a number of sleight-of-hand tricks—in fact, packed away in my old quarters on Clapham Road. I had a good bit of magical apparatus. Just—just parlor stuff, at best. And the booking agent just off Haymarket—Lionel Trotter was his name—was wanting a magician for the East End—at four pounds the week. And so—"

"A magician? You mean—a ventriloquist?"

"No, sir. A—a magician. I see you are in some way confused by—by that ventriloquial effigy. No, Mr. Calthorpe, that effigy in your hands belonged to a chap named Cyril Kane. Who died in Middlesex Hospital in—in—1927—of—of an intestinal perforation—due to—to ulcerated colitis. He was on the same cheap circuit as me. Pardon me—as *I*. At the time he died, we'd been rooming together. In—in a rooming-house—the King Edward it was called—in Juniper Street—near—near the Shadwell Basin. Yes, off the Thames. He had nobody—so I took over his two ventriloquial dolls. Which of course I couldn't personally utilize." Filkins swallowed a bit embarrassedly—at least he made his Adam's Apple bob with proper energy in his neck—and, if he were a ventriloquist, the complete voluntary control over his Adam's Apple would have been his. "But shortly after, I brought them to America with me. Right after, in fact, I—I was egged—yes—egged!—in the Bucket of Blood Music Hall—in Stepney—and found only two pounds in my envelope—instead of the four pounds promised me. For that, sir, was when I decided that a good butler making five pounds a week and room and keep was a thousand times better off than a poor artiste—slaving before a lot of—of ignorant uncouth egg-throwers." He shook his head firmly. "No, it was Cyril Kane who was the ventriloquist. Not I. And I brought his two dolls with me. To America. Where I sold his Negro doll with no trouble at all. For all ventriloquists here, it seems, use a Negro dummy. But the finer one you have there—it may interest you to know, sir, that it has no less than 2163 pearl buttons sewed on it to make up its unique costermonger costume—I never could sell it—for no American ventriloquist, don't y' know, can talk the extreme Cockney—the costermonger Cockney—that such a doll—in such a costume—would logically have to talk."

I gazed at Filkins from under lowered eyebrows. There was a peculiar speciousness in his whole discourse—more particularly, an exactitude of detail as to places, persons, dates, and conditions—that made me more suspicious than ever that I had caught a master liar.

I held up the cap.

"Where did you get this cap?"

"That, sir?" He raised his eyebrows in admirable keeping with the tone of his voice. "Why—it's—it's mine, sir. A sacred memento of the great night that I myself played Sherlock Holmes—in the play made so famous by William Gillette himself. True, I but understudied the lead—but the star of our provincial company, Mr. Reginald Ponderly-Gruddidge, was ill that night. So—so I played—the Great Holmes. Just the once. But I shall never forget it! 'Twas in the town of—of yes—of Stoke-Upon-Trent—in Stafford."

I heard him all the way through, frowningly. And asked:

"Well then—why the devil is this cap damp—and fishy?"

"Why, because, sir, I—I got it out this morning. And sprinkled it well. From the cold water faucet. And but by George—the water is fishy this month, isn't it?"

"Come, come, Filkins—Why in hell's-bells should you sprinkle a cap—like this?"

"Why, sir—to iron it out. To press it out. For only last week I passed Maurice L. Rothschild's great haberdashery for men—in particular, the little narrow window, if you know of it, which fronts just on Jackson Boulevard—and they had the whole window full of these identical caps—grouped with canes—and cravats. And a sign which read—well—something like this: 'These'—yes—'these will be the mode for the well-dressed American—with English tastes— by Christmas.'"

He paused momentarily, as one desiring me to complete the explanation myself. Then went on apologetically:

"And so, sir, since those imported caps in that window were priced at $5 apiece—and I do, sir, so long to dress in an English fashion—I got mine out—and prepared to press it up."

"And be right in the mode, eh?"

"Quite, sir."

Again I looked at Roger Pelton.

And again he looked at me.

I turned to Filkins. "Filkins," I said, "If I've done you wrong here tonight—will you accept my apologies?"

"Quite, sir. We all, at different times, become the victims of our own errors in judgment."

"Yes. And how much, Filkins, would you charge—would you require—for sitting right where you are—tied up exactly that way—till late tonight—say—midnight?"

"Tied up? This way? Why—sir—if it's in line with my duties here, I would be happy to—"

"Would $5 an hour pay you?"

"I should say yes. That would be handsome remuneration—for so simple a labor."

"All right, Filkins," I returned, though still suspiciously.

"Consider yourself hired then—at five bucks an hour—to stay tied right there in that chair—where you now are—and the way you are."

"Thank you, sir. And in case you and Mr. Pelton are going to repair to the parlor, to continue your conversation, I'd—I'd be awfully happy, don't y' know, if you would turn on the radio over there on the mantel—very softly will be sufficient—to alleviate my tedium."

"I will," I assured him. "And right now."

I stepped over to the mantel, where Pelton's small Gothic-arch-shaped radio receiving instrument sat.

"What do you like, Filkins? Opera?—jazz?—Amos and Andy? Kate Sm—"

"I would like sir, if you don't mind—if you'd just put on Ed Wynne. Yes. The Perfect Fool! I would like so much—to hear the Perfect Fool."

"Maybe, Filkins," I said dryly, as I turned the dial to WGN, "that you have the Perfect Fool right here in front of you now!"

CHAPTER XXIII

A REVELATION

Washington Square is a small public park on Chicago's near-North Side. Not far, in fact, from Mrs. Winterbotham-Higginsbottom's rooming-house where I reside. An even block square, it is crossed by two long diagonal cement walks, lined with benches each side, the walks connecting the opposite corners of the quadrangle, and intersecting in the middle. Where a fountain plays. By day Washington Square is occupied practically solely by nursemaids and their charges who come there to enjoy a breath of clean, moist, grass-scented air; and by old gentlemen living on their married daughters, which daughters, driven to distraction by the presence of the said old gentlemen about the house, have sent them scuttering to the park to line the benches like crows, and gaze mistily through rheumy eyes over palsied hands crossed atop canes. After 6 o'clock at night, however, Washington Square is no longer Washington Square; it has become the notorious Bug-House Square, and from then up to the hour of 9 p.m.—at which time all meetings are dispersed—wild-eyed anarchists atop soap boxes under the different street lights on the edge of the square, shoutingly exhort variously sized multitudes as to what's wrong with Congress, the President, the capitalistic system and what not; while food faddists prove to smaller crowds that eating cornmeal mush and caviar at the same meal makes cyanide of potassium in the stomach; and long-whiskered exponents of nudism argue to small but salaciously inclined groups that evil is only as evil dangles; and Free Love exponents prove that marriage is archaic and outmoded; and all the while painted and powdered-up boys ramble about the edge of the park seeking conquests of other like boys; while short-haired women in tweed jackets and trouser-like skirts pick up acquaintanceships with other short-haired women. Thus, Bug-House Square. To and up till 9 o'clock at night. At which time the police come, waving batons, and the bugs all adjourn to the famous Dill Pickle Club, off Tooker Alley, down Dearborn Street. Washington Square by day; Bug-House Square by night. And, during the last few months, not even Bug-House Square by night—for even bugs—lightning or otherwise—have to have light to exhort by. And, as I had tried to convey to this Milo Payne—if Milo Payne it really had been who had talked with me on the phone—the Chicago Small Parks System had ripped out all the light poles in the park—and about its four edges—in order to install a new lighting system, only to have its directors discover that all their mistresses had seen their wives wearing new fur coats—and had to have new fur coats likewise. Or something like that. So Washington Square was left, in the meanwhile—and would be so left, the papers had said even before I went to the Philippines, till January 1st, next—without the sign of a light in it or around it. And with the dozens and dozens of tall leafy trees studded over it, and the immense bushes with their thick foliage, it was darker than the innermost of three coal mines all fitted one into the other.

So when I dismounted from a taxicab at 11 o'clock this night, at the southeast corner of the square, I gazed rather dubiously towards its black interior. And rather longingly back of me toward the two dimly illumined gateposts of the once grand old brownstone Union Club on Delaware Place—now a Salvation Army Home for Girls. In my breast pocket was the twenty thousand dollars which Roger Pelton had given me to redeem the skull—but which I had little hope of redeeming. In my hip pocket was the eleven-shot Severignac revolver which, thanks to John Barr, had arrived wrapped, and in the hands of an A.D.T. boy, in plenty of time at the Pelton home—but alas, thanks to the absence of its special calibered French bullets, it would better be called tonight a zero-shot firearm!

For a moment I paused at the corner of the square. The first ten or twelve feet of the walk that led into the park was visible—thanks to the fact that most of the young ladies in the Salvation Army Home were going to bed—and the windows, though covered with shades, were lighted. But after that first ten or twelve feet—blackness, impenetrable. However, I had my plans. And that blackness helped them. And so I forged in.

A damp wind was blowing in from the lake; and with the absence of any moon whatsoever, or even any stars, the night seemed immeasurably chilly. And from the absence of any subdued conversation or glowing cigar ends—I was fully aware that the Square was practically deserted.

Twenty feet from the entrance I came across the first bench. I had to move to the right-hand edge of the walk, and reach out to make sure that it was a bench, and not the framework of a mastodon—or a grape arbor. After that I kept to the right, and kept my arm out. To count as I touched. An empty space of eight or nine feet, seemingly filled with bushes, followed the first bench. Then came the second bench. At the third one, however, I had progressed far enough inside so that it was no longer possible, from even that short distance, to distinguish a bench from a bush.

So I groped ever so carefully now. Up, that is, until I reached the seventh bench. At whose outer end I stooped over, quickly, detached from my vest pocket the package of money, and folding it double, slipped it, by the sense of feel alone, under the cast-iron hind leg of the bench. Take that, Milo! (That is—if you're not floating face upward somewhere in the lake.) I've been slugged by better men than you! I resumed my journey. It was like going into a bottle of ink. And thus passed the eighth bench, the ninth, the tenth, the eleventh, the twelfth, the thirteenth, the—And then I stopped, as out of the darkness where the fourteenth bench should have been, came a voice.

"'Ave you got the bloody time on you, Mister?"

"Eleven bells," I said. And pausing but the thousandth of a second, added: "Eleven bells—Payne."

"Good! Sit down. 'Ere—'ere's the bloomin' bench. I'm at the right-'and end. You've the 'ole rest o' the bench—if you likes."

Alas for my fine theories about the floating Milo! And his "murderer" Filkins—whom I had left, scarcely more than a quarter of an hour ago, tied up snug and tight in the Pelton library... For here my appointee sat, and gazing quite impudently up at me too—since against the whitish blob of his otherwise manifestly smooth face the typical snugly compact "Lunnon shopkeeper's" mustache, with its curled-up—and probably waxed!—ends, showed blackly. Bright red, I hypothesized on the instant, that mustache must be—and my guess was based solely on the cockiness in its owner's voice; and bright red, in fact, I was to find ultimately it was!

I groped about in the vicinity of my knees, and found the bench. Found the very cast-iron connecting piece, in fact, that marked its middle. And sunk down on the seat, well to the left of its middle. For I didn't want this fellow to try any foolishness until he at least learned the utter uselessness of such. And I leaned back against the cold damp back-rest of the bench, waiting for him to speak.

"Well," he began, very businesslike, his red mustache—jet black in the deep gloom—bobbing up and down as he spoke, "since you know me bloomin' nyme, I tyke it you've come from Roger Pelton. Eh, wot?"

"What makes you think," I inquired curiously, "that I'm not a police officer?"

"Orficer, 'ell!" he said easily and confidently. "If you towld me you wuz that, I'd—I'd s'y 'sausage.'"

"Sausage?" I queried. "What—"

"Yuss. This 'ere long sausage. Wot th' nyme of it means a bird's spoofing."

"Oh—baloney! Oh, I see. You'd say baloney—if I told you I was a police officer? Oh, yes, I see. So you're fairly confident that Roger Pelton isn't taking the police in with him?"

"Nar, o' course 'e 'int. 'E 'int burnin' up in an electric chair, or sweatin' 'is 'ead 'orf in prisink for the rest of his life up in Mich'gan."

I said nothing.

"You're a young 'un," he commented. "I can tell by your voice. Up so close like as wot it is. Too bad 'e sent you. A—a older man would 'ave more sense. But 'ere you are—and 'ere you be. So wot's— but first, 'oo are you? An' do you know wot this is all about?"

"Yes," I told him. "I know everything. And I'm Roger Pelton's son-in-law—that is, son-in-law—to be." I had no cause to hold this fact back. More particularly, if Filkins were the fellow's confeder- ate—and had handed this, as well as other information, out. And if Filkins hadn't—then I still had the best of reasons for advancing this particular item. "Going to marry his daughter."

"Oh, I see. Love birds a-goin' to be 'itched. Well now, you love birds wouldn't want to see the old 'un makin' shoes in prisink, would you? Or fried in th' h'electric chair?"

"That all depends," I said cryptically. "You know—he's got a candy factory!"

"Oh—ho," he said. "Hum. Well—fancy that nar."

The covert meaning back of my words seemed to floor Sherlock Holmes. And that he had on his Sherlock Holmes cap, I was now pretty more than certain. For my eyes, in the meanwhile, had got- ten a bit more used to the blackness, and I could make out not only that the whitish blob atop his head was a cap, but that it was bril- liantly checkered as well. I was even certain, as he turned his head now and then off-wise, that I could catch the suggestion of the cap's long beak. But that was the chief thing about Sherlocko's dress that was certain. Unless it was his high collar—of the old-fashioned choker variety—whose whiteness gleamed like the cap. And the broad white silk ribbon badge—for obviously that was what it must be—pinned to his coat lapel; a badge undoubtedly dropped—as I then figured—in a hotel lobby somewhere by some delegate to one of Chicago's countless daily conventions. Those three things were, as I say, the chief discernible points of Sherlocko's dress. For in that lightless park, under that starless, moonless sky, the nearest street light on the other side of Clark Street, a half block away, and screened by countless trees and bushes as well, his face was almost more a voice than a face. A whitish vague blur, at most, pierced with two eyes, and eclipsed by his "shopkeeper's" up-ended mustache—a blur that told nothing more about him except that he was otherwise smooth-shaven—and not even the closeness with which he shaved. I found myself wondering whether, if he should ever commit sacrilege, and shave off his mustache, he would turn out otherwise to be a homely devil? Or to be good-looking? And whether he was in his late 20s—or his late 30s. Or what. And was he married—back in England? Or single? And—but he was speaking.

"Well," he said gruffly, "let's us get down to business. 'E sent you. An' 'ere you be. Wot's 'is answer? On that twenty thou?"

"What answer did you expect?" I equivocated.

"Cash," he said calmly. "'Ave you got it with yer?"

"'Ave you got the bloomin' skull with yer?" I asked.

"S'y," he said, darkly. "Are—are you tryin' to himytyte me?"

"I beg your pardon," I returned. "Unconscious himyno—imitation. I'll try to hold on to my h's." I paused. "But have you got the skull?"

"Listen—you," he asked harshly. "I'm arskin' you if you got the cash?"

"Yes," I said. "I have. But I have something else. In case you have any naughty thoughts whatsoever." And fumbling in my right-hand hip pocket I drew forth the revolver John Barr had sent me. "Friend Payne," I invited, "reach out your hand towards me—the one that's nearest me—so's you can at least feel the muzzle of this thing I have with me. I won't hurt you. I just want you to feel its muzzle. So you'll know I've got it. Don't grab it. It would go off if you did that. Just feel it." He seemed either a game beggar, a thorough one, or a curious one. For feeling around in semi-Stygian darkness for the muzzle of a gun that can blow a hole through the palm of your hand is not a pleasant occupation. If it had been loaded, I don't think I would ever have risked his getting hold of it. But since it wasn't loaded, I had to squeeze the last ounce of bluff out of the fool thing.

But nevertheless he waved his palm about, as I waved the muzzle of the gun about. For suddenly I felt the muzzle's nose pressing against the soft surface afforded by that palm.

"Ow!" he said, though pleasantly and genially. "Feels like the mouth of a French '75!"

"It is French," I retorted. He withdrew his hand. "And you only have to give it mental suggestion—to get results. It's like—like the German housewife who used to get pregnant if she only went to bed in the same room with her husband's pants."

"Come orf it!" he said. "'Ow—'ow could she get pregnant—with h'only a pair o' pants in the room? It—it can't be did."

"Oh, that's just a joke," I said wearily. "I forgot about you being English."

"Well," he said, "let's get down to bus'ness. You got a gun—and I mybe 'ave got 'un an' mybe 'aven't. Mine is loaded—if I 'ave it. An' 'int loaded if I 'int got it. That's logic, 'int it? Yours is loaded, 'cause you got it. Or—or is it loaded?" Damn his shrewdness. For there was just that in his tones that made me think he guessed I possibly wouldn't go through the streets with a loaded revolver and risk a night in the Detective Bureau and a hundred-dollar fine.

"Yes, it's loaded," I lied faithfully. "Eleven times."

"Well, wot' the bloomin' idea back o' all this confab, anyw'y? You shoot me—an' you've shot yourself, your pop-in-law an' your woming all into the p'ypers. For this 'ere w'ite silk badge wot I'm wearin' says as 'ow I'm a delygyte from Lime'ouse to th' British H'Isles an' Colonial Possessings Convenching o' Skyte-an'-Chips an' Jellied Eeels Purveyors, to be 'eld in Vancoover, British Columbiar, three weeks from tomorrer. An' seein' as 'oo I am, shootin' me wouldn't be good-like. No! For I've left a few notes in me 'otel drawer—an' me delygyte's pypers—in case o' accident like wot. So wot's keepin' us from gittin' down to business? You s'y you got that twenty thousand dollars? Orl right. P'y it over—like as 'e towld you you was to do."

And now came my stalling act. For tonight only. For I had decided to abandon that foolishness about the Day and Night Bank refusing to pay out money at night. That could be checked up on too easily by Milo Payne. I had a sounder one.

"Roger Pelton," I said slowly, "gave me twenty thousand dollars. No—it's not on my person. So don't you go shooting—for you'll shoot the only person who knows where in this whole park it is. Sure—I came into the park first and stowed it someplace. He told me I was to redeem that skull with it. If you haven't got the skull with you—then I don't know what I can do, myself. I'm not him, remember. You can get in touch with him tomorrow—on the phone." That him would be again me, I told myself, behind two thicknesses of silk. "Maybe," I held forth shrewdly, "he'll go so far as to pay you the money on trust. For later delivery of the skull. But I'm only the messenger. I dare not pay. Till I get the skull. Is it in your possession? On you?"

"Did yer think," he asked cuttingly, "that I'd be sittin' 'ere with the rummy thing on me lap, singin' a sweet chune to it—to put it to sleep? An' 'avin' one o' Roger Pelton's gunmen stickin' a gun on me—and tykin' it aw'y—from me. Strike me pink! Am I barmy?"

"In short language," I said, "you came here tonight without the skull. While I've come with the twenty thousand. The idea was that I would get nothing in exchange. Well, Roger Pelton is simple-minded and would have played with you on just that basis. He believes in everybody. But I can't. See? It's not my money."

That would checkmate him. For that made me the monkey wrench in the machinery—and not Roger Pelton at all.

"But you act'ally got that 'ere sum with you?" he queried grumpily.

"I said I had. But not on my lap either. For the money is somewhere in the park. And no monkey-business I warn you. Shoot—and you can spend the rest of the night searching for it with matches—and you'll have all the coppers on the North Side helping you."

"Not so bloody good!" he said frankly. "Well, 'ell's bells—you got your end—I got mine. What th' 'ell are we gassin' h'about? Suppowse we h'exchynge goods, eh?"

It was hard to believe that this fellow was such a simpleton as to deal for the first price accepted, when he could run it up to a hundred thousand. And more. At least so far as he thought—not knowing about San Do Mar! He had me frankly puzzled.

"You've the skull—hidden near by—under some bush?" I queried.

"Yuss. That's jest wot I 'ave."

"Wrapped up? And tied, I suppose?"

"Yuss."

"You'll—you'll allow me to examine it?"

"Yuss. If you shows me your coin—at the syme time." He had me checkmated. I was absolutely certain he was not the simpleton he made himself out to be. And yet—

"I'll tell you," I ventured. "Let's—let's make another appointment for tomorrow night." If he was a simpleton, he would fall for that.

"But you said you 'ad the money 'ere tonight?"

"Yes. I have. Every penny of it. But—"

"Then 'old them buts. Now listen' ere. I knows a bloke when he tells the truth. You're scared, buddy, o' bein' wot you H-Amerycans calls double-crossed. If you didn't 'ave the money with yer, you—you wouldn't ack so dam'd jumpy-like. On a strick bus'ness deal like as this. I sorter likes yer, damn' if I down't. Yer voice, anyw'ys. So I'm goin' to tell yer a story—not a long one, neither—and w'en I'm finished, not only will yer put that money in my 'ands and be glad o' the chanct ter do it—but yer'll be 'ible to marry that girl with your 'ead h'erect—and keep it that w'y for the rest of yer life."

"And what strange narrative can accomplish such a miracle as all that?" I asked skeptically.

"Only this," he said quietly. And I noted with surprise that his Cockney speech had suddenly ceased entirely. "Phil Walmsley, my dear sir—and remember that you haven't told me your name yet— Phil Walmsley, my dear sir, was never murdered. Nor is there any such person as Milo Payne. In fact, you're talking now to Phil Walmsley himself!"

CHAPTER XXIV

"BELIEVE IT OR NOT"

I stared speechlessly toward him—or at least toward the particular section of semi-blackness which enveloped him, and from which came his voice.

"Why—why—" I stammered, "how can that be—why, man, I've seen the skull of—"

"No matter what you've seen," he replied—and a little testily, too, I noted—"I tell you again that Phil Walmsley is talking to you right now. And not in Cockney any longer either, if you'll notice. I'm—"

"But," I broke in, "Roger Pelton told me the whole story of those early years, including the details of that camping trip, the exchange of the money belts, the trip in the canoe, the shot fired directly in the back of Phil Walmsley's head. So—so how do you explain those facts? To my mind, they're incontrov—oh, yes—my name? It's Calthorpe. So back to those facts. They're incontrovertible, I'll say. They—"

"Incontrovertible?" he echoed. "Facts? What are more deceptive in life, Thorpe, than—"

"Calthorpe," I corrected. "Not Cal Thorpe."

"Oh—beg pardon. Calthorpe. What are more deceptive in life than facts? It's facts that hang innocent men every year. And it's just the facts you've stated that would have placed Roger Pelton in the

227

electric chair. Or in a sunless cell over in Lansing Penitentiary, Michigan. Depending on where he would have been tried and convicted. But he would never have 'burned'—as the crooks put it—nor would he have remained long in that sunless cell—for long before all that came to pass, in order to have me come forward and save his worthless life—or get him out of an existence worse than death—he would have paid over to some attorney of my own choosing the precise price I asked tonight.

"So let's look into these—ah—facts!

"So he told you, did he, about those early days of his and my life? In which case he undoubtedly told you I was an embezzler from the Berkeley State Bank of this city. True. Ten thousand—all lost on horse races. No chance in the world to make it good. None whatever. And a tough customer, I'm telling you, that Berkeley State Bank. Absolutely merciless when it came to prosecuting errant employees. 100 per cent merciless! There was ten years in Joliet Prison just staring me in the face. So—"

"He said," I put in, "that you forged a check on a big bookmaker. Did he lie—to me?"

"Lie to you? No—not at all. I did exactly that. The fellow's name was Humphrey McGeoghan. The check was for $35,000. And stamped as cashed personally by me at my window. That's what made it go past the bookkeeper without any trouble. That—and McGeoghan's continual cashing of huge checks. Poetic justice in all that. Humphrey McGeoghan was a bookie. Me—a loser on the horses. Only—McGeoghan didn't have to take the $35,000 loss. The bank did. Naturally."

He paused.

"Yes, if I had to go to prison, I was going to go for $35,000—and not for $10,000. For there was no difference, you see, in the respective sentences for the theft of two such amounts. Only—I didn't intend to go to prison at all! I never intended even to return from that camping trip. I had several weeks before McGeoghan would receive his monthly statement. So I went to Rapid River with Roger—as we'd planned. For I had a little plan of my own to make it appear that I'd been drowned. Swept into Hell's Rapids and torn to pieces. Sucked into the Devil's Whirlpool. And ground up some more. And—but did he tell you about those two diabolic stretches of water?"

"Yes."

"Well—they were my plan! I'd go down river a ways. In the canoe. Alone. To fish. And neither canoe nor rider would ever be seen again. Back in my rooms—in Chicago—for benefit of the bank detectives—I'd left an account book—a long affair—showing the names of horses for months and months back. Winnings and losings. Losings and winnings. Total losses: $35,000. Suicide—or murder? Let the bank worry!

"Then what? Roger himself helped my very plans. Yes and no. No and yes. For when one thief steals another thief's stealings—well—however, the fact is, that he did and has helped the plans—of the inner man. The better man, Calthorpe. Did I get the name right that time? Good.

"London was where I was going. Wonderful London—city of my dreams. Soho—Mayfair—Hyde Park—Kensington Gardens—Hampstead Heath on Bank Holiday—all places that held a magic in them from the first books I ever read on the place. And from Arthur Morrison's *Tales of Mean Streets.* And I—but I say—do I bore you—rhapsodizing?"

"In God's name—no," I said. "Rhapsodize all you want. I'm so damned glad that you aren't dead, that I can listen all night."

"Good. And thanks so much—don't y'know!" It was plain that this fellow had reached his dear London all right—and stayed there a good length of time. "But you won't have to listen all night. Five more minutes—that's all."

He paused a bare second.

"So now let's get to this murder—of poor Phil Walmsley!

"When we—Roger and I—hit the North Woods, I had my money divided into two piles. Five thousand in an oilskin wallet. Twenty thousand in a chamois-skin money belt. Kept it on me, you know.

"It was on the second day we were there that we went in swimming. We didn't swim far—no—from where we'd cached our clothes and money belts. No farther, in fact, than where we could keep our eyes on the place. The water was cold. We came out. Dressed shiveringly. And loaded up our canoe preparatory to starting up river and pitching a new camp. Water too swift where we first pitched. Roger went into the woods to retrieve the axe—and that's where, I guess, he found he had a belt on him with twenty thousand dollars in it. I didn't dream there'd been a mix-up. Not till it was all—well—over.

"On our way up river I sat in the prow of the canoe. Paddling of course. Roger in the stern.

"I was smoking my pipe when I saw him—ready to murder me. You're too young—that is, you must be, if you're going to marry his daughter—to remember the old ten-cent-store mirror pipes. Just a square upstanding corncob bowl with a piece of mirror glued on the inner face. So the smoker could admire himself, I guess. Or maybe so the American ten-cent-stores could sell corncobs for ten cents. I don't know. I was gazing into the mirror facing me in my pipe— no particular idea in my head—pondering, I guess, over one or two details of my scheme for appearing drowned, when—

"Whooie!

"I noticed Roger—in the back of the canoe, raising his repeating rifle and leveling it directly toward my back. The first thing that came over me was the thought that his jealousy of Doris Penfield, the girl with whom both of—"

"Oh!" I broke in. "And—and that accounts, then, for the picture signed 'Doris'—and with her love thereon—which was found in the Palmer House after you left there?"

"Yes," he replied. "For twenty-one years I've carried about the world with me the picture of Doris Penfield—the girl whom Roger afterwards married. God, 'twas the only thing of all my possessions that I sent on to London—ahead of myself. It lay for weeks and weeks in the General Post Office there—waiting for Milo Payne to call for it. But that picture—we'll reach that when we reach that.

What say?" And without waiting for my answer he hurried on. "To continue, I heard the warning click of the rifle hammer as it slowly raised. I knew absolutely and positively that the second click would mean my death. Quick as a flash—a bare thousandth of a second before the report—or maybe at the very report itself—I'm not sure—maybe he actually fired and missed—for that canoe was pitching pretty lively from stern to bow—I rolled straight head over into the water—found myself sucked instantly into that swirling current—and twenty feet back of the canoe as soon as you could say Jack Robinson. I guess he was afraid to look back. At first. I only know that I flopped over on my back and floated. I knew if I made a move I'd get all the bullets in that rifle. And thus I floated till I was around a bend in the river. Where I swum like—like hell to the bank. The opposite bank, too, from the side where Roger and I had pitched camp. The first thing I did was to feel for my oilskin wallet. Safe! Currency and all. I searched my money belt. One hundred and forty-five dollars! For Roger, you see, had the belt with the twenty thousand in it.

"Well, there was no doubt in my mind then what his motive had been for attempting to kill me. I crawled up onto a wooden knoll—dried my clothes—and thought and thought for two long hours what to do. If I went back and denounced him—it meant imprisonment. He knew now that I was carrying twenty thousand dollars on me. He'd call the sheriff. Now that he'd tried to kill me, it was war. He'd see that I got sent up. And I knew he wanted that girl badly—oh so badly. Yes—the cards were stacked.

"At last I decided that I'd have to take it on the chin. Let the cards lie as Fate had tossed them. And I wasn't sure at that that I wouldn't settle with him some day. At least one thing was certain now—I had an 'official witness' to my 'accidental death.'

"So I made my way cross-country northward on foot. Got a hat from an old scarecrow. By the time I reached Lake Superior, I looked like a tramp. An iron-ore steamer took me all the way down through Whitefish Bay—the Sault Ste. Marie Straits—Lake Huron—to Detroit. No such things as wireless on iron-ore ships back in '20, you know! I laid up in Detroit. Bought myself a new outfit. Got access in the public library to all the back Chicago papers. Which told of my death by drowning. And how my accounts at the bank had been short thirty-five thousand dollars. And no mention, of course, of any restitution on Roger's part. He'd kept quiet about the twenty thousand—which was to be expected. And reading 'em all up, as I did, I came to the story of how he gave that Cormington rifle No. 1,000,004 to the Chicago Historical Society the very second day he got back. Couldn't stand the sight of the thing, I guess. And—but did he tell you of that?"

"Yes," I said. "And I don't yet underst—but I'll—I'll let you tell it."

"Good! I made my way to the seacoast by train. On cushions. Like a gentleman. But no passenger line across the ocean! No—sir. No passport, you see. I had to work it—just like an ordinary hobo—on an oil tanker. For my round-trip passage. And me—with five thousand dollars in my jeans.

"Well, the tanker finally sailed up the Thames. London at last! And I deserted. Naturally. As the purser of the tanker expected me to do. Which gave him half of my wages. And at last I breathed easy for the first time. But I watched my step. I commenced to learn English right off—no, I don't mean English as you speak it over here, but English as only an Englishman speaks it. I had to become an Englishman, you see. For if any immigration official should have had reported to him about some American who kept staying in England on and on and on—well—that would be just too bad! For me. So I rented me a room above a shop on Whitechapel High Road. And hobnobbed with British sailors, cockneys, costermongers, till I actually thought in their language. And I rented me another room too—thorough, I was—out in Hammersmith—a little new de-luxe suburb something like—oh—like your Southport Avenue district here in Chicago—and lived there every other week, and buckled down to talking Oxfordian English with the long 'A'—to thinking and acting every bit the Englishman.

"Well, now I was Milo Payne. Cockney or gentleman—as and

when I wished. Safe, all right. But I wasn't happy one bit. I couldn't forget I was a thief. A man who had fled his own land with money which would have to be made good. And to keep from going sheer crazy—I took up the study of medicine. At the college of Physicians and Surgeons—near St. Thomas's Hospital. On the Thames. Oh, not the actual study of it—for I was permitted to enroll only in the medical preparatory course. I had about umpty-ump years' work ahead of me.

"But no go! My heart just wasn't in what I was trying to do. Old Mr. Conscience was beginning to get in his fearful work. And I began to realize that I'd never be happy again until somehow, in some manner or other, I got together that thirty-five thousand dollars—and made restitution to the Berkeley State Bank far across the ocean. But—and here was the rub!—Roger had gotten twenty thousand of that loot. And if I showed up with any part of it, my tale of his attempted murder of me would be laughed at. And from a knowledge of him gained through a lifetime acquaintance—I knew he wouldn't disgorge from any sense of justice or fairness. So I felt then.

"It happened that one day I strayed into a class room where they were having a lecture on cerebral operations. And sat down in the rear. And an idea—a startling, unique idea—grabbed hold of me. For I'd been reading you see, in the London *Times,* the previous week, about a young American named Goddard—Calvin Goddard—who had established a new criminological science—who could prove conclusively that a bullet had came out of such-and-such a gun and that one only. And sitting there in that lecture, my big idea came to me. And this was it: When I was a youth of about twenty-one, I suffered what is known as an intra—"

"—dural hemorrhage," I put in for him. "A fall from a motorcycle. On Ashland Avenue. I've talked with old Dr. Max Prior. All about your case. Or all about Phil Walmsley's case."

"Well—well—well," he said. "Now I'm the one who's surprised! Well, then no need for me to rehearse it. You know how my skull was opened, the hemorrhage drained, and an etched plate put in my skull. And that was the pivot of my idea. Which was scintillating, to say the least. For it was just this: that if ever a skull were found up there around Rapid River, having in it just such a silver plate as was in my own—etched identically, that is, and far below stream where Roger and I had camped years before—and with a bullet hole in it—and a lead pellet in the brain cavity corresponding, by all the tests of the new science of criminal ballistics, to that identical gun he'd had—"

"Wait!" I said. "It was a big idea. But please—please—a question! And here 'tis: How in the devil could you ever get hold long enough of that gun that was locked up here, 5000 miles away, in our Historical Society, to fire a bullet through it—through that much bone, in fact—a bullet, moreover, of the same colorshifting lead that that bullet was made of—and, last but not least, a bullet which our famous ballistic expert, Calvin Goddard, could get up in court and swear was fired—"

"Get hold of—that gun?" he echoed. And his tone was one of amusement. "I didn't even need that gun. I had the bullet. Already. Yes—of brass-alloyed lead. And fired from that very gun—yes. And having it, I just about had Mr. Roger Pelton right in the palm of my hand!"

CHAPTER XXV

THE PROPS!

I stared towards his place in the darkness. And the confused facial blur that was coolly handing me the most surprising tale I had ever heard in my life.

"You—you had the bullet—already? How—"

"Yes," he put in calmly. "The very gods themselves were with me. With my plan, that is. For I had the bullet! Right on me. Had been carrying it, in fact, for luck, ever since I left Roger Pelton." He paused. "Simple enough, however. The very first evening that Roger and I camped up there, I jeered him about his new rifle. Told him he couldn't hit a wolf skull—stuck in a crotch of a tree—at ten feet! And the wolf skull was there at hand, too. Some huge timber wolf—who'd died there in the snows the winter before. And the maggots that came in the spring had cleaned him. Roger indignantly repudiated my aspersions on his marksmanship. I stuck the skull up in the crotch of the tree. He drew a bead on it. Fired. Knocked it right off onto the ground. A little while later, while he was broiling the bacon, I got to wondering just how much momentum those high-speed brassy-nosed bullets he used in that rifle had. I picked up the wolf skull and examined it. The bullet had bored right through the first thickness of bone—the top of the skull—but hadn't come out again. In fact, it rattled forth into my hand. I put it into my pocket. To show him later. And forgot. And it wasn't

235

until I reached Detroit and changed clothes that I found the pellet. And realized that it probably was my good-luck piece—had saved my life. And so I kept it. And had it still in London—when my great idea came to me."

I started to speak, but shut up. This was a story utterly unlike anything I had ever heard or read. And he seemed more than anxious to give it all to me.

"Well," he went on, "I happened to know that my cranial operation was fully described. In certain records. And that there were photographs to boot. In fact, Dr. Prior had shown them to me. A few weeks after I'd left the Alexian Brothers' hospital. Here in Chicago. He had said that one typescript volume of his work would go to the library of the medical school in London where he had studied his cranial surgery. I had to locate that medical school. It took a bit of trying. But I found it. It was the Royal College of Physicians and Surgeons off Kensington Gardens. I found the book. In the library. I recognized my own case quite plainly by the initials 'P. W.' And the occupation—that of bank clerk. And the circumstances of the injury. And the librarian made me photostats of all the photos. Only a shilling apiece."

"And now," I put in, "you got hold of a skull?"

"Not exactly. It was a human head when I first got hold of it." He paused. "I went through the dissecting rooms of the college where I was enrolled. Searching carefully. There were stiffs galore available. That's what the pickled dead corpses for dissecting purposes were known as—commercially—and by the studes. Stiffs! And I wanted a skull with perfect teeth. Like my own. I musn't fall down, I knew. On some small detail. Some lucky defense attorney for Roger Pelton might—well—unearth the fact that in life I had had perfect teeth. And that my skull had bridgework—or missing teeth! And I finally found what I wanted. An American stiff. Not even the whole stiff. For nothing but his head was left. His body had been dissected about all to pieces. The copious history ticket wired to his scalp told a little about him. He'd been a steer wrestler. If you know what that is! Came to London—from Wyoming—with a small American traveling rodeo. Had fallen ill and been taken to Guy's Hospital. And died there. He had nothing—no relatives in America, even, according to his entry papers into Britain—the rodeo had gone on to Berlin—and so he had wound up pickled—in a medical college. The head—the last of him—as was shown by the notations on the back of the ticket, had been all through the works. The studes in opthalmology had chopped his inferior oblique eye-muscles in two—and pulled his eyeballs partway out, and stitched his superior recti muscles into new places outward on his eyeballs—for cyclophoria. His neck—what there was of it—had been all opened up in goiter excision practice. Some student in the rhinology department had taken out the turbinates in his nose—and the whole rhinology department, judging from the notes, had taken turns finding and irrigating his sphenoid sinuses—the most difficult sinuses in the human head to reach. Or to treat. Studes in the ear department had operated on his ear-drums, and practised sounding his eustachian tubes through his nose. In the surgical-neurology, they had severed most of his facial nerves for tri-facial neuralgia the poor Wyomingite never had had, and never would have: Oh, he'd gone through the works all right. All except brain surgery. He'd escaped that somehow. And he nearly escaped me, too. For when I got around to getting him for myself, the old porter in the cellar was just swinging him, black hair and all, in a shovel, into the crematory. And he cost me all of two shillings!

"I took him home and boiled him. With a chemical in the water that's used in medical colleges to expedite the clearing off of human bones. Boiled him clean. And scraped him with a piece of dull metal. For Abner Sprigge, ex-steer-wrestler, was going to be me. Abner Sprigge was—"

"Whoa—Tilly!" I ejaculated. "Abner Sprigge, eh? Then—then in addition to being Phil Walmsley—and Milo Payne—you are also 'Abigail Sprigge'?"

CHAPTER XXVI

PAST WANSTEAD FLATS

I had evidently tossed a bombshell into his lap—judging from the stunned silence with which he greeted my words. Finally he seemed to collect his wits—at least enough to answer me.

"'Pon—'pon my word—my friend—you surpr—Say, will you kindly tell me how in the dev—"

"Well, you are 'Abigail Sprigge'—are you not?"

"Yes," he said, quite freely. "I am. But—but how could you know that? Yes, I am Abigail Sprigge. It's a literary pseudonym I have used for years—on little poems that I've dashed off here and then. That is, 'Abigail' when the poem was sung from a woman's point of view. And 'Abner' when it had an out-and-out man's viewpoint. I don't know how to account for it, but my conscience has always bothered me—the way I used that poor Western ranch-hand. Abner Sprigge! And I felt that the least I might do for him would be to give him credit—for what little effusions I turned out."

"But which meant, I take it," I said, "foregoing the money for them—or did it not?"

"Money?" he retorted ironically. "For—poetry? Why—the amount of money obtainable from writing poetry you could hang on—on one of your eyelashes! And you could—however, you haven't explained yet—but I think I get it now. You've seen, perhaps—and liked—at some time—in one of our magazines—one of my

Abigail—or Abner—Sprigge verses?"

"Well," I admitted, to avoid a long involved explanation at this point, "I *did* see one—yes—a little humorous couplet—except that it was just one submitted to a publisher—and I liked it. And didn't exactly forget the name—you see! However, what may be of more interest to you is that I also saw another one—also one that wasn't in print. And I—well—it's too long—and too complicated—a story to expound fully at this point—but, in brief, I happen to be in personal touch with a man who's starting a poetry magazine. And he had both of these verses."

"I don't doubt it," was Walmsley's answer, "seeing that I submitted both to him. Whoever he is. For I merely submitted to some room number and address on—on Federal Street—yes. No name, either, of publisher or proposed magazine was given in the ads calling for material. But about this man—is he really on the level—guaranteeing to pay what he does?"

"Yes, he is. He may go bust—yes. And probably will. But he's on the level—while his money lasts. Incidentally—" Again I saved myself a lot of words. "—he knows that the humorous verselet you sent in under the name 'Abigail Sprigge' is from the same pen as one sent in under the name 'Miss O. M. Lee.' In fact, thanks solely to you, I had a glorious—and expensive—cab ride today, visiting the grave of 'Miss O. M. Lee' in Restvale Cemetery. Wurra—wurra—what a ride!"

He chuckled audibly. I know he couldn't help himself.

"I'm awfully sorry, my friend. But if he sent you out there to look me up, I'm afraid you'll have to look to him for your taxi fare! But I am sorry, though. Yes, it occurred to me that a man offering to pay that much money for poems—in case it wasn't some queer new kind of a racket—would want more concrete evidence of the real existence of Abigail Sprigge. Which in the past I have never given—to any magazine or newspaper. For the simple reason that the president of the Berkeley State Bank has been for years head of the American Poetry Association. And even in those years long ago—when I was only a bank clerk there—he knew I was a budding poet—for we once had an argument over the legitimacy of using a certain peculiar meter. Which I often use—for Abigail! And, peculiarly, I've always had a fear that, scanning the magazines for new young poets, he might become interested in Abigail—and, as president of the A. P. A., go to see her. Or worse—have a long, long memory—and suspect that that supposed illegitimate meter which crops up in her work so frequently is no other than his young bank clerk—come back to life. Hence—no address, ever, with Abigail! I couldn't very well risk it. For the few dollars which, at best, I might get from her."

We were both now silent a moment. So I invited him to continue.

"Well," I said, "when we broke off, you—you had boiled Abner Sprigge's skull clean. There in London. And scraped it. And then—what?"

"Yes. Well, that done, I then purchased from an old Jewish secondhand medical instrument dealer on Lambeth Road—near the school where I was enrolled—the two instruments I required. A Peloux rotary trephine. Electrical. With a No. 5 cutter. And a Kronjedt beveler. All mentioned in Prior's case history of Operation No. 82. I had to adhere strictly to the technique of the original operation, you see. Also I got me a wooden bowling ball, and—"

"A bowling ball? What for?"

"Wait. A bowling ball—and the upper half of an old skull. I had to do some practicing!

"In my room I practised trephining. I trephined that bowling ball till it looked like anything but a ball. Then I trephined that old piece of skull till it looked like—like one of those discarded clamshells from a Muscatine, Iowa, button factory—after about a dozen pearl buttons have been drilled out of it. By this time I felt competent to operate on my steer wrestler.

"To tell you the truth, it was really absurdly easy. He was as dead—as Yorick himself—and held tightly in a vise besides. No blood and serum spurting all over—no scalp drawn away in clamps—no grave-faced nurses hovering around holding ether cones. Easy, really. I took out the disc of bone exactly of Number 5 shape. Beveled the opening with the Kronjedt beveler. Inserted a correspondingly beveled disc of German silver which I had painstakingly etched myself—slowly—in a vise after rephotographing onto a silver film deposited on its surface the very letters on that life-sized photostat. Photography was a hobby of mine.

"I drove it in. Well in. And the substitute Phil Walmsley was trephined! Now for the bullet hole! I shopped around London to get a good whirling high-speed bullet. About like what Roger had used. And a few points larger caliber for good measure. I got such, and a rifle to shoot it with—somewhere on Fulham Road. And the next day I took the skull out to the country. 'Way 'way out—even past Wanstead Flats. I was careful, too, in the way I rigged it. Tied it tight to a fence post. Wound a band of thin pliable leather around its base in black. That was to be my scalp, see? I didn't want to split my handiwork. I wanted conditions identical in every respect.

"I aimed. Same distance. No, I didn't take any chance of the gun wobbling—I propped it up in two forked sticks. I worked a half hour on that aiming. I didn't want to do that job all over again.

"Crack!

"When I went and examined the skull, I saw that my bullet had whistled through beautifully. In fact, it dropped right out into my hand. Through what's known as the occipital foramen. Where the vertebral column, in life, joins onto the human head. The bullet was mushroomed a bit at its nose, of course. I promptly threw it away. And tried the mushroomed nose of my own bullet in the hole. The bullet, that is, that had been in my possession ever since I left the States—the one that had gone through the wolf's skull. It passed through just—and nicely—thanks to the few points larger caliber. And with that I was done. Took everything home. Wrapped the precious bullet in cotton, so as to preserve those valuable microscopical ballistic markings—and put everything away.

"For now I had Roger Pelton in the electric chair—any time I wanted to put him there. But I didn't want him there yet. For I had work to do.

"I gave up the fool medical course. Indeed, I hadn't even struck the rudiments of it yet. I saw that it would be years and years before I could hang my shingle on Harley Street. Much less make a living. I didn't fit, in fact. And now I had an ambition. To make up my share of my stealings. To make it all up.

"I went to work in London. At a lot of different occupations. Worked on salary. On wages. Ran little shops. Tried lots of things. Failed at a lot, too. Even had a jellied-eel restaurant once in Pentvonville Road. Near King's Cross. And finally, after five long years, I returned to the States. To New York, that is. By the most stringent of self-denial over those five years—by shutting my eyes to luxuries and pleasures of all sorts—I'd succeeded in doing nothing more than hang on to my original five thousand dollars—and run it one thousand higher. And five years were gone!

"I must get ahead faster, I saw that plainly. And London was not the place to do it in.

"Again I tried my hand—in a country that was now zooming with post-war prosperity. Salaries bigger; opportunities greater. I tried my hand once more. At everything. Bookkeeping. Accountancy. Ran an A. and P. store in Brooklyn. Opened a number of little businesses. Some I sold out. Some failed. Made money. Lost money. Came '28. Had $7500 then. Everybody getting rich on stocks. And jeering at those who stayed out of the Market. And in I went, too. Though cautiously. With half of my $7500 only. In September, '29, the half of it had a paper value of $10,000. I was nearly ready, I saw, to spring on Roger. But something sprang on me! The crash. Of '29. When it was over, I had just $3750. And ten years gone!

"Sometimes I used to get the letter out. And read it, wonderingly, discouragingly, too. The letter from the president of the Berkeley State Bank. To one Jethro Appercut, a lawyer in London—only they call them solicitors over there—in Chancery Lane, near Lincoln's Inn Fields. For I had such a letter. Got it just before I left England. So's I'd know where I stood. I'd gone to this solicitor. Gave the name of Aldershot Wyndham. Pretended I was thinking

of marrying a distant girl cousin in an American family called
Walmsley. And that one of the tribe—chap named Phil—had been
in trouble in America. Filched some money from a bloomin' bank,
don't y' know! That my Mama wouldn't permit my marriage—
unless this American stain on the 'scutcheon was cleared up! How
much would it take—of our family's fortunes—to clear it up—so
I could marry into the family? The president wrote my solicitor a
very nice letter. The theft, so he said, had been written off the books
long ago. It had been settled partly from a special bank fund—partly
by insurance. Thirty-five thousand doilars. A return of the
$35,000—American money or British pounds sterling to that
extent, at current rate of exchange—would settle it in full. No interest. For the defalcation had been written off. Prosecution would be
waived entirely for that sum. Even if Phil Walmsley were alive. In
fact, he gave my solicitor a complete letter to that effect. And the
solicitor turned it over to me. He was English. Like I was! He under-
stood how an English mother feels—about her son marrying into an
American family!

"Well, back I went to the fray. And God—what years followed
that crash of '29. The Great Panic! Save money? Why—you couldn't
hold on to it—let alone save it. By '30, my stake had slipped backward to $3250. '31—back to $2900. Slipping, slipping. Not gain-
ing an iota. By '32, down to $2501. By '33, down to $1910. Then
came a man called Roosevelt. You've heard of him. The tide was
turned. By '34, prosperity was coming back. By '35 it was back.
Total resources now: $2000. And fifteen years gone. Fifteen—
years—gone!

"I came on to Chicago. I knew it would be quite impossible for
anyone who had ever known me to recognize me now. And I wanted
to study Roger Pelton at closer range. He'd come up in the world.
Smart! When people wouldn't pay $1 a pound for candy any more—
he put out a huge line of weird confections at a nickel. Smart. He—
he made me grit my teeth. And decide to fling myself back into the
battle. At least, I wouldn't be plucking a skinned chicken—when
I went after him. If the time ever came. Only thing bothered me was

his daughter. If he died, it seemed as though I'd have to go after her—threaten an exposure of her father. But darn it—the kid—I saw her once—at the Ravinia Park Opera—she was the living likeness of her mother. Whom I loved. Well, I just prayed that Roger Pelton wouldn't die, that's all.

"But, as I say, the tide had turned now. Money came. But it stayed. Invested a little in Chicago real estate as it was going up. And got out—when it contracted. But stringent self-denial—as before. Strict foregoing of all the expensive pleasures of life. Shutting my eyes to luxuries. God, man, you don't know how slow money comes—when you have to save it. But my one-time desire had become an obsession—to make good with that Berkeley State Bank—to be able to walk the streets and not have to turn away from my own reflection in cigar store mirrors!

"Each night I used to say, wearily—as laborers do—another day—another dollar. And I came nearer and nearer the coveted amount. And finally—ten days ago—added the last five-dollar bill to my accumulation, which now brought it up to $15,000. Now it was up to me to slave for another ten years—fifteen years—twenty years—or else to get the balance of that $35,000 from the man who, to all intents and purposes, stole it from me.

"Which further slaving I didn't intend to do, of course. With the result that, a week ago, I took a trip up to Rapid River, Michigan. And looked over the old scenes. With fishing pole and rifle. And incidentally buried that skull and lower jawbone, which had been encased now in a box of dirt for two years, getting a proper shade to the bone—and a proper tarnish to the plate. I buried it in a tongue of land below Hell's Rapids—a tongue that looked as though it was made of silt. A couple of days later I got a boy in the near-by village to accompany me. To tell me the history of the place. Tommy Huckins was his name. Official witness, see? And whilst we were on that tongue of land I decided to fish. And forthwith dug for some worms. Tommy didn't think I should dig where I was digging. But then—I wasn't digging for worms! I struck the skull, of course. 'Well—what's this?' For I wasn't a Cockney up there. An upper-class

Englishman, yes. And up came Mr. Skull. I cleaned off enough of the plate with saliva to ask Tommy if there was any doctor—or even native—named Prior around the country. No, there wasn't. And Tommy was now able to identify the skull in a court of law! I rattled out the bullet. Made Tommy cut off a piece and put it away—to identify it by later. Told him he'd doubtlessly be a witness in a murder trial eventually. Get a chance to take a trip. Have his name in the papers. Tickled stiff, the boy was. Will have to send him a five-dollar bill one of these days, I guess, to salve his disappointment. Where was I? Oh—yes. Well, I took the skull and bullet. To my hotel. And cleaned 'em well up.

"I called up Dr. Prior in Chicago. Just as a matter of record. To show how Milo Payne would have connected with Phil Walmsley's brother—Peter Walmsley. With Prior, I was an upper-class Englishman again, not a Cockney. Then I hammered out a letter on a typewriter to my brother, Peter Walmsley, for years a rector here in Chicago. I said—"

"I know," I put in quietly. "Roger Pelton read the entire letter. Surreptitiously. You might as well know it."

"Oh-ho," he said. "I do get plenty surprises tonight! Well, then you know what I wrote. So that's that! And I told him I'd be at the Palmer House on such-and-such a date—which date was day before yesterday—and if he'd come at 6 o'clock in the evening, sharp, I'd give him what I'd found. Would have it all packed in a bag for him. I hated to tax him—my own brother—for the cost of that bag—but I had to cover my identity as Milo Payne, you see. I—"

But listen," I said. "Weren't you running a big risk? Of his recognizing you? Your own brother, you see—and only twenty—or twenty-one—years elapsed—or did you come right out and tell him you were—" I broke off.

"Recognize me? Why, man, it has been more than forty years since my brother has seen me. And I was but a few years old then. And he about thirteen. No, we'd been separated, you see, as boys. Our parents died. One of us had to be sent to Colorado to live with one uncle. That was he. I stayed with an aunt. We corresponded for years.

Like brothers. But never met. Always going to—yes. But never did.

"So he came all right—to the Palmer House. And mighty grateful to me—for what I'd done. Told me all about the affair—which I already knew. Declared he'd always distrusted the story Roger Pelton had brought back from that camping trip; was suspicious as to how Roger had financed the purchase of a certain decrepit candy factory. He'd always half believed, he said, that Roger might have killed his brother—maybe to get some of the stealings that could conceivably have been on his brother's person. Sagacious, Peter always was. Anyway, he said he was going to place the whole affair—evidence and all—into the hands of the State's Attorney next morning, have the gun at the Historical Society taken up immediately by the S. A.'s office, have this Tommy Huckins of Rapid River subpoenaed—for I told him frankly I wasn't staying on here—that I was heading on for India—and send Roger Pelton to the electric chair—or to life imprisonment in Michigan. Ferocious to avenge my death, Peter was. Poor Peter!

"Then he left. I got out of the hotel pronto. My work was done. I didn't know how fast Peter would work. And I didn't want to get subpoenaed into a murder trial that would be blazoned over the whole country—and a trial for my own murder, to boot! I got out so fast, in fact, that I left behind me the thing I prized most in the world—and carried always with me—the picture of the girl Roger and I loved—but whom Roger married. I've often wondered if her child is like her. If, for instance, she writes like her. Handwriting, you know—its general character, that is—is often inherited. I don't expect you to believe it. But—"

"Yes," I said. "Doris Pelton's handwriting is sure like her mother's. And—how! As I've just found out. But don't bother to convert me to that theory. I'm already converted!"

"Good. Well, about my poor brother. He never got the traveling bag even as far as his rectory. For a chap—regular dumb-bell, he must have been—accidentally made an exchange of his own bag with that bag on a Broadway car. Going north. And the following evening the late newspapers reported Peter's death in a train wreck near

Spotts Forks, Nebraska. Where, as it seems, he was going to visit a sick sister. Not a blood sister, you understand. Peter's foster sister. From his boyhood days in Colorado. Dead. Poor Peter! I'm sure glad I saw and talked with him once before he died, though."

He was regretfully silent a moment. Then he forged on.

"Well, I could go further with this story—but what's the use? You've heard enough. The skull came back to me; that's obvious— or I wouldn't have been back on the job again. But now I no longer had Peter to put everything through for me. And suddenly—to tell you the truth—I began to realize that Roger Pelton has suffered a lot in all these years."

"He has indeed," I said. "More than you, I'll wager."

"That's about what I concluded. It suddenly came to me—that is, when the skull came back to me—that this whole thing was all part of a gigantic plan of Destiny—a plan to save me. The great Ouspenskian truth suddenly dawned on me that everything that confronts each of us individually is created by each of us individually; in short, I had, virtually, shot at myself up there on Rapid River. Roger was only my own tool. For I stole that money. Tossed temptation into his way. He shot at me. Hence I created my own attempt—at my own murder. But if I stole that money, what caused me to steal it? Crooked horse-racing. And economic injustice. Paying a teller $21 a week! And I traced back and back. And I damned near got back, I tell you, to the Garden of Eden. And the original sin. Between Adam and Eve. And I began to see that we're all enmeshed in a plan. I was no longer bitter at Roger. I was a bit grateful to him, to tell you the truth. I saw, in a flash, that if I'd succeeded in getting to London with all of those stealings—I'd have been dizzy with all that money—and would have lost it all at Epsom Downs. For the horses were in my blood at that time. But because I was frightfully bitter at the double-crossing I got—and because I had only five thousand dollars between me and a British almshouse—I held on to that thousand pounds. Desperately. It saved me from gambling with it. And Roger's act put the $20,000 into his hands and helped him to get a candy factory. And to conserve it. To make it ready for me—

THE RIDDLE OF THE TRAVELING SKULL

whenever I should get together the other $15,000. While, in the meantime, the factory employed hundreds of people. For years. Helped 'em to marry. To have babies—"

"To suck on our No. 11—or Midget—lollypops," I said. "But go on."

"Yes, to suck on your lollypops! And grow up and populate the earth. It was all a huge divine plan—if I may use that word divine. In the twinkling of an eye I stopped hating Roger: I saw that he and I together were but a mechanism to produce good—not evil—and that he, moreover, was a lever within the mechanism—to save me. All very complicated, apparently—but not so at all in reality. But of course I had to put on a hard front tonight—when I talked to him on the phone—in order to get my issue across. He would have to learn the Ouspenskian truth—in other ways—later. He would—but I'll stop philosophizing. And now, without my going on any further with either philosophy or story, and without additional wearisome explanation on my part—do you see the justice of my stand? I made Roger Pelton—with that 20,000 dollars. I've paid bitterly myself— for my original theft. Scrimped and fought and struggled to get it all together. For twenty long years. So haven't I the right to that money you've got with you tonight? Since I'm not a blackmailer at all? But just a man—trying to get right with the world again?"

CHAPTER XXVII

ALL'S SWELL THAT ENDS SWELL!

Phillip Walmsley's story had amazed me—and at the same time delighted me. It was evident now that Doris could never suffer the shame of being called a murderer's daughter. Nor would Roger Pelton have to spend his life in the Republic of San Do Mar—much less in the penitentiary at Lansing, Michigan.

But there was still a slight obscurity that puzzled me. And another matter on which I wished to be positively assured. So I spoke up quickly.

"Yes, I'm willing to admit, Walmsley, that this money belongs to you—providing that you're going to restore it to the Berkeley State Bank—as you claim. And on that point I naturally want to be completely satisfied. And then, in addition, I haven't got things quite clear in my own head yet. About this skull.

"So, as to the first-named matter—how will you guarantee to me that you'll restore the money to the bank people, and not lope off with it—if we exchange my currency and your goods—although your skull now has for me a purely academic value. The next-named point, the point of obscurity, is this: When you followed the Chin— but first, it may surprise you, but I'm the man who got the Reverend Peter Wamsley's bag on the Broadway car."

"Indeed?" The tone of his voice indicated that he was quite flabbergasted. I could make him out stroking the pointed ends of his mustache troubledly.

"Yes," I added, "and not because of my dumbness, as you hypothesized a while back, but because of the dumbness of a German conductor."

"Well—well! Then do accept my apologies, won't you? I fear I spoke out of turn!"

"Quite all right. Let it pass. But I'm the man who was knocked out that night. On Lake Shore Drive. By the Chinky whom you subsequently followed. It was this way: A few minutes after I got into my upstairs room, at 1515 North Dearborn Parkway, from that Broadway car, I learned I had the wrong bag. But I managed to open it up, nevertheless, with an old valise key on a bunch I unearthed. And found the skull and jawbone in it. And after looking 'em well over, I put 'em back into the bag again, and locked it tight. And set it on the floor near my window. Went out to hunt me up an expressman, got detoured by a movie film, and when I finally got home I went straight to bed. At about 1 in the morning I got a ring on the phone. To come, with the bag, over to 1870 Lake Shore Drive. Being the original Mr. Sucker from Suckersville—or else falling like a ton of bricks for a lot of Bible stuff and hooey that was handed to me, I wiggled into my clothes, grabbed the bag up off the floor, and hiked over there. To No. 1870. The very house you were watching. And watching, I take it, from the dark parkway across from it. And there, in the vestibule of Number 1870, I was knocked galley west. By Ichabod Chang. Whom you followed. And whose booty—that selfsame bag—you dug back up again, after he buried it on the Oak Street beach. And Ichabod—"

"P-lease—just a minute!" he said. "I'm—I'm floundering. Trying to—to collate all these facts. But that name—Ichabod, did you say? Ichabod Chang? Did I get you right—on that name?"

"Yes."

"Ichabod Chang, eh? Well, my dear fellow, did you read tonight's papers? Or tune in around mid-afternoon today—on any of the radio news broadcasts?"

"Read the papers?" I echoed bitterly. "Tune in—on radio news?

Hell-fire, man, I haven't seen a single newspaper or heard a bit of radio news since I hit this city since, in fact, I left the Philippine Islands weeks ago. Where I happened to be. Not even a single news story—outside of one that I read on the front page of a noon *Despatch* out in Hyde Park. The story of a cracksman who blew your brother's safe to get—phooie!—last Sunday's collection. News? My God-amighty—for all I know of what's going on in the world, we might be at war with Germany. Or France. Or Russia. Why—all I've done is rush madly about like a hen with its head cut off—and sleep the sleep of the dead between times. News? I don't even know who's Mayor of this town. News?" I know I actually snorted.

"However," I went on, after a brief pause, "it—but what brought all this up? About news? And my not getting a chance to read any? Oh, yes—I was talking about an Ichabod Chang, and you—"

"Is he a Chinese crook—who's known to the police as 'The Bible Spouter'?"

"He undoubtedly must be. For he spouts the Bible. And did even to me. And there wouldn't be but one Ichabod Chang in the entire world. But now—this news—what's this news—concerning Ichabod Chang?"

"Just," he told me calmly, "that he's dead!"

"Dead? The devil! How—when—"

"All I can give you is what came in today on a radio I have in my place. Where I live. The account was plenty graphic enough— even coming in that way. It seems that this Chang went over to Chinatown about 2 o'clock today, and stuck a pistol against the stomach of an old Chinese pawnbroker on one of the side streets over there. Old fellow known as Ong Jin. With a teakwood safe, and about ninety years old. The Chinaman—not the safe! Chang told him he had to have money—and he'd shoot Ong Jin through the stomach unless the latter gave it to him. But alas—Ong Jin's place was bristling with Suey Sing tongsmen—all hidden—for there'd been threats of a rival tong, the Bing Kongs, against Ong Jin—and he was afraid of a tong raid. And when this Ichabod stuck his pistol in old Ong's tummy—the place just naturally riz up all over with tongsmen who shot Ichabod from twelve directions. And cleared out.

"When the police from the Peking Station—I gather that's the station on South State Street near Cermak Road—the one covering Chinatown—got there, Chang was laid out on the floor—still breathing—but going fast. They recognized him right away—as 'Bible Spouter'—an ex-convict—from Joliet. One of the plain-clothesmen leaned over him, and rather brutally said: 'Bible-Spouter, the Suey Sings got you! And you're checking out. Can you dig up a verse to cover that, Bible-Spouter?'

"'Yes,' said this chap Chang. 'Jeremiah-XVIII-18!' And promptly rolled over dead."

"Jeremiah-XVIII-18?" I echoed. "Now I wond—"

"Yes—so did I. The news broadcast had just broken off short—so that the Wishy-Washy Dishcloth could be described for Chicago housewives—and so I looked up Jeremiah-XVIII-18—in a pocket Testament I have. And it runs: 'Come, and let us smite him with the tong!'"

"The tong? Why how—Oh, yes—the tongue. Let us smite him with the tongue—with the tong—by God, not bad, not bad, for a Chinky—dying on a floor!" I was silent. "So Ichabod Chang—is dead?"

"Quite, it would seem," Phillip Walmsley replied laconically.

"Well, then," I said, "that brings me back again to my two problems. First, how I'm to be guaranteed 100 per cent that you'll turn Roger Pelton's money back to the bank, if I turn it over to you. And second—you haven't recounted the details of how you dug up that bag that Chang buried? After he knocked me out? For that—"

"That's the second time you referred to my digging up a bag. I didn't dig up any bag! Didn't even know one was buried."

"You didn't? Well—Chang buried it on the Oak Street beach after he knocked me out. And up until you called today—and I put Roger Pelton next to the underlying facts—Pelton didn't know for a positive certainty whether some kid had dug the bag up and took it home to his father—or whether the stake marking its location simply got blown over with sand."

"Hm? Well, maybe he never will know."

"How's that? Didn't you dig it up? If not, how in the devil did you get that skull?"

"Well," he replied, "that's a curious story—all in itself. And one which shows that truth is a hundred times stranger than fiction. And that—but about that guarantee. As to that money going back to the Berkeley State Bank. I think I can provide you what you ask. And I'll take that up in a minute.

"But about how that skull finally got back to my hands, eh? Well, remember I warned you that truth is stranger than fiction. For the human threads that make up the web called Life mesh together in patterns more startling and more bizarre than they even appear on the surface to do." He paused. "But first, did you ever do wrong to a woman?"

"Did I ever do—well—hrumph—yes—no—it all depends. It was years ago. A girl. Brunette. But I offered to go with her to the minister's and get married. And she said, 'Don't be sil. The Dark Ages are over!'"

He laughed in spite of himself. "No, I mean have you wronged any woman recently—in recent weeks?"

"In recent wee—well—no, heck no—but there's a woman— lives down in Texas or Arkansas or Oklahoma, or someplace like that when she's in America—her name is Sophie Kratzen- schneiderwumpel—she's a missionary—and has a bug that different men have proposed marriage to her. She's known on the Pacific Ocean as Suing Sophie. I parted from her in 'Frisco, about five days ago. Now if you asked her, wherever she is today, she might say I had proposed marriage to her and loped out—except that I really didn't do anything of the kind. Her bug, you see?"

"A bug, eh?" There was a slightly skeptical tone in his voice. But it partly fell away, as he resumed speaking. "Well, maybe so. I know nothing of that. But would it surprise you any if you were told that she had a brother living right here in Chicago who was once a professional hypnotist, known on the cheaper vaudeville circuits as Herr Professor Hypno, that he was now many years retired, and that—though named Otto—he goes by the name of Otto Schmidt—and not Otto Kratzenschneiderwumpel?"

"Well—no—it's not impossible."

"Or would it surprise you if I were to say that I knew this Otto well, from 'way back in a flat in Hammersmith London where we both roomed—or that we've kept in touch all these years—or that he runs to me with the complete story of everything that happens to him?"

"Well—no—I guess it wouldn't surprise me. I—I guess anything's possible."

"Well, would it surprise you then, if you were to learn that this woman telegraphed her brother from San Francisco to carefully watch a certain man in Chicago whose name and address was in her possession—and whom she believed might be a friend or acquaintance of another man who had made violent love to her on a Pacific steamer, proposed marriage to her, and who was now wriggling out?"

"Not a damn bit! She's—she's done it to five other men—not telegraphed to anybody—no—but cooked up in her brain that they proposed marriage and jilted her. Damn it, it's—it's her bug, I tell you. I never even—"

"Well, calm yourself. I'm only trying to show you the fallacy of paying $2.00 for fiction books written by professional novelists—when Life teems all about you! Well, it seems that so far I haven't even jolted you. So I don't presume you'd be in the least surprised, would you, if I were to tell you that this Otto, with the thoroughness of the true German, moved right into the place where this chap lived, or that he made instant friends with him, or that he watched him day and night to get onto the trail of whoever should come to see him—"

"Me, in short! Of all the cursed, damnable luck. Which—which friend of mine is this Otto camping next to?"

"Have you a friend living on East Superior Street? Near the Lake? A fellow who had an operation this morning? On his larynx—or rather, his vocal cords?"

"Yes, I have. Barr is his name. John Barr. Except that he didn't have the operation this morning. He was only going to have it this morning, that was all. In actuality, it's to be tomorrow—at 2 o'clock in the afternoon. And it isn't his larynx—and it isn't his vocal cords— it's the removal of a pair of tumors—an—an angioma—and—and a nodule—whatever they are—from—well, now, maybe at that it is from his vocal cords!—he's the last person on earth to be specific enough about anything—that I could worry about it. However— your information—obviously from this Otto—is a little skewgee."

"No, it's you who must be wrong. Positively. For this John Bower—"

"Barr," I said. "As in cocoanut bar."

"Barr," he corrected, "came home in a cab around noon today. With his beard and mustache shaved off. And his throat all wrapped around with gauze. And a flat open-and-shut statement to the man living in the room next him that his vocal cords had been operated on. And that—but have you ever heard that local anes- thetics, injected deeply into tissues, can be made to retain their anes- thetic powers twice as long if suggestion under hypnosis is added?"

"Yes, I have. And I'm beginning to see some kind of a stinking plot against him. And against me, too. By this kraut-eating German hypnotizing son of a—But I'll leave you to elucidate it. As for his— this Barr's—having had the operation and giving out today, as he did, that he hadn't—that's John Barr. Hates people fussing around him—asking how he is—sending flowers. Yes, I see now. But still I don't get the connection between this spying, prying, snooping bastard of a German hypnotist, and the skull, and—"

"Well, it's certainly plain that you don't like Otto Kratzen- schneiderwumpel. But don't get peeved at me." He paused. "Well, would it surprise you—but I don't suppose it would, eh?—if I should say that Otto persuaded your friend to let him put him under a short hypnotic-sleep to double the number of hours under which the anesthetics would retain their power? The anesthetics, that is, that were injected into his throat tissues—and, I would sup- pose, his vocal cords, too—and so forth? Or would it surprise you if

I were to say, that under the deep one-hour sleep Otto put him into, he got to talking? Actually babbling? And that he told a lot of detailed stuff—and in an absolutely altered voice, to boot—to the effect that—"

"You tell Otto," I said scornfully, "to cease peddling baloney! Even if he is a bum ex-hypnotist. Neither he—nor any of his brotherhood—could ever make me think a hypnotist could change a man's voice. Tell—"

"I believe the same as you do," Walmsley said. "However—if such a phenomenon as that really took place—I don't believe an explanation of it, based on hypnosis, is even necessary to account for it. For instance: If the tension of your friend's vocal cords—both of them—were lessened by the surgical removal of some sort of a growth on each, then the fundamental pitch of his voice—its very distinguishing quality—would be changed completely. Remember the laws of our high school physics? About the change in pitch of stretched vibrating wires—with any changes in their mass or tension?" And without waiting for me to comment, Phil Walmsley went on. "And again, if your friend were—say—allergic—as thousands of people are—to some of the new synthetic products for local anaesthesia—particularly those having a hemostatic, or blood-clotting, capability too—and his sinal membranes, because of the delicate vaso-motor mechanism of the lining of the human nose, swelled temporarily up, cutting off some of his nasal and head cavities—changing the size and volume of others—cavities such as the ethmoidal caverns, the sphenoidal chambers, the maxillaries, and so forth—well, wouldn't that change the entire resonance of his voice? For remember, again, our experiments in high school physics on resonance: Different-sized or shaped resonating chambers—different resonance! Indeed, doesn't a violin-shaped volume of air, held in a violin, resonate quite differently than—say—an oboe-shaped volume of air—held in an oboe? I think so! And if your friend's natural resonance were changed, the timbre of his voice would be altered. And, with pitch and timbre of his voice both changed, he would be a man with—at least for a few days—a brand-new voice. Would he not? Remember, I have not only studied elementary physics—but I have studied at least the rudiments of medicine. And if you accept my naive theories—then you'll at least have the satisfaction of feeling that you're robbed one dogmatic—as well as perhaps egotistic—German of thinking he achieved something super-wonderful—merely under hypnosis!"

"Well," I asserted, "your theories sound convincing enough to me. If they're good only to prick this guy Otto's bubble—and let some of the air out! But what's he—no, not this damned Otto-on-the-job—but my friend—supposed to have babbled?"

"Well, would it surprise you to learn that in that one hour sleep he babbled that in his lower bureau drawer was a skull, with an attached jawbone, and—"

"He—he had a skull? And a jawbone? Where did he—"

"Wait! You might as well know the truth. That he filched them from your bag. When he was waiting in your room. As I understand it, he went up there—the night you arrived home. Did you wire him or something—that you were coming?" But without waiting for my answer, which was unessential anyway, he went on. "Anyway, he opened your bag. Had a master key with which he could do it. As I understand it, he's in the bag business. Or something closely allied with the bag business. Anyway, he filched everything in it. And tossed in a pair of your own heavy-soled shoes, that he found in your closet, to give it a fairish weight. And he—"

"Listen," I said furiously, and the blood was pounding in my temples till they throbbed, "this—this is a filthy, German, Teutonic, scurrilous, rotten lie. This is a—Listen, if this damned, lousy, German hypnotizing son-of-a—Listen—if he tells you that John Barr did that he—"

The virulence of my attack seemed to stagger Phillip Walmsley.

"Well," he remarked, placatingly, "it must be true, don't you think—considering that the skull and jawbone—came back to me?"

"No, it musn't," I shot forth. "That German is covering some monkey business of his own up. No, don't ask me what—for I don't know. He must have stolen an impression of John Barr's master bag-key. When he first breezed in there to live and got acquainted with him. Before even I had hit Chicago. The square-head probably thought it was a master key for all the bags in the cosmos! And that I might be carrying some sort of evidence—when I arrived here—that would help his sister's case—against me. He must have gotten into my room. After I got here. By some subterfuge. I don't know. But it doesn't matter what he told you. I tell you that this man John Barr, whether drunk or sober, stinko or blotto, mesmerized or hypnotized or in a state of catalepsy, or even in a fit of downright absent-mindedness, would not go into a bag of mine."

"Well, you're a loyal cuss all right. But, frankly, what do you know of the veracity of one Otto Kratzenschneiderwumpel? Nothing, do you? So let's analyze the situation. To see if we can't make everything jibe." He paused a second. "To give the devil his due, your friend, after all, didn't go into a bag of yours. 'Twas a bag of someone else's, wasn't it?"

"Sure. Of course. But he couldn't know that."

"Well, from the way things have come to me, that isn't quite the case. As I understand it, he recognized, on the metal framework of the bag he saw there in your room, some kind of a convexity, a thing called a Billy—a Billy—a—now what the dev—"

"A Billy Bulger Bulge," I said bitterly. "This damned Ger—"

"—man," he finished for me dryly, "will have to run sixty miles an hour if you ever see him first! Isn't that so?" And without waiting for my emphatic assent, he went on. "Well, what you term this convexity is what it's called, I guess." He paused a second. "However, as the story does, your friend realized from the presence of this Bully Bilger Bilge—or whatever the fool thing is named—that the bag sitting there in your room wasn't one that could rightfully be in your possession. For no bags with that on them—as I gather it—had yet been sold to the trade. So he wasn't entering your bag at all. And knew he wasn't. He entered it because he—"

"I get it all now," I put in quickly. And a bit relievedly, I will admit. "My landlady had told him a weird story about a Chinaman with long mustaches and a knife in his hand following me that night. He knew that that bag could well be the reason. And decided to investigate. But why didn't he tell me subsequently, I wonder, instead of spilling it all later, in a hypnotic-gabfest, to this damned snoophound of an Otto Kratzenschneiderwumpel? Whose schnozzle I intend to land on, I don't mind telling you, if I search out all the Otto Schmidts in Chicago!"

His reply, I confess, made me a bit angry, as it seemed like a terrific, though clumsy, attempt to protect his German friend.

"Oh—Otto?" he said, in a troubled tone of voice. "Well now—um—er—about poor Otto—remember, please, that I only asked you if you'd be surprised if—if there was an Otto. And—and if he did thus and so. I didn't at any time, if you'll go back over all my words, say that there was such a person. In fact," he added triumphantly, "you—you supplied me yourself just a few minutes back—with the name—Kratzenschneiderwumpel. To tell you the truth, I—I really wanted to show you how easy it is to—to construct dramatic fiction plot—what a racket these damned fictioneers have!—so that never again will you pay $2.00 for a mystery novel." And he added, with an attempt at facetiousness: "So that you can just—roll your own—as the saying goes."

"I'll—I'll roll Otto into the gutter, before I'm done," I fumed. "For you can't cover him up that easy. I'll—but say—now look here. Now—if none of these bags had been sold to the trade, I don't see—"

"Head buzzing with questions now, eh? And still looking for that guarantee about the $20,000? Well, I've got something I'd like to show you. Got a match about you? If not, I think I can dig one up. You see, this chap—your friend—recognized that that bag in your room was none other than the one I had given to the Reverend Peter Walmsley in the Palmer House, a few hours earlier. So he took measures—immediate and quick!—to regain that—"

But I had found the match he had just invited me to use. And drew it sharply across the side of the box which had contained it. With a hiss and a sputter, it flared up. And I held it above me and grumpily surveyed the man to whom I had been talking all the while in the profound darkness. And the questions that buzzed in my brain ceased entirely to buzz there.

For the white silk ribbon convention badge pinned to his lapel was not a badge at all: it was a short clipped newspaper story taken—as I was subsequently to find—from that night's *Chicago Brevities*. And reading, as I was also later to find:

WOMAN WITH WORLD'S LONGEST NAME MARRIES MAN WITH WORLD'S SHORTEST!

Love Inevitable, Under Such Conditions, Say Numerologists.

Miss Kratzenschneiderwumpel, woman missionary, weds well-known Oklahoma City clergyman named D.D. Zy, D.D.

Met him yesterday—wed him today—couple to do missionary work in Philippine Islands.

But, with my match burning away, I was of course scrutinizing not the improvised paper badge—but the man behind it.

Smooth-shaven he was, and not wearing a "Lunnon shop-keeper's" mustache at all—as I had supposed. For the mustache, two dabs of adhesive wax showing on its inner surface, was now held in his upraised fingers—and it was as false as it was red. Nor was he wearing a high collar, either, as I had also supposed—for his throat was swathed in gauze. And his kindly eyes were laughing—laughing at me! John Barr—himself!

THE END

ABOUT THE AUTHOR

A lifelong Chicagoan, Harry Stephen Keeler (1890–1967) began placing stories and serials in pulp magazines while still in his teens. His first novel, *The Voice of the Seven Sparrows*, was published in 1924. Successive works established what Keeler called his "webwork" plotting, which wove wildly disparate coincidences together into dizzying narratives. Upon its release, his 1932 book *The Box From Japan* achieved some notoriety as the longest mystery novel in the English language—"perfectly adapted to jack up a truck," as Keeler boasted —and was notable for its use of color television as a plot element. Even as Keeler's readership increased, his eccentric artistry kept pace: he wrote "documented novels," odd conglomerations of telegrams, poems, Chinese jokes, photographs, and the like. Several novels written around 1940 include rambling, hammily accented dialog that lasts for hundreds of pages, without any narration intruding. Dutton dropped Keeler in 1942; he moved to Phoenix Press until 1948, and began airily inserting his wife Hazel's stories into his novels. His last English-language publisher, in Britain, abandoned him in 1953. Keeler continued to write, and had a few books published in Spanish, but much of his late work has never been published at all.

English As She Is Spoke
by José da Fonseca and Pedro Carolino
Perhaps the worst foreign phrasebook ever written, this linguistic train wreck was first published in 1855 and became a classic of unintentional humor. In the preface to an American edition, Mark Twain wrote "Nobody can add to the absurdity of this book, nobody can imitate it successfully, nobody can hope to produce its fellow; it is perfect."

"This book has made me laugh so hard it almost hurts... Should be experienced by anyone who loves our language."   —*The Washington Post*

To Ruhleben—and Back
by Geoffrey Pyke
In 1914, Geoffrey Pike made his way across wartime Europe on a false passport, a pretty good German accent, and sheer chutzpah. He was eventually captured and ended up in Ruhleben, a horsetrack turned prison. After an escape in broad daylight and a nerve-racking journey across Germany, Pyke wrote the first eyewitness account of a German internment camp. In print for the first time since 1916, his extraordinary book is a college student's sharp-tongued travelogue, an odyssey of hairsbreadth escapes, a sober meditation on imprisonment, and, as Pyke intended, a ripping yarn.

"The war will produce few books of more absorbing interest than this one."
                                                              —*The New York Times*

Lady into Fox
by David Garnett
Another lost classic from the Collins Library: David Garnett's haunting 1922 debut novel, the story of a man, a woman, a fox, and a love that could not be tamed. Hardcover, bound in foxy orange cloth, and illustrated with woodcuts by Garnett's wife.

"It is the most successful thing of the kind I have ever seen... flawless in style and exposition, altogether an accomplished piece of work."
                                                              —Joseph Conrad

"Magnificent... write twenty more books, at once, I beseech."
                                                              —Virginia Woolf

For more information and future titles, please visit
www.collinslibrary.com and www.mcsweeneys.net.